About the Au

This is me kissing DDD on Dunkery Beacon, Exmoor, Devon
On our Golden Wedding Anniversary May 2013
fifty-one years after our first kiss in the same place

To know more about my writing read
Fortunes of Love
Pocket Books
Of my Light and Dark shaded Poems
Published Spiderwize 2016
The Fisherman's Story
A New Testament Fictional Novel
Published Olympia 2017
The Joyfinder
My Extraordinary Autobiography
To be published

The Go(o)d Year

Simon Boreham

The Go(o)d Year

Olympia Publishers
London

www.olympiapublishers.com
OLYMPIA PAPERBACK EDITION

A CIP catalogue record for this title is
available from the British Library.

ISBN: 978-1-78830-457-3

This is a work of fiction.
Names, characters, places and incidents originate from the writer's
imagination. Any resemblance to actual persons, living or dead, is
purely coincidental.

First Published in 2020

Olympia Publishers
Tallis House
2 Tallis Street
London
EC4Y 0AB

Printed in Great Britain

Dedication

For DDD
Our children
DG, CR & JP
Our grandchildren
E, L & D
Who mean so much
And
All my *Dear Friends
Who know who they are
Or if they would like to be

Acknowledgements

To, Lynn Crisp,
Who was brave enough
To be a reader

To Kristina and Co at Olympia Publishers
Who helped make this second book
As good as it could be

Remembering

Claire Kempster and Mark Haseler fell to their deaths roped together, whilst having their picture taken by Michael Wigney on the summit of Aiguille de Bionassay, on the 22nd July 1997.

I read about the tragic deaths of Claire and Mark in the Sunday Times (10.08.97), which described the fall as witnessed by the second group, and occurred when Kempster, standing on the summit ridge, lost grip of her backpack and toppled over the edge trying to grab hold of it, dragging Haseler with her.

I was struck with how one moment of exquisite pleasure felt at conquering the mountain peak, turned instantly into the terrifying knowledge that one was about to die falling from it.

I wrote a poem. The poem has two parts, the five narrative climbing stages, with six interposed inverted comma exhortations, that demand memory of that moment.

The Accursed Mountain

"What happens when we die"
Three by three friendships roped tight
Joining hill snow in the night
Footsteps shadowed by moonlight
Climbing up the dizzy height
Give strong determined words to write.
"Is not for me to say"
Three by three friendships roped tight
Heartbeats breath outpacing fright
With expectations rising bright
Of hidden summits of delight
Give longing hopeful words to write.
"But when I die, as die I must"
Three by three friendships roped tight
At last stand fast on mountain might
To greet dawn's coming into sight
And sense this moment's thrill is right
Give laughing thankful words to write.
"Will someone shout hurrah?"
Three by three friendships roped tight
Share breathless time to know souls' flight
And what future next may sudden blight
That mortal proves frail lifelines slight
Give tears to stain the words I write.
"And remember that I conquered once"
Three by three friendships roped tight
Departed from the sacred site
To face a loss without a fight
And keep a silent memory quiet
Give prayers to calm the words I write.
"Aiguille de Bionassay"

Go(o)d

Consider this. God[1] is a figment of human imagination. God that is beyond human experience cannot exist. The word God that describes a being beyond life and a life after death is meaningless. Blind faith, that is a necessary prerequisite for a belief in a God requires, first and foremost, a human decision. Every manifestation and ritual that has ever been attributed to God by mankind must now be attributed to human beings. This is reflected by all shades of humaneness, from the bad[2] to the good[3], which in turn is subject to the power of reason[4], and choice[5]. As the historic value of God has been for the supposed benefit of mankind, it would be better if God had been spelt Good. Past, present and future considerations of good thoughts and deeds now attributed to mankind, only require choice exercised by reason. The selection of good, if left to mankind's self-perpetuating interest, can rely on mankind's need for universal manifestations of human goodness. Historic examples of this human goodness are given in the past lives of great sages, and poets, and the inspiring talents of artists, artisans, and scientists. Better this reality, than the sectarian interests of religious dogma that, under the gaze of a personal God, hide from universal scrutiny and responsibility. Furthermore, the creation of, and justification for a God, to explain a reason for human existence, and balance the inequalities of life opportunities suffered, that can only be justified in a life after death, must now be seen as nonsense, with the acceptance that no one is born equal, or to have equal opportunities. And that without the interference of mankind, and the exercise of the power of goodwill by mankind, there is absolutely no possibility of equality happening. So it is only by denying the existence of God, that the greatest level of equal life opportunities for all can exist, and be allowed to grow and flourish. The developed laws established from the time of Moses, will always be needed for every new generation's potential to transgress in their lifetime's cycle. But evidence of expressions of goodness, repeated continually in so many varying ways and degrees, from the smallest to the greatest of gestures, exists. *From goodness comes belief in the possible, hope for the better, and knowledge of love in all its forms and manifestations, that can be both given and received. There is no God. There can be no good luck. But with good there is the possibility of benefitting from good thoughts and good deeds as a joyfinder.*

[1] *"God" superhuman being worshipped as having divine power over nature and humans.*
[2] *"Bad" worthless, inferior, defective, not valid, incorrect.*
[3] *"Good" having the right qualities, fertile, commendable, worthy, proper, kind.*
[4] *"Reason" motive, cause, justification, human intellectual characteristic, sanity, sense.*
[5] *"Choice" act of choosing, decide between alternatives, power of choosing.*

Gemini

1

The twins were born in 2001 at the Maimonides Medical Center, Borough Park Brooklyn, during the aftermath of the September 11 attacks on the New York Twin Towers.

As the terrorist attacks were unfolding in New York, Washington DC and near Shanksville, Pennsylvania, a hurricane was spinning off the north-east coast. A weather satellite image showed Hurricane Erin 500 miles east-south-east of New York with the smoke plume from the World Trade Center twin towers after they were hit. Winds out of the north-west blew smoke and debris from the disaster in Lower Manhattan into Brooklyn. Hurricane Erin would not make landfall in the north-east as the westerly winds gave Erin a final east-north-east shove.

How different circumstances might have been on the fate of the Twin Towers and perhaps on the astrological chain of events affecting the birth of the twins if Hurricane Erin had taken a different path and made land fall over New York.

As it was the twins' birth only added to Borough Park's title of 'the baby boom capital of New York City' in a small way. In every other they contributed very little to the total pool of happy relieved delivered mothers, as their mother Myriam Cohen, utterly exhausted by her ordeal, only managed to cradle them briefly in her arms before she suffered a massive bleed, dying shortly after they were snatched from her to allow for the frantic efforts of the maternity staff, struggling to save her life.

Myriam's husband, Abel Cohen, believing that he was not the true father, was absent and therefore unaware of the tragedy. So it was not until the police found him in his money lending office that he was forced to confront the reality of parenthood without a mother's support and the love that comes with the ties of blood. Fortunately, he had money, and the knowledge of borrowers who had little, and so within the time it took him to pay his target indebted couple a visit and part with a hastily negotiated sum up front with the promise of future payments to the new surrogate father, "in cash to avoid all the messy tax implications, you understand", the twins were residing in their first home within a Jewish tenement block off Lower East Side. The only stipulations Abel made were that the wife would give up her domestic cleaning job to look after the twins full-time and that he would have access to the twins whenever he saw fit to check on their welfare. Sadly for the twins this interest did not include their emotional welfare, rather an opportunity for him to check on how his money was being spent. After all they were not of his loins, so why should he feel love for them? And if it was a mother's love that was needed, the childless woman to whom they were entrusted was surely a sufficient proxy, even if her saloon bar glass washer of a husband would treat her roughly following his periods of excessive drinking.

The foster couple were both small and slight, the man called Asher, meaning, 'the fortunate', for indeed he was always finding enough money for drink and the woman,

Evelina, 'life-giving', for although barren did give of herself to the lives of the twins.

On Abel Cohen's instructions, the twins took the couple's surname of Schiff.

There was another issue that cemented Abel's rejection when he saw the twins for the first time. For whilst he had Middle Eastern curly black hair and dark brown eyes, the girl twin was blonde haired and green eyed, a genetic possibility he considered that could only have come from their mother's stock linked to his suspected cuckold's seed.

So apart from the hospital record of their birth, the twins' story would have had no further connection with their estranged birth mother and would live without shedding the tears that should have flowed from the knowledge of her last desperate cries of "My babies! My babies!", as they were wrenched from her unwilling grasp, were it not for Myriam's 'diamond' ring returned to Abel from the hospital along with her personal clothing.

Now holding the ring, which had come from his sideline interest in Herkimer 'diamonds' found within the dolostone in Herkimer County New York, Abel was very aware that Myriam's 'diamond' ring was not actually a diamond as the 'diamond' in the name suggested, but a crystal possessing the visual brilliance of the real thing because of its double-terminated quartz crystal shape of exceptional water-clear clarity.

But what was lost to Abel was that Myriam's wedding Herkimer 'diamond', in not having a diamond's indestructibility and so needing tender love and care to survive the possibility of being smashed to smithereens, perfectly reflected Abel's true feelings for his wife in the shattered brittleness of his love.

2

The twins were fraternal twins and although not similar in colouring, as she was fair skinned and blonde, he coffee coloured with brown hair, their green eyes and facial features bore a striking resemblance to each other. Later the boy would suffer from an overcrowded mouth as his second teeth appeared requiring him to have extractions and braces to overcome crooked teeth, whilst the girl, with her bigger jaw, would have perfect teeth. His face was without blemish. Hers had a small cross-shaped birthmark in the centre of her forehead that would fade over time.

They were named by the Schiffs: David 'the beloved one', and Ruth, the 'heartbreaker'. Their names, green eyes and characteristics may well have been just coincidence to the random selection of time, but for all anyone knew their DNA could have followed the bloodline legacy of Jesus suggested in *The Fisherman's Story*, with their names pondered by Jesus as he sat upon his Capernaum rock ,thinking that if his child was a boy he would call him David, and if a girl, Ruth, for the great book said Ruth begat Obed who begat Jesse who begat David, who was also the ancestor of Joseph who was the husband of Mary and would be the legal father of Jesus.

Born on Tuesday 25th September the twins fell under the sign of Libra, the symbol of the scales based on the scales of justice held by Themis, who as one of the oracles of Delphi became the goddess of divine justice, the inspiration for the modern depiction of Lady Justice, but which in the irony of fate would only tilt towards the rough end of it.

Being Tuesday's children, they were also 'full of grace', but then are not all the newly born babies full of grace, if not of opportunities?

By the time they were six the twins' characters were formed, and the pattern of their early lives established. Evelina was an attentive stepmother, if rather weak, allowing herself to be dictated by the will of the twins, or rather by Ruth's will in particular. David, with his sweet nature, had also become his sister's willing slave.

But now at six they were to be separated for the first time, by attending the different-sex schools for Borough Park's Hasidic families, a local Yeshiva school for boys for David, and a Bais Yaakov school for girls for Ruth, which Abel Cohen, who was part of Hasidic Judaism, said he would pay for.

It was over the next four years that the abuse of the twins by Asher took place.

You could say that it was the trusting nature of the twins' babyhood and their gentle early childhood handling by Evelina with her submissive attitude to Asher's participation at bath time, feeding and playtimes that contributed, or the natural beauty of the twins' faces and forms that seduced those that saw them smile and laugh and gambol, or the untimely death of their mother, or the decision of Abel Cohen to reject them and place them with strangers. You could say that it was the fault of God in allowing any or all of these. What you could not say was that it was the fault of the twins themselves. They were just pawns in the life of chance. What you could definitely say was that by the age of ten they were marked by the abuse. David had become withdrawn, submitting to the escalating demands of Asher, and whilst Ruth's rebelliousness had avoided them, they had both built up frustrated feelings for their stepfather, anticipated fear by David and bitter hatred by Ruth. For as much as Ruth strove to keep David with her, she was no match for Asher's cunning in the way he divided them for his private David time, encouraging Evelina to go out with Ruth during non-schooldays and suggesting Ruth and Evelina share drug-induced sleep together at night, leaving David alone for him to ply his grooming and flattery, granting his favours, performing his unpleasantnesses, and hear him say when he was finished, over and over,

"You dirty little Jew, you dirty little Jew."

This could have continued longer were it not for one fateful day when, following Abel Cohen's routine payment for the twins' upkeep to Evelina which was then requisitioned, as usual, by Asher, Asher rewarded himself with enough drink to cause him to fall down the stairs and break a leg. His subsequent confinement and restricted plaster-cast movement allowed Ruth to have more time with her brother, and eventually learn from him the detailed nature of Asher's unpleasantnesses.

And it was this information that Ruth wrested from David that would now bring about the reckoning and the retribution.

So as David wept his confession in her arms, Ruth planned her revenge.

"Look," she said holding him close and whispering into his ear, "I will make him stop. But you must do what I say, and promise me that you will never tell anyone what we have done."

And as he nodded his relief, she told him what she planned.

3

The police hammered on the tenement door early in the morning. It took several attempts before Evelina answered it with her dressing gown wrapped about her.

"Are you Mrs Schiff?" the sergeant asked.

Evelina nodded still trying to bring herself out of her deep sleep.

"Can you get Mr Schiff mam?"

The detective sergeant and the woman detective waited patiently whilst Evelina went to find him.

Shortly Evelina returned and said:

"He's not here. Why, has something happened?"

"Perhaps we could come in," the sergeant answered, and without waiting to be asked pushed past, leading the way into the front room. When the three of them were together again he continued:

"Where is your husband?"

"I don't know," Evelina replied. She was thinking *Where was he?* Asher had taken to sleeping in the front room. With his leg in plaster he would do his drinking there and then fall asleep, taking over the bedroom when she got up in the morning to attend to the children.

"Is there anyone else in the house?" the woman detective now asked.

"Just the twins," she said. Evelina felt faint.

"Do you mind if I check?" asked the sergeant, leaving his detective with Evelina. He was back shortly. Looking at the detective he said:

"They are both sound asleep. They didn't respond to my voice or touch. Seem drugged to me."

Looking at Evelina he asked:

"Have you given them something?"

Evelina shook her head.

"We all had hot milk before we went to bed. They were asleep almost immediately. I read for a bit and then turned my light out."

"What about your husband?" probed the sergeant.

"He doesn't like hot milk." She gave a nervous smile. "Prefers whisky, which he helps himself to, before sleeping it off in the lounge."

Evelina felt helpless.

"Has he been depressed recently?" This time it was the detective.

"Why, what's happening?" Evelina sank down into a chair.

"Just answer the question, mam," the detective pressed.

"I don't know about depressed, but he has been drinking for some time, which led to his falling down the stairs and breaking his leg." She looked pleadingly at the police.

The sergeant looked at the detective and nodded unperceptively.

The detective left the room and proceeded to call social services.

The sergeant pulled up a chair and sat facing Evelina. Leaning towards her, he said:

"You must prepare yourself. We think your husband has been killed. A man was found dead in the outside basement of this tenement block early this morning. He appeared to have fallen from the roof. He had a plaster cast on his right leg."

The woman detective re-entered the room.

"They're coming," she said to the sergeant.

Evelina sat in her chair white faced, shaking.

"Do you understand what I am saying?" the sergeant asked Evelina.

She nodded her head dumbly.

"Look," the sergeant went on, "we have called in the social services to take care of the twins whilst you come with us to identify the body. Are you up to this?"

Again she nodded.

"Let me see the twins," she blurted out, trying to get to her feet.

Gesturing to the woman detective he said:

"Jody will come with you, and help you get them up and give them some breakfast, and stay with them until the social arrive. You must then come with us. OK?"

As they left the room Jody asked Evelina the names of the twins.

"Ruth and David," she answered.

"Nice names," Jody said.

The sergeant followed them, but spent his time looking round the rooms of the tenement and then checking the staircase leading to the roof. He saw the baseball bat and the glove and the ball. He noticed the unlocked door onto the roof, and the signs in the dirt of something being dragged across the roof space towards the edge, and a piece of torn garment caught in the top rail. Perhaps where a body went over, he thought? And then there was the face-down fall of the man, and the damage to the back of his head.

"Get the forensics onto that," he mused aloud.

Despite the repeated denials of the stepmother, and the blank-faced silence of the twins, the facts spoke for themselves. There was clear DNA evidence that the baseball bat had been used to make the blow to the back of Mr Schiff's head, a blow that may or may not have killed him, with the bat returned to its place with the glove and ball, its handle wiped clean of prints. The piece of torn garment found on the rooftop rail had come from the jacket that Mr Schiff had been wearing. All of them agreed that Mr Schiff had been last seen in the sitting room drinking on the night of his death. Mrs Schiff had drunk her hot milk with the twins, and having settled them down, had gone straight to sleep until the police came knocking. She remembered it had been a particularly deep sleep. No, she had no idea why her husband would go onto the roof, or how he came to fall off it, particularly as he would have been drinking and had a leg in plaster. No, she didn't think he was suicidal and how he got a blow to the back of his head, she had no idea.

The police agreed privately that Mrs Schiff was an unlikely killer. Sure, she was intimidated by her husband, perhaps abused by him, but she lacked the mental and physical strength to carry out a murder and at the very least she would have needed help to manhandle the body. And she confirmed that the twins had heard nothing.

Now the ten-year-old twins were something different. They behaved as if they were one body, giving the same answers, telling the same story. The girl Ruth was obviously the leader, and whilst the boy David would look at her, she would clutch his hand and look defiantly at the questioner as if daring the questioner to challenge her. And when the twins were separated for questioning they would both refuse to give answers, saying only that they wanted to be with each other. And another thing, whilst they would cling to the stepmother whenever they were in her presence, they showed no emotion whenever their stepfather was mentioned. If anything there was a veil of hostility in the way they would look at each other and violently nod or shake their heads to any questions about him.

All except for when they were asked if they had loved their stepfather. Then they stood stock still, returning a mute stony look of hatred.

A physical examination of the twins gave its own story. The girl resisted strongly, and had to be restrained for the check to her virginity. The boy was quite docile and allowed himself to be handled, although unhappy at the examination to his anus, breaking down and crying when touched in this sensitive area. The social services agreed that, whilst the girl was probably untouched, there was evidence of interference to the boy. When questioned about this the stepmother did admit that there were times when the boy had been left alone in the company of the stepfather.

So the combined speculation of the police and the social services was that the boy had been abused, that the twins had lured the stepfather onto the roof, knocked him unconscious and, having dragged him to the rail, somehow managed to push him over to lie dead or dying in the basement below and that they had drugged their stepmother's hot milk before enticing the stepfather onto the roof.

Furthermore, that they were unlikely to get a confession from the twins, that the twins would need to be referred to a family support agency such as the Jewish Board of the Staten Island Family Services, that the twins' interests would be best served by remaining with the stepmother providing their estranged father Abel continued his financial support and that, subject to periodical reviews, this would remain in place until they were eighteen.

4

Life for the three Schiffs continued as before, but with the tension of the stepfather's presence now absent. In fact, it was quite noticeable to the trained therapists of the Staten Island Family Services allocated to the Schiffs that the mood of the twins had changed from withdrawn to outgoing and friendly. But however hard they tried, in their subtle way, to elicit what really had happened on that fateful night, they failed to unlock the suspected truth from the twins. What did become apparent was that they were happy together, and that Ruth was the dominant figure in decisions that affected daily meal choices, outings, schooling and friendships, in particular David's friends. Ruth had become her own surrogate mother to David, with Evelina now included in Ruth's family and controlled by Ruth in her role of conduit between the twins and Abel Cohen with regard to his allowances, additional special money requests, and their welfare news.

Any private enquiries from Abel to the stepmother would also, in the end, have to be dealt with by Ruth.

"Tell him such and such," Ruth would say.

Once when the stepmother had, on behalf of Abel Cohen, tried to broach what had happened on 'that night', Ruth had said, firmly looking her stepmother straight in the eye,

"Neither David nor I know anything. Like you, we were both asleep."

Relieved that she didn't have to face any disturbing information, and content to hide behind the will of Ruth, she answered:

"Yes of course dear. I will tell him that."

And another noticeable thing for the therapists was that the school results of the twins were now in the top five per cent, and as they grew into adulthood how good they were at sport, with the very competitive Ruth excelling at baseball, emulating the left-hand pitcher and slugger 'Babe Ruth', and David growing into 'gridiron football' as a formidable quarterback. Such was their sporting confidence that there was the memorable occasion when Ruth, similar in height to David, disguised with a helmet and shoulder pads took his place and ran onto the pitch during a game. Taking a snap pass she proceeded to run a quarterback sneak, throwing a pass for a touchdown before being knocked out by a defence tackle. Having been carried off the pitch, imagine the surprise of the attending medic when the helmet was removed revealing Ruth's blonde pigtails.

"Well I'll be doggarned!" said the medic. "I ain't never seen anything like this!"

5

At the age of sixteen, two things happened that would propel the twins into a totally unexpected future.

The first was that Abel Cohen wished to marry his long-time secretary Louise, or rather was forced into marriage by her contrived pregnancy.

Louise was aware of the arrangement for the twins, but apart from knowing where Abel's money-lending skeletons were buried, felt the need to protect her inheritance more securely and what better way than with a child?

"I know the pregnancy is unexpected," she told Abel, "and that I am a little on the old side, but I have always wanted to give you a child of your own. Now that the twins are almost old enough to look after themselves you should be able to reduce Evelina's allowance when she finds herself a job. And with the business doing well, you can afford to give us a more comfortable home."

The second and more pressing event was the unexpected death of Evelina from a heart attack, discovered by Ruth when she returned from class one day.

Realising the scrutiny their stepmother's death would bring upon them, she immediately contacted the emergency services and then Abel, asking him to notify David's school and the Staten Island Family Services. She deliberately did not touch any of Evelina's things, including her purse, made herself a mug of coffee and waited for David to join her when he returned home. She knew she was now fully in charge of managing her and David's future, and was determined that she would be viewed as trustworthy and responsible by the Staten Island Family Services to keep them together, come what may.

Following Jewish tradition, the burial of Evelina took place as quickly as possible, with the funeral service at the nearest burial ground. As Evelina had no known living relatives, the attendance was confined to the twins, Abel Cohen and a representative of Staten Island Family Services.

The responsibility for the twins now rested with Abel, and seeing them standing at the graveside, Ruth's blonde hair and green eyes brought back his negative feelings for them stronger than ever. Now he would not only have his own family to care for, but also the bastard children of his first wife, Myriam. It was time for him to free himself of their burdensome responsibility. After all he had been more than generous. He would speak to them, and tell them of his plan for them. And then they would be out of his life for good.

Several days later Abel sat with his estranged children and their social worker, and said:

"You know that I have provided for you and your stepparents ever since your mother Myriam died giving birth to you. And I did this despite knowing I am not your true father. You can see this for yourselves by looking in a mirror." He paused to give himself time to ease his slight conscience before continuing, "I have been more than generous. You have had a roof over your heads, food on the table and a good education. Had your stepmother lived I would have been prepared to continue this until you reached eighteen. But that's not what has happened. You cannot continue to live here on your own, and now that Louise is pregnant and I have my own family to take care of, you cannot live with me."

The twins said nothing and stared at him. Ruth took David's hand protectively and they continued to wait. The social worker also remained silent, as she knew what had already been agreed with Abel.

"So," he went on, "this is what I am prepared to do. Provided you will do what I say, and go where I want you to go without fuss, I will continue to provide for you both for the next two years. But it cannot be here, here in New York. I have decided that it must be in Israel on a kibbutz, where you can experience the kibbutz way of life, learning new skills and how to live in a community with other Jews. They will become your new family."

After a silence Ruth asked:

"When?"

"When I have received your passports and booked your flights," replied Abel. "I have been in touch with a kibbutz. They will meet you at the airport and take you to your new home. In the meantime you will remain in the care of the Staten Island Family Services."

He looked at the social worker who nodded her agreement.

"As long as we stay together we don't care where we go," said Ruth, squeezing her brother's hand.

Ruth had passed through her puberty, becoming a lovely young woman with strong legs, rounded hips below a narrow waist, and small breasts between wide shoulders. Her beautiful face with the large green eyes, framed by the extraordinary blonde hair was further transformed when she smiled, showing white even teeth framed by a full-lipped generous mouth. But how all this could change if she or her brother were threatened, when she would present a snarling, narrow-eyed, thin-lipped look that dared to fight. Flight was not in her vocabulary. And despite interest by both sexes she was still untouched, although not unaware of the attraction chemistry she possessed or that possessed by others.

David was temporally disfigured by his braces and the acne of puberty which, when finished with, would leave him with a near spitting image of his sister save for his skin colour, voice, young beard, thicker frame, and of course, her cross-shaped scar. He was also developing in confidence and could be relied upon to get things done. He was still a virgin and due to his abuse likely to remain so for some time. It would take the discovery of being 'in love' to unlock the door to his private, hidden sexual desire.

Their strength lay in their interdependency, she in her need to be allowed to be the first and to protect him, and he in his need for his sister to be the substitute for his mother's missing love.

So in their sixteenth year, the twins were to be referred for the third time, first to their stepparents, then to the Staten Island Family Services, and now to an unknown kibbutz community.

Strike
6

First there was the muezzin call.

Then the dogs howled, the cock crowed, the shell whistled, the explosion roared, the silence paused, people screamed and the ambulances wailed.

Many dead lay quiet.

Allah had not granted them their earthly life.

They will have to make do with Jannah, or a version of the afterlife that befits the extent of their goodness on earth, including all those that had denied the Prophet and would be damned.

But then Abdallah, whose name meant servant of Allah, did not care. He did not believe in a God. He believed in revenge. And today, with his radio transmitter, he had called down vengeance on all those that attended that Friday Adhan in the Great Mosque of Gaza.

Now he must escape the strip, so much more difficult that the strike had happened and every point of exit would be on full alert.

Much more difficult than his entry when his fake passport and ID papers, his Palestinian *thobe*, *keffiyeh* dress and headscarf, his electrolarynx or 'throat back' device, and the special reason for his visit that had eased him through.

But this didn't concern him. He just had to disappear.

And he did.

For Abdallah the act of disappearing was not difficult. He just had to become a woman. And this was easy because he really was one, and a woman of significance. Her name was Myriam, Myriam with the dyed brown hair and the dark brown contact lenses, Myriam who was a trained operative with ISIS.

Not the bloodthirsty Islamic State of Iraq and Syria ISIS, also called Daesh, a Salafi jihadist militant group that followed a fundamentalist Wahhabi doctrine of Sunni Islam, proclaiming itself a worldwide caliphate with religious, political and military authority over all Muslims worldwide, but the cold-blooded ISIS of the Israel Secret Intelligence Service.

The year was 2028.

7

Retaliation to the strike from the east was swift. A barrage of short-range Qassam rockets was fired into Israel.

Although they served their purpose of indiscriminate targeting of the general population and would be intercepted by Israeli's 'Iron Dome' defence system, this attack was designed to detract attention from the Palestinians' hidden motive of firing their recently acquired long-range missile at the Temple Mount, a hill located in the Old City of Jerusalem, one of the most important religious sites in the world venerated as a holy site for thousands of years by Judaism, Christianity and Islam.

This act of Islamist self-harm was breathtaking in its purpose. It desired a reaction from Israel that would be completely disproportionate. It sought a major retaliatory strike response that would be judged to be totally unreasonable to eyes of the world's Arab Jewish watchers.

8

The Knesset, located in Jerusalem's Givat Ram, was convened.

The Prime Minister of Israel spoke to the assembled.

"First, I must make it clear that our missile attack on the Great Mosque of Gaza was a justified response to Hamas taking yet another hostage of a valued member of our Israeli Defence Forces.

"Second, it is clear from the response of world leaders that, despite the Palestinian missile attack on the sacred Temple Mount that followed, Israel will be blamed for this outbreak of hostilities.

"Third, there is a burning desire by our Islamist neighbours for retribution against Israel, and itchy fingers twitch upon their triggers.

"Fourth, time is short for us to decide how to make a response that not only shows our impatience at becoming embroiled in tit for tat reactions, but at the same time demonstrates that we are ready to defend our sovereignty to the last drop of our blood.

"Fifth, I have a plan that I wish to discuss with our generals.

"Sixth, I ask that you put your trust in me, and allow me to act as I think fit, and as we have so little time, that you will give me your agreement now, by a simple show of hands."

The Prime Minister raised his hand and waited for their assent.

An earthquake in the magnitude of six on the Richter scale occurred in the Sinai Peninsula with its epicentre on the peak of Mount Sinai, the summit of which has a mosque used by Muslims, a Greek Orthodox chapel constructed on the ruins of a sixteenth-century church that encloses the rock considered to be the source for the biblical Tablets of Stone and Moses' cave, where Moses was said to have waited to receive the Ten Commandments.

Several things were unusual about the earthquake. Records of earthquakes in this area were not recorded in modern times. Apart from the seismic evidence, there was the displacement of a large volume of rock from the top of the 7,500-foot Mount Sinai and the distant sound of an explosion preceded by a ball of intense light, followed by a large expanding mushroom cloud.

So it was not long before the world's media were transmitting the story that a nuclear device had been detonated on Mount Sinai, and that it was equivalent to the sixteen-kiloton atomic bomb that had been dropped on Hiroshima.

9

Following the furious partisan responses of leaders in the Middle East, a knee-jerk movement to General Nuclear Response for a mutually assured destruction scenario with potential for all-out nuclear attack took place between the USA and Russia.

A scrambled call between their presidents followed.

"You need to exercise your influence with Egypt, Syria and Iran," said the US President, "and stop any possible retaliation towards Israel."

"And you need to sit on the permanent members of NATO," said the Russian, "and find out what is going on between Israel and Palestine. Has Israel gone rogue?"

"Just threatened," replied the American. "Now, as neither of us will be prepared to blink first," he continued, "will you agree to take your finger off the button while we find out? And let's both keep an eye on North Korea. There is so much at stake here."

"Perhaps the heads of the world's various faiths should be encouraged to meet to show solidarity for peace?" asked the Russian, always looking to lead.

"Sure," said the American. "Everything that acts to put a break on this situation has got to be helpful in slowing things down. You talk to your Patriarch, and the representative imams. I will get messages to the Chief Rabbi, and the heads of the Catholic and Anglican churches."

"What about Eastern faiths? Should they be included?" asked the Russian.

"Let us divide Asia up. I will do India, Pakistan, Bangladesh and Japan, you China, South Korea and the Malayan Peninsular. What do you say?" answered the American.

"What a mess!"

"You can say that again."

"There must be a better way to sort out our differences. The world is just too small a place for the problems in one place not to be felt everywhere. Social media makes sure of that," said the Russian.

"And with the skill of hackers, secrets are hard to keep." The American grinned down the phone. "Perhaps when this is all over we should have a drink together. I know what yours is!"

"I have bottle of the best green vodka waiting to convert you," the Russian laughed back.

"I will if you will try our best bourbon?"

"*Za zdaróvye*," said the Russian.

"You too buddy," said the American.

Truth to say, neither of them drank much.

But despite the hidden relationship between these two powerful men who shared a selfish, if different, path to power, it was still no laughing matter.

The world teetered on the brink.

10

At a secret place a meeting took place between the Pope:

His Holiness Bishop of Rome, Vicar of Jesus Christ, Successor of the Prince of the Apostles, Supreme Pontiff of the Universal Church, Primate of Italy, Archbishop and Metropolitan of the Roman Province, Sovereign of the Vatican City State, Servant of the servants of God, noted for his humility, emphasis on God's mercy, concern for the poor and commitment to interfaith dialogue, and with his less formal approach to the papacy choosing to reside in the Domus Sanctae Marthae guesthouse rather than the papal apartments of the Apostolic Palace

and the Archbishop of Canterbury:

the spiritual leader of the Anglican Communion recognised by convention as primus inter pares, or first among equals of all Anglican primates worldwide representing the evangelical tradition within Anglicanism, who resided at his official London Lambeth Palace residence on the south bank of the River Thames, a stone's throw from the Houses of Parliament on the opposite bank where, as a member of the House of Lords, he sat on the panel of the Parliamentary Commission on Banking Standards.

The climate of the meeting between the incumbent elderly Pope and the younger Archbishop was influenced by their pledges to press on towards the full reunification of the Roman Catholic and Anglican churches and heal the split between the two churches which had emerged in the convulsions of the Reformation five hundred years earlier, while still admitting that they "did not yet see" a solution to differences over the female clergy and sexuality.

An emissary of the Archbishop of Canterbury had been sent to the Pope to arrange the meeting about a most delicate but as yet unconfirmed subject, and at a mutually convenient venue. The invitation simply said that the topic would be introduced at the meeting, and that it would be of great interest to the Pope. The Archbishop had been quite specific as to the restricted attendance at this meeting when he had requested that it would be just between the two of them, and for the need for absolute secrecy on the topic when it was disclosed.

When the room had been swept for bugs and they were locked in, comfortably supplied with light refreshments, and they had completed their pleasantries, the Archbishop said:

"My intention for our meeting was that there would be one item for discussion. Now with the recent events in the Middle East and the request by the Russian and American presidents to participate in a gathering of religious leaders to influence a peaceful resolution to the troubles, there must now be two. But, because the two items are in a way connected, with your permission I would like to lead with my intended item, and follow it with this latest unintended one."

He looked at the Pope, who nodded.

"Thank you. I wish to discuss 'the definition of God'."

The Archbishop allowed the Pope time to register this before continuing,

"You will be aware from the report by the Pew Research Center, that as of 2010, Christianity was the world's largest religion with an estimated 2.2 billion adherents, nearly a third of the 6.9 billion people on Earth, with Islam second with 1.6 billion. Further, because Muslim populations are concentrated in some of the fastest-growing parts of the world, as the world's population rises by the middle of this century Islam could grow more than twice as fast as Christianity, ultimately equalling Christianity worldwide before possibly continuing to overtake Christianity by 2070. Here I am not considering the impact of hidden growth opportunities from 'silent' believers in large population countries, such as China. So, despite the overall belief in God increasing with the growth of populations, UK Christian adherents, measured by attendance now below a million, may continue to fall, as they are less likely to be affected by population growth. So perhaps the reason for this decline should be considered."

Looking at the Pope he paused to let him digest his opening statement and then went on:

"The reason could be that despite the search for answers to the big questions of universal fairness and justice, an increasingly secular world in the West is rejecting religion because it is failing to inspire people in a traditional belief in God to bring this about. Further, that the UK trend could be taken as a model for all Christian growth or the lack of it, as negative Western values about religion are spread and absorbed worldwide."

He saw the Pope's eyebrows rise slightly.

"So whilst the essential income to do our Church's work may remain sufficient at present through tax-efficient gift aid, modern management cost-control measures and asset sales, its future income from believers could be at risk, continuing to decline with its membership unless steps are taken to address the issue of an acceptance in God, that whilst still recognising that Christ's 'good' teachings remain relevant, Christ's association with the historical image of a God in a heaven may not. And if the combined wealth from Christianity in its billions were to be considered by believers, questions could be asked as to its value for money in carrying out its good works."

He was watching the Pope closely now for his reaction, but saw he was happy to see where his argument went, which would now go beyond the point of no return. He took a breath.

"Therefore, consideration should be given to a redefinition of 'God' that retains the power to inspire and restrain human nature, without the need for a link to the abstract nature of God and the Devil, and the blind faith required to believe in them. This redefinition could also help to attract other faiths' believers, influenced by secular thinking encouraged by education and the dissemination of information through the Web and social media, to consider a Christian message that can satisfy a present need without first acceptance, by an act of faith, of an invisible God."

He waited for the Pope to speak.

"Is this a crisis in your faith?" the Pope finally asked.

When he heard this question, inferring the continuance of their conversation, the Archbishop knew that the Rubicon, the Pope's Italian frontier river, had been crossed, so he continued.

"What I believe is not germane. The heart of the problem of blind faith is that it competes with a science that aims to explain everything to its roots, against a church that needs to grow a willing congregation that will continue, despite the question of its relevance in a world that demands greater economic equality of choice and share in the world's riches."

"So, do you have a suggestion?" asked the Pope carefully.

The Archbishop answered:

"I do. The starting point would be to change the word God, so that its meaning is more tangible and then redefine it. In English, God could become 'good'. The abstract and remote upper case 'G' would be replaced by a common, of-the-people lower case 'g', and the single absolute and omnipotent 'o' replaced by the expanding double 'o' symbolizing its power to resemble the sign of infinity. The definition of 'good' would be 'having the right qualities', and be 'adequate to the fair goals aspired' in an ever-changing world, perhaps 'not without end', but towards a 'means to an end'."

He paused.

"To ensure we have a common understanding of the symbol; may I digress here?"

The Pope nodded, with a half-smile playing on his lips.

Paraphrasing from a source of research, the Archbishop said, "The infinity symbol, sometimes called the lemniscate, is a mathematical symbol representing the concept of infinity introduced into mathematical literature by John Wallis in 1655, in his *De sectionibus conicis*. Although the reason for explaining his choice of this symbol is not clear, it has been conjectured to be a variant form of the Roman numeral for 1,000, used to mean 'many', or of the Greek letter omega, the word omega literally meaning 'great O' which, as you will know, is the last letter in the Greek alphabet. Interestingly its shape of a sideways figure eight appears in the cross of Saint

Boniface, wrapped around the bars of a Latin cross. The Swiss-born Leonhard Euler, a giant of eighteenth-century mathematics, used an open variant of the symbol to denote his *absolutus infinitus*. And in mathematics, the infinity symbol is used more often to represent a potential infinity, rather than an actually infinite quantity, where the variable grows arbitrarily large towards infinity rather than taking an infinite value."

He glanced at his notes.

"May I go on?"

"You may as well finish," said the Pope dryly, used to the extent of detail that the Archbishop offered when making his points.

"In areas other than mathematics, the infinity symbol may take on other related meanings. For instance, it has been used in bookbinding to indicate that a book is printed on acid-free paper and will therefore be long-lasting. The infinity symbol also appears on several cards of the Rider Waite tarot deck. In modern mysticism, the infinity symbol has become identified with a variation of the ouroboros, an ancient image of a snake eating its own tail that has also come to symbolize the infinite with the ouroboros sometimes drawn in figure-eight form to reflect this identification. The well-known shape and meaning of the infinity symbol has made it a common typographic element of graphic design. For instance, the Métis flag, first used by *Métis* resistance fighters in Canada before the 1816 Battle of Seven Oaks, where its horizontal figure of eight symbol on the flag represents the faith that the *Métis* culture shall live on forever. In the works of Vladimir Nabokov, including *Pale Fire* with its poem explicitly referring to 'the miracle of the lemniscate', the figure-eight shape is used symbolically to refer to the Möbius strip, a surface with only one side when embedded in three-dimensional Euclidean space and only one boundary with the mathematical property of being non-orientable. In modern commerce, corporate logos featuring this symbol have been used, including Room for PlayStation Portable, Microsoft Visual Studio, Fujitsu, and CoorsTek. Finally, the symbol is encoded in Unicode. So, you see, the symbol has a history and recognisable present meanings which would help in its acceptability as a God substitute."

"Yes, yes, yes, I am trying to follow you, but I am not sure how this helps," said the Pope.

"Well," said the Archbishop, "it is a matter of shifting from one form of description of God as the absolute, to another of the potential of infinite good, giving consideration to the idea that all past good works traditionally credited to God could now be explained and accepted as a naturally evolving Darwinian expression of human talent, work and benevolence developing over time, with the inspirational motive to do the good works already inherent in the genes, as is the beauty of nature waiting in the bud for its time to flower, combining to fill the well of goodness for the benefit of all mankind."

"Do I infer that that you consider God comes from the imagination of man?" asked the Pope. "And that despite human being's history of cruelty and oppression over his fellow, human beings can be trusted to self-manage behaviour to do good?"

"Yes," the Archbishop answered. "I am suggesting that it is in human beings' self-interest to do good, however small, and with each small good combining to replenish the well of goodness. I call it 'The Practical Philosophy of Incremental Goodness'. Of course, the 'well of goodness' may also receive the acid poison of hate, and have to have it neutralised with an alkaline of love. That would be our role, we that perform the role of religious practice."

The Pope took a deep breath.

"There will great resistance to this change for fear of the loss of religious power and wealth, even if the sense of it is in our hearts."

"It is easier for a camel to go through the eye of a needle than for a rich man to enter the kingdom of God," sighed the Archbishop.

The Pope reflected on this, grappling with the implications. Finally, he said:

"All right, so whilst I follow your arguments around the word 'good', is this not lost when 'good' is translated into other languages, *bene* in Italian, *bien* in French, *gut* in German etc?" queried the Pope.

The Archbishop replied:

"If all the 'good' word substitutes for God take on the same meaning and qualities, then a common understanding of what God as 'good' means could over time be achieved."

"I wonder at how the power of 'good' would produce the same results as 'God' and the 'Devil' in controlling the actions of people, and in influencing the volume of their gifts?" the Pope mused. "I wonder at how the message that 'God' equals 'good' could be conveyed and then presented to the faithful? I wonder at the reaction of Islam to Christendom's denial of the traditional God, and the consequence to their increasing membership?"

He paused again.

"But I do accept that serious consideration needs to be given to the prospect of a greater and greater loss of faith in

Christianity's historic understanding of God driven by fear and poverty, and that without catastrophic events to frighten people or inexplicable miracles to draw them, there will be questions asked leading to doubt and the erosion of traditional faith."

"The clock is ticking," said the Archbishop, "and if you are in agreement that something needs to be done, the sooner a start is made to consider this argument, the better prepared we will be to protect Christ's message and build back his following."

The Pope said, "Let us agree a code word for this subject that we can use to alert the other when further communication is required on this particular matter."

"What about 'good year'?" the Archbishop asked, "for do we not live in the perpetual hope that every year will be a good year for humanity, even if the unpredictable nature of the air, the water, the earth and disease may still conspire to harm mankind?"

"Why not, it is also a tyre, round, full of air and when inflated bounces back no matter what the condition of the road it travels," said the Pope.

At which they both laughed.

"And now, about the second item?" the Pope queried.

"Well," answered the Archbishop, "perhaps we should take council, and arrange a separate meeting when things are a bit clearer as to the responses from our fellow religious leaders to the invitation and then what will be involved and the part we will be required to play."

They nodded and smiled at each other as they parted, silently agreeing that the first would take time, whilst the second would not wait.

Invitation
11

Despite the presence of 'The World Council of Religious Leaders', an independent body that existed to bring religious groups to support the work of the United Nations in a common quest for peace, organising a convocation of the world's spiritual leaders was easier said than done.

First, there was the framing of the message of intent, to be conveyed to the five main religious groups of Buddhism, Christianity, Islam, Judaism and Unitarianism that would not offend them, or presume that any of the separate religions were not in themselves up to the job of sorting out the problem of achieving world peace.

Second, there was the logistics of getting everyone together in one place on a particular day, and attending to their individual securities, diets and sleeping arrangements.

And third, there was the getting of a common agreement to the stated outcome of the convocation.

The first and the third were linked of course. Start with a goal everyone could accept and the agreement should follow.

The American President had canvassed opinion within Christendom, and the Pope had been suggested as a contact starting point to represent Christianity. That in turn had brought in the Archbishop of Canterbury, and from the Archbishop had come the idea for a common definition on the meaning of God that suggested all religions' belief should be centred in goodness.

The invitation was addressed to the most senior title within each religious denomination, hence forth referred to as the Representative:

Dear Representative.

In the knowledge that a nuclear bomb has been detonated on Mount Sinai, and that the American and Russian nuclear weapons have been placed on a high state of readiness, you are invited to attend a meeting of religious leaders to present a unified message to world leaders calling for them to restrain from mutual destruction. To underline unity, you are asked to consider presenting a common definition of the meaning of 'God' that is centred in the English meaning of goodness. Implicit in the definition of goodness is 'that which does no harm'. This focus on a message of goodness is to replace all partisan forms of prayer and to be conveyed as a simple human entreaty from one human being to another, using the communication channels of each faith from its leadership to its followers to do so.

Details of the place and timing of the meeting will be given to each of the invited representatives in a personal way, using the code word 'goodyear' to verify the sender.

May the kindness of humanity offered to you in this message be received by you with an open heart.

Signed
Under the joint offices of the Pope and the Archbishop of Canterbury

The work collating the list of potential representatives, with contact addresses and telephone numbers and the submission of the invitations was managed and coordinated by an Anglican bishop and a Roman Catholic cardinal, working from a specially chosen office within the Vatican, supported with selected telephonists and typists. The funds to cover the administration of the office, travel and accommodation arrangements for the representatives would be drawn from an account set up in the Vatican Bank located in the Tower of Nicolas V, and in turn made available from deposits received from the office of the President of the United States of America.

Because of the urgency in assembling the representatives of the religious denominations, a second message was sent forty-eight hours later. It served to detail the place and timing of the convocation, which would be fourteen days hence within the Vatican City walls in Rome, where accommodation, meals, medical support and security could be assured, and certain points of procedure detailed that would satisfy the idea of equivalence for the different religious forms and presentations grouped together in one place at one time.

The arrangements included special carriages to be available on trains and seats on helicopter flights, to ferry representatives directly into the Vatican City Railway Station and Heliport. Individual bedrooms would be provided in the five-storey 106 suite Domus Sancatae Marthae guest house, with a secure meeting area in the Apostolic Palace complete with dedicated toilets and self-service catering facilities. The Pope would relocate to his papal apartments within the Apostolic Palace together with the invited Archbishop of Canterbury. Each representative would be allocated a member of the Vatican staff to act as a guide and mentor, and a personal bodyguard escort from the Vatican's Swiss Guards. The guest house kitchen would cater for any specified dietary requirement, and a medical team would be on standby in case of a medical emergency. There would be an office with secretarial support, and private booths for restricted telephone and email use.

The language to be used would be English, and so it was imperative that the representative sent had a full command and understanding of the English language. It also needed to be clear that the representative chosen would represent, and could speak for, all the countries that came within the reach of the faith represented.

The particular point of procedure proposed to achieve equivalence was that all representatives, including the Pope and Archbishop of Canterbury, would wear similar golden-coloured gowns whilst they attended the meetings. Outside of the meetings each representative would be free within the confines of the Vatican to enjoy its gardens, courtyards, colleges, churches, chapels, the Vatican Radio, Lourdes Grotto, Belvedere Casino, the Tower of the Winds and the Borgia Tower, St Peter's Basilica, etc. wearing the clothes of their choice.

Other points were that there would be no identification badges, and that lots would be draw to provide the sequence number to be placed on the meeting table for each representative to speak in their turn, if they wished. The meeting would be chaired by an atheist with impeccable credentials, who would play no part other than to advise on the order of speakers, their time taken, the proposed breaks required, and the use of the single telephone. No mobiles would be allowed. The time allocated would be approximately five minutes per speaker, progressing from one speaker to the next in a continuum until it was clear that there was nothing further required to be said.

The presentations on the first day would include the meaning of God as it appeared to each of the representatives. The second day would hear suggestions for the form of words to be used and posted onto whiteboards by the chairman with, on the third day, the final agreed text to be produced as a written proclamation signed by every representative also posted on the whiteboards and then presented to the press for broadcasting to the world.

The swept and secure meeting room would be locked and guarded from the outside, and no one allowed to enter or to leave during the meeting period, other than the representatives and the chairman.

A further two days following the three would be available for any representative who wished to remain longer to meet and converse with other delegates.

Every detail was reviewed by a group of skilled intelligence operatives carefully selected from the FVEY intelligence alliance, which now included Ruth Schiff.

The second message was introduced by the code word 'goodyear' and ended, as with the first with:

May the kindness of humanity offered to you in this message be received by each of you with an open heart.

Kibbutzniks
12

Ruth and David Schiff became kibbutzniks, fitting into the collective community ideals of a modern form of the so-called renewing kibbutz model, whereby each member's income consisted of their individual income from their kibbutz work and sometimes income from other non-kibbutz sources. They had to learn the concept of kibbutz sharing, coming together at mealtimes in the communal dining hall. This was not difficult between the two of them, but whilst David was open and generous minded to a fault, Ruth found it difficult to give up any extra income she earned.

After a period of adjustment, they were assessed for their suitability for work and further education. David, with his easy non-confrontational manner fitted into the physical labour duties on the kibbutz, whilst Ruth was quickly deduced to be questioning and assertive, singled out for further education and marked for university.

They were not required to sleep in male and female designated areas and so shared a room together, that is until David fell in love with Hannah.

Hannah was from a Black Hebrew group that came to Israel from the US in the nineties, and as a result of being orphaned at the age of three by the death of her parents in a car crash, adopted by the liberal-minded Kibbutz in 2003 when Black Hebrews were granted permanent resident status. Because of her mixed blood she was honey-coloured and grew up to be a pretty brown-eyed curly haired soft curvaceous girl, and the minute she set eyes on David, he had no chance. She used all of her female guile to capture his attention, including the delights of her full willing mouth, soft rounded breasts, and the irresistible, but forbidden, access to the secret hidden depths of her silky supple thighs.

The meeting of Hannah and David came about at the twins' seventeenth birthday party, when Hannah had found David standing alone transfixed by the unfamiliar array of Jewish food that had been specially prepared for them, and which included an array of pickles, chopped herring, borscht, golden chicken soup, fish patties, bagels with cream cheese, stuffed cabbage peppers and vine leaves, whitefish, roasted meat, Challah bread, noodle kugel, strudel, filled cookies with black poppy seed paste, fruit compote, fried doughnuts, assorted fruit preserves, figs, dates, grapes, wine with honey, and local beer.

She had looked at him, came close enough for him to be aware of her, then, slipping her hand into his led him back into the happy dancing and singing throng, where in the joyous milling two like minds and hearts were joined in the exquisite sensation of first love.

But there was a problem. The irresistible offer of her soft arms came at a price, for another of her suitors, a tall strong young man called Isaac, who had been brought up on the same kibbutz with Hannah, had grown up with her to think that he would have first call on her charms. And he didn't like his displacement one little bit, not holding back his seething resentment by telling David exactly what he thought of him, David, and of David's misplaced entitlement to his, Isaac's, long-term girlfriend.

But David's love of Hannah blinded him to the danger of his situation. In fact, he went out of his way to placate the injured feelings of Isaac, thereby exacerbating the hatred Isaac felt for him.

As Isaac stood in stony-faced silence David said to him as reasonably as he could:

"I understand how hurt you must feel, and if there was any way I could spare you, I would. But you must see how much Hannah and I love each other. That we are meant for each other, that we are soulmates. That the love we share is right, and so whatever love you thought you had with Hannah cannot possibly compare with ours. The proof is that Hannah does not love you in that way anymore. Of course, she still wants to be friends with you, as I do, and we are both sure you will get over her and in time find the right person just for you." Smiling at Isaac, he insisted, "You will you know; time really is such a great healer."

So, as Ruth struggled to come to terms with her displacement by Hannah for David's attention, Isaac was plotting revenge for his replacement by David for Hannah's favours, revenge with consequences that would bring Ruth to the attention of the Mossad.

It was one evening when David, returning late from a day in the orange grove and content with the fruits of his labour, was thinking of the presence of Hannah waiting for him, her joyous smile at the sight of him, how she would rush at him, hug him and lead him to his shower, when, having washed away the day's sweat, they would find a comfortable chair for him to sit in, taking her onto his lap, his arms about her, hers about his neck, their whisperings intermingled with embraces and endless kisses, their need for each other building with the contact movement of her wriggling hips on his pushing groin when at last she would fend off his straying hand and push herself away firmly saying "no" for the umpteenth time, leaving them still desperately wanting (except for that one time when the chair selected was without arms and Hannah had sat facing David with her legs on either side of his, and she had led their hips in a thrusting frenzied sexual dance, before she gasped out her climax into his ear as he burst forth leaving two secret damp patches in their clothing); then ravenous, run together to the dining hall for whatever food remained to delight them and later walk together hand in hand speaking in soft tones of the day that had been and of the days that were yet to come, that the blow took him suddenly and unexpectedly.

They found him unconscious, and carried him back to the sanatorium. As his clothes were removed it was clear that, that having taken a blow to the head, he had fallen onto his front and then been given a kicking to his side and face. His nose was smashed and his jaw broken.

But although he would lose his spleen that he could live without if he was careful, his liver compensating for its loss, and his nose could be remodelled and his jaw wired, he would recover and, David being David, he would not bear a grudge.

Hannah had raised the alarm when he failed to join her at their evening rendezvous. Such was David's regularity and dependability in meeting up with Hannah, and displaying their love birds' presence, there was no hesitation in other kibbutzniks responding to her anxious concerns on his whereabouts, and for volunteers to join her in going to find him.

So whilst Hannah fretted about David and went with him to the hospital, senior kibbutz members discussed the assault, and knowing the background to the relationship between David and Hannah, the name of the jilted probable culprit, Isaac, was soon suggested.

The police were called.

Ruth meanwhile wasted no time in confronting Isaac who had appeared earlier, and was now standing around in his outdoor clothes and boots, pretending his innocence and concern.

Standing close to him with her eyes boring up into his, she said, spitting her words into his face:

"Did you do this?"

He stood looking at her, glaring back.

"No," he said, "but he had it coming to him."

What happened next would be run in the *Jewish Chronicle* and become part of kibbutz folklore.

13

The *Jewish Chronicle* was on the reading list of a *katsa* field intelligence officer of the Mossad, and it was in its latest copy that the front-page picture of a beautiful blonde young woman as much as the article that followed that caught his attention with the intriguing headline of:

LOVE SPAT ON THE KIBBUTZ

In an extraordinary twist of events a suspected lovelorn man accused of a revenge attack on a rival is floored by the rival's twin sister. Twins Ruth and David Schiff, recent newcomers to their kibbutz became entangled with a longstanding childhood couple Hannah Weiz and Isaac Kranz. Despite Hannah and Isaac growing up together on the kibbutz, it was love at first sight for Hannah and David, leaving Isaac out in the cold. Unable to stand being jilted, Isaac has been accused of attacking David, putting him in hospital with concussion, flattened nose, busted jaw and severe bruising from a kicking to his torso. With the injured David unable to respond at the time, his sister confronted Isaac, challenged him, then with a one-two punch knocks him out cold, the first blow an uppercut that weakened his knees, the second a left cross that struck his temple on his way down. Now Ruth has joined her brother in hospital with both of her hands damaged. With no witnesses to David's attack, and no charges brought by David against Isaac, the suspicions against him are not being pursued. Despite many witnesses to Ruth's retaliation, charges have also not been brought against her. It seems that there is general agreement that rough justice has been served, and with Isaac leaving the kibbutz, David and Hannah continue to be an item.

Ruth said, "I don't regret knocking his [Isaac's] lights out. I would do it again. I will always stand up for my brother."

But while David and Hannah have no plans to leave the kibbutz Ruth, who has been assessed by the elders as exceptionally intelligent and very athletic, wants to continue her education at a science- and engineering-based university.

There shouldn't be any shortage of offers.

The *katsa* intelligence officer for the Mossad filed the copy. *No harm in doing an in-depth background check on the girl,* he thought. *We need to keep an eye on this one as a possible future recruit.*

14

The Mossad is Israel's intelligence agency specialising in collecting and analyzing information, which is then provided to the Prime Minister and his cabinet to aid in their decision making.

Their motto, based on Proverbs 11:14, is:

Where there is no guidance, a nation falls, but in an abundance of counsellors there is safety.

Referring to itself as the Israel Secret Intelligence Service or ISIS, it defines its mission as, 'collecting information, analyzing intelligence and performing special covert operations beyond Israel's borders.'

Coming into existence in 1949 its image and reputation has become that of a deadly organization involved with the liquidation of its enemies, with a number of successfully targeted assassinations in which terrorists, nuclear scientists and Nazi War criminals have been killed.

The Mossad's job description of a *katsa*, a Hebrew acronym for a 'collection office' is, as in other intelligence services, a person referred to as 'case officer' or 'handler of agents', its male and female officers indispensable to the agency's fieldwork of spotting, approaching, recruiting, running, defending and babysitting the agents required to provide information.

These officers belong to a department known as Tsomet or Junction.

A second operational department is Keshet or Bow, which is in charge of target surveillance as well as break-ins into places of interest.

A third department is Caesarea, which encompasses the Mossad's most specialised field agents. These are the operatives who infiltrate enemy countries such as Syria, Lebanon and, the most dangerous, Iran. Within this department is Kidon or Bayonet, whose agents carry out select operations where violence and wet work may be necessary.

If selected, a candidate must go through and pass the Mossad training academy, the Midrasha, located near the town of Herzliya, which also happens to be the official summer residence of Israeli's Prime Minister. There, for approximately three years, trainees are taught the tradecraft of intelligence gathering. The main priority of the training is to teach *katsas* how to find, recruit and cultivate agents, including how to clandestinely communicate with them. They also learn how to avoid being the subject of foreign counter-intelligence, by avoiding car and foot surveillance, by killing, and by preventing foreign agents from creating traps at meetings. Once training is completed, trainees will spend an apprenticeship period working on varying projects before becoming fully fledged *katsas*.

And so, it was on a hunch that she would excel at 'special' assignments as a *katsa* officer that led to Ruth Schiff being picked for future training and development.

Ruth, or Myriam, the name of her deceased mother she had chosen to be called whilst operational, sat opposite her handler, his question lying suspended in the air between them.

"Have you any other secrets about your past that you would like to tell me?"

Ruth flushed. Her path to this moment had been an emotional one. It had involved the 'accidental' meeting with her handler Peter, during her second semester at the Weizmann Institute of Science, and the intense affair that followed, during which she had revealed many of her most intimate inner thoughts, but not her secret of secrets about Asher which she shared with her brother and expected to take to her grave.

Her hesitation before she answered "No" gave her away.

Peter smiled at her.

"You have nothing to be afraid of from me," he said.

Does he suspect me over Asher's death? He must know something, she thought. They will have done their checks.

"No," she said again, regaining her composure.

He seemed satisfied with this.

She understands the game, he thought. *She knows how to lie.*

"Let's leave things there for now, and continue tomorrow," he said.

But whilst Ruth's love affair with Peter would fade for her in time and be replaced, Peter could not get over being the first with Ruth, and the intense feelings he felt for his beautiful young virgin recruit remained, spoiling him, despite other affairs, in finding his 'one and only'.

15

Peter Chorack was born in Israel in 1993.

He was the only son of Simon and Ania Chorack whose Polish Jewish parents had fled Germany in November 1938 following *Kristallnacht*, 'Crystal Night' or *Reichskristallnacht*, 'the Night of Broken Glass', when a pogrom against Jews throughout Nazi Germany was carried out by Sturmabteilung paramilitary forces and German civilians. The name *Kristallnacht* comes from the shards of broken glass that littered the streets after the windows of Jewish-owned homes, stores, hospitals, schools and synagogues were smashed and ransacked.

In the preceding August, the German authorities had announced that residence permits for foreigners were being cancelled and would have to be renewed. On 28 October in the so-called *Polenaktion* more than 12,000 Polish-born Jews, among them the philosopher and theologian Rabbi Abraham Joshua Heschel and future literary critic Marcel Reich-Ranicki were expelled from Germany on Hitler's orders. They were ordered to leave their homes in a single night and allowed only one suitcase per person to carry their belongings. As they were driven out their remaining possessions were seized as loot by the Nazi authorities and their neighbours.

The deportees were taken to railway stations and put on trains to the Polish border, where Polish border guards sent them back into Germany. This stalemate continued for days in the pouring rain, with the Jews marching without food or shelter between the borders. Four thousand were eventually granted entry, the remaining 8,000 forced to wait.

A British newspaper told its readers that "*hundreds are reported to be lying about, penniless and deserted, in little villages along the frontier near where they had been driven out by the Gestapo and left. Conditions in the refugee camps were so bad that some actually tried to escape back into Germany and were shot.*"

Peter would be formed by the passed-down stories from his grandparents who were among the four thousand granted entries into Poland and would ultimately escape to Israel.

There was also the escape from the concentration camp Treblinka in August 1943, by men of his grandfather's age and of one in particular with a similar name, and how that story of hopeless desperation and extraordinary heroism, the report of which he read again and again, produced in him a mixture of burning rage at man's inhumanity to man and weeping triumphalism from the meaning of courage and sacrifice that had to be endured by events of the Holocaust. All of this would combine with Peter Chorack's intelligence, aptitude for languages, physical prowess and vengeful attitude as he preceded Ruth in joining the Mossad.

This is what he had learned from the records of Treblinka. *Treblinka was an extermination camp built by Nazi Germany in occupied Poland during World War II. It was located in a forest north-east of Warsaw, two and a half miles south of the Treblinka train station in what is now the Masovian Voivodeship.*

The camp operated between 23 July 1942 and 19 October 1943 as part of Operation Reinhard, the deadliest phase of the Final Solution during which it is estimated that between 700,000 and 900,000 Jews were killed in its gas chambers, along with 2,000 Romani people. More Jews were killed at Treblinka than at any other Nazi extermination camp apart from Auschwitz. Managed by the German SS and Trawnikis, also known as Hiwi guards, the auxiliary police enlisted from Soviet POW camps to assist the Germans, the camp consisted of two separate units:

Treblinka I, a forced-labour camp or Arbeitslager, whose prisoners worked in the gravel pit irrigation area, and in the forest cutting the wood to fuel the crematoria, resulting in more than half of its 20,000 inmates dying from summary executions, hunger, disease and mistreatment, between 1941 and 1944.

Treblinka II, an extermination camp or Vernichtungslager where a small number of men who were not killed immediately upon arrival became its Jewish slave-labour units called Sonderkommandos, and were forced to bury the victims' bodies in mass graves, later to be exhumed in 1943 and cremated on large open-air pyres along with the bodies of new victims.

The killing process at Treblinka differed from the method used at Auschwitz and Majdanek, where the poison gas Zyklon B (hydrogen cyanide) was used. In fact, after visiting Treblinka on a guided tour, Auschwitz commandant Rudolf Höss concluded that using cyanide at his camp was superior to the exhaust gas used at Treblinka, Sobibór, and Bełżec, where the victims were considered dead after thirty minutes' silence in the chambers from suffocation and carbon monoxide poisoning.

According to Jankiel Wiernik, who survived the 1943 prisoner uprising and escaped, when the doors of the gas chambers had been opened, the bodies of the dead were standing and kneeling rather than lying down, due to the severe overcrowding. Dead mothers embraced the bodies of their children. Prisoners who worked in the Sonderkommandos later testified that the dead frequently let out a last gasp of air when they were extracted from the chambers. Some victims showed signs of life during the disposal of the corpses, but the guards routinely refused to react.

Gassing operations at Treblinka II ended in October 1943 following a revolt by the Sonderkommandos in early August. Several SS Hiwi guards were killed and 200 prisoners escaped from the camp, where almost a hundred survived the subsequent chase.

What happened was, in early 1943, an underground Jewish resistance organisation was formed at Treblinka with the goal of seizing control of the camp and escaping to freedom. The planned revolt was preceded by a period of secret preparations. The clandestine unit was first organised by a former Jewish captain of the Polish Army, Dr Julian Chorążycki, who was described by fellow plotter Samuel Rajzman as noble and essential to the action. His organising committee included Zelomir Bloch, Rudolf Masaryk, Marceli Galewski, Samuel Rajzman, Dr Irena (Irka) Lewkowska, Leon Haberman, Hershl (Henry) Sperling from Częstochowa, and *others. Chorążycki, who treated German patients, killed himself with poison on 19 April 1943 when faced with imminent capture so that the Germans could not discover the plot through torture. The next leader was another former Polish Army officer, Dr Berek Lajcher who had arrived on 1 May.*

The uprising was launched on the hot summer day of 2 August 1943, a Monday and regular day of rest from gassing, when a group of Germans and forty Ukrainians drove off to the River Bug to swim.

The conspirators silently unlocked the door to the arsenal near the train tracks, with a key that had been duplicated earlier. They stole rifles, hand grenades and several pistols, and delivered them in a cart to the gravel work detail. At three forty-five p.m. seven hundred Jews launched an insurgency that lasted for thirty minutes. They set buildings ablaze, exploded a tank of petrol, and set fire to the surrounding structures.

A group of armed Jews attacked the main gate, and others attempted to climb the fence. Machine-gun fire from about twenty-five Germans and sixty Ukrainian Trawnikis resulted in near-total slaughter. Lajcher was killed along with most of the insurgents. About two hundred Jews escaped from the camp. Half of them were killed after a chase in cars and on horses. The Jews did not cut the phone wires, so hundreds of German reinforcements were called in from four different towns and set up roadblocks along the way.

Partisans of the Armia Krajowa, the Polish Home Army, transported some of the surviving escapees across the river, and others like Sperling ran nineteen miles to be helped and fed by Polish villagers.

Of those who broke through, around seventy are known to have survived until the end of the war, including the future authors of published Treblinka memoirs, Richard Glazar, Chil Rajchman, Jankiel Wiernik, and Samuel Willenberg. Among the Jewish prisoners who escaped after setting fire to the camp, were two nineteen-year-olds, Samuel Willenberg and Kalman Taigman, who had both arrived at Treblinka in 1942 and had been forced to work there under pain of death.

Taigman died in 2012 and Willenberg in 2016.

Taigman described his experience. "It was hell, absolutely hell. A normal man cannot imagine how a living person could have lived through it. The killers were natural-born killers who, without a trace of remorse, murdered everything."

Willenberg and Taigman migrated to Israel after the War and devoted their last years to retelling the story of Treblinka.

Escapees Hershl Sperling and Richard Glazar both suffered from survivor guilt syndrome and eventually killed themselves.

16

Ever since the *Jewish Chronicle*'s piece about her, Ruth's path to her assessment meeting with Peter had been predictable. Not to her, of course. Her vision of her future was measured in the individual steps it took for her to decide on a science degree at the Weizmann and, with her natural aptitude for languages, courses in the 'local' languages of Hebrew, Yiddish, Farsi and Arabic, and in addition Russian. In her fresher's year she was recruited into the student council that ran a variety of social, cultural and extracurricular activities throughout the year, and into the David Moross Fitness and the Shirley and Meyer Weisgal Sports and Recreation Centres' programmes.

She also enrolled for Sambo, a Russian martial art and combat sport, which integrates the techniques of judo, ju-jitsu, catch wrestling and other native Turkic wrestling-style martial arts. Israel's interest in Russian sports had survived the destruction of the Maccabi sports club and other Zionist organizations by the Bolsheviks after the 1917 Revolution, and Jews had continued to participate actively in the athletic life of the Soviet Union on many different levels, with impressive achievements.

Ruth was sponsored in her further education by her kibbutz, which in turn was underwritten by the Jewish state. So without realising it she had already become a servant of Israel. But in her mind, she considered the source of funds to come from her 'father', supplemented with the paid work she did on the kibbutz.

Whilst Ruth pursued her privileged fast-track career into the national intelligence agency of Israel, David continued his work on the kibbutz, learning land management and the all-round day to day operation of the accommodation and catering needs of its residents. This included an element of tourism through the renting out of kibbutz rooms, classes in the farming techniques used, assisting in harvesting and fruit picking, bird and nature watch activities, enjoying community meals and entertainments, and understanding how meals were prepared in the kosher tradition. These traditions were shaped by the detailed and complex Jewish dietary laws, or *kashrut*, for Jewish festivals and the Sabbath, and the cooking styles of Ashkenazi, Sephardi, Mizrahi, Persian, Yemenite, Indian, Latin-American Jews and Jewish communities from Ethiopia to Central Asia.

So, from the shy introverted young man who had arrived, and having recovered from his beating with the dedicated nursing care and attention lavished on him by his Hannah, David learned the ways of the kibbutz, and developed into an easy-going social adult, comfortable in his own skin. He was now part of an established Jewish couple, planning marriage and children.

But the essence of David was his natural ability to forgive any slight against his person. Even the not so insignificant deception and assaults perpetrated by Asher his substitute

73

father, which started innocently enough with warm cuddles and soft words any young boy might receive and treasure from a loving father, but turned into the eventual incomprehensible demanding and painful embraces of a sex-starved deviant. Even then, when afterwards he was left alone with the stink of sex about him crying himself to sleep in his bed of shame, he would let the experience go, believing that tomorrow would be better. And had it not been for his sister's probing that finally brought these dark actions into the light, he would have continued to defend himself by insulating the physical acts from his thoughts, bearing up against the unpleasantness of the moment with a numbing belief that it would soon be over, and that the bitter now of now would pass to be replaced by a better now of tomorrow.

He would forgive Asher, and then his sister her anger and her vengeance against Asher, in which he played a reluctant part, and let his memory of that time fade until it became as invisible as a childish scar. David was just incapable of bearing a grudge. He was a lovely human being, easy to love, and with an infinite capacity to give out his love.

Ruth and David were granted Israeli citizenship under the Law of Return, which granted all Jews the right to immigrate to Israel and almost automatic Israeli citizenship upon arrival in Israel, provided that the Jew did not practice a religion other than Judaism willingly and would serve their Mandatory Military Service at eighteen. Ruth for her eighteen-month term and David for his three years. As trained soldiers they would be entrusted with the safety and security of the Jewish homeland, always on standby to be called up at a moment's notice, and required to refresh their knowledge and skills as necessary.

In all of this David too would be sponsored by the kibbutz underwritten by the Jewish state.

Because of their different paths, save for moments of respite from their respective duties and obligations for family and social get-togethers, including the marriage of David to Hannah and the births of their children, it would be another five years before the lives of David and Ruth were to come together again in a significant way.

By then Ruth would have passed out top of her class with a science degree, and a silver belt in Sambo to become a fully-fledged katsa within the Caesarea department, and part of Kidon, travelling to the USA, Europe and Russia on intelligence-training missions.

David would now hold a junior executive role in the kibbutz, and have become a corporal in the Israel Defence Forces' military reserve force, which included special training on Israel's missile launch programmes.

And so, it was David's likable character and valued kibbutz and IDF team membership that would lead to Israel's furious retaliatory response to his hostage taking.

Intelligence
17

As one of the principal members of the US intelligence community, the CIA reports to the Director of National Intelligence and is focused on providing intelligence for the President and Cabinet.

In addition, the CIA obtains information from other US government intelligence agencies, commercial information sources and foreign intelligence services.

Because of her US citizenship Ruth was seconded for the later stage training of student operations officers at the classified Camp Peary, near Williamsburg, Virginia. As such she was required to undergo a polygraph examination, which she passed despite questions that probed into the cause of death of her stepfather Asher Schiff. She had been Mossad taught and had a natural aptitude for beating the test. She knew about stimulating her heart rate, respiratory rate, blood pressure and sweat level while answering the innocuous 'control' questions with white lie answers, ensuring that the 'control' lie blip was exaggerated, so that other blips to following questions that could be true, were smaller by comparison.

At Camp Peary she was briefed on 'Five Eyes', or FVEY, the intelligence alliance comprising of Australia, Canada, New Zealand, the United Kingdom and the United States, countries bound by the multilateral UKUSA Agreement, a treaty for joint cooperation in signals intelligence, described as a 'supranational intelligence organisation that doesn't answer to the known laws of its own countries'.

Through FVEY she found herself connected to the UK's domestic counter-Intelligence Military Intelligence Section 5 (MI5), directed by the Joint Intelligence Committee (JIC), and the foreign intelligence secret Military Intelligence Section 6 (MI6), accountable to the Foreign Secretary, which, with UK's Government Communications Headquarters, (GCHQ), and Defence Intelligence (DI), supplied the British government with its intelligence.

Little did she realise how her association with Five Eyes, would give approval to her future suitability for a critical world peace assignment.

It was during an R and R period at Camp Peary that Ruth arranged to visit her surrogate father Abel, still living in Brooklyn, to pursue a burning question about her and her brother's past.

Having been introduced to Abel's second wife, Louise, when she arrived, and having exhausted the catch-up small talk, once they were left alone together Ruth confronted Abel over the issue of her and David's natural father.

"The last time we were together you said 'you know that I have provided for you and your stepparents ever since your mother Myriam died giving birth to you and I did this despite knowing I was not your true father. You know this from the mirror'."

Then came her question:

"Well if you aren't, who is?"

She waited, looking at him with her tight face and fixed stare.

Caught unawares he reddened at the challenge.

"Your mother and I had not been close for some time. Whilst I was developing my business, she got a job at the Fulton fish market, when it was at the Manhattan site and pretty much under the control of one of New York's Mafia families. She was a beautiful woman in the Grace Kelly mould, but with crocked teeth. Despite this she came to the attention of a Mafia lieutenant who was a British-born Catholic, with blond hair and green eyes. He was a man called Patrick. I met him once when he paid me a visit, saying he knew all about me from Myriam and that, as I was family, he would ensure that I would be properly taken care of for a small consideration. I knew what he meant, so I did what I was told and kept my mouth shut."

"What did he want you to do?" asked Ruth.

"Better you don't know," replied Abel, "but knowing my money lending business, you should be able to guess. Anyway, once your mother died he faded out of the picture to disappear suddenly without ever seeing you, his children."

"Do you know what happened to him? Is he still alive? Could I find him?" Ruth pestered.

"Maybe, but you would have to get the answers from the Mafia, and that might expose you to some unwelcome attention from some pretty unpleasant people, so perhaps it would be better if you just let it go," Abel said, doubting that she would.

Ruth considered this, letting her mind sort out her options. She changed track.

"Where did Myriam, our mother, come from, and how did you come to meet her and marry her?"

Abel took a deep sigh.

"I will tell you, but not today. Can you come and see me again? When you do I will also have something of hers to give you." He did have the time, but he wanted to consider his answer and anyway it was a good excuse to see Ruth again. The lure of the keepsake and more knowledge of Myriam would ensure her return.

"Yes," she said, "but it can't be for a few weeks."

Ruth wanted to set the wheels in motion as soon as possible to trace her father, but whilst her mother's story wasn't going anywhere, she could wait a little longer. After all she and David had avoided this sensitive area of their past up to now. But however unreasonable, the stirring up of the rejection issues that came with their mother's death, the blame they felt towards her in leaving them to the tender mercies of their stepparents, still persisted. She got up to go.

As her father rose with her, he put his hand on her arm.

"I did my best for you and David," he said helplessly. "Are you all right for money? Let me give you your fare."

"That won't be necessary," said Ruth. "Stay here. I'll let myself out."

Ruth made the call to her handler.

"Peter," she said. "I found out from my surrogate father Abel Cohen that my real father was a man called Patrick. He works, or worked, in the Manhattan Fulton fish market. I don't know his surname just that he was a Catholic and was part of the Mafia."

"What makes you think he is your real father?" asked Peter.

"He had, has, blond hair and green eyes," answered Ruth.

"I see," said Peter. He saw very well as he already knew this. "Why do you want to find him after all this time?" he probed.

"Well I am here and I do," said Ruth. "I need you to get this information for me, to give me back mine and my brother's past."

Peter knew there was no point in arguing the issue. He knew how determined Ruth could be.

"Sure," he said. "If the answer is out there, I will get it for you."

"How long?" pressed Ruth.

"A few days," he said.

Three days later, there was a note for Ruth to ring 'P'.

"Well?" she asked when she heard Peter's voice.

"He's still alive, living in Dublin," he said. "He had to leave the US in a hurry when the Feds closed down the market's Mafia operation."

What he didn't tell her was that Patrick had received a tip-off to get out of the US from a total stranger, who having told Patrick his 'life story' as an introduction, had also told him that an Aer Lingus flight had been booked for him from JFK to Dublin the following day, and that if he wasn't on it he should say goodbye to 'life, liberty and the pursuit of happiness'. What clinched it for Pat was a passport with his surname and a sum deposited in a Dublin bank waiting for him, but only if he agreed to return a benefit in kind. He realised there would have to be an 'if', and his was that he could expect a call sometime in the future to request a favour, which it would also be in his best interest not to refuse.

Oh, and another thing. He needed to stay put in Eire for the foreseeable future, and not to worry about the contact finding him, because he or she would. G2 would take care of this.

The Directorate of Military Intelligence, or G2, was one of the most secretive intelligence agencies in Europe, so much so that the Irish government and defence forces rarely alluded to its very existence. But what was known was that its tentacles reached everywhere and that, like those of the sea box wasp jellyfish, one of the most deadly creatures on the planet, its tentacles carried darts full of venom causing intense pain and death from cardiovascular arrest, if shock had not occurred first, leading to drowning.

Ruth's second visit to Abel Cohen would probably be the last. She didn't feel beholden to him. Better for her and David to cut this link to their past for good, once they had the information they needed.

When she entered his study, she was momentarily distracted by the fist-sized slate grey jagged block of rock full of holes that rested on top of his desk, and the sparkling diamond-shaped crystal that twinkled at her from one of its blackened hollows.

Seeing her interested look, Abel picked it up and offered it to her to hold.

"It's a Herkimer diamond. There is a connection to your mother," and he went on to explain his interest, and the origin of the crystal. "Keep it," he said as she sat down nodding her thanks, surprised at the sharpness of its flinty edges and dry roughness of its volcanic surface, before letting it rest in her lap.

Abel had sent Louise and their child out. He wanted to be free to speak to Ruth without the possibility of interruption. A tray of cups and instant coffee had been put out for Ruth's morning visit.

Having served them, Abel started:

"Did you have any luck in tracing your father?"

"Nothing so far," Ruth answered, and then went on immediately. "You said you would talk about our mother Myriam." She waited.

"Well," said Abel, his coffee untouched, "our families were both second-generation immigrants from Germany, and we shared the same synagogue here in Borough Park. She, your mother, was a beautiful young woman, and could have had her pick. I think she chose me because I made her laugh, and perhaps because she thought I would keep her well provided for. My family were moneylenders, and I was good at it, making interest from small loans, or pawned items to collage kids and hard-up wives. At college I was nicknamed Shylock, you know from Shakespeare's *Merchant of Venice*," trying to make a joke of it. He paused weighing up his words. "Anyway, after we got married it soon became clear that I was failing her in the bedroom department, and she started to look elsewhere. I put up with it until her behaviour became public gossip, and had no choice but to tell her to go."

"You kicked her out, is that it?" demanded Ruth.

"Well, as I said, I had no choice. I did find a room for her, paid for it, and opened a bank account for her with a cash deposit. She didn't have to behave like a common whore. I think I was more than generous in the circumstances. Here, let me show you the special Herkimer diamond ring I got for her, which I have kept for you." And he took a small pouch from his pocket putting it on the table before sitting back defensively with his arms crossed.

Ruth took it and pulled open the drawstrings letting the ring fall out onto her receiving palm. Wondering at how the ring came to be with Abel, this first and only possession they would ever have of their mother, Ruth sat forward, her elbows on the table again nodding slowly, confused feelings swirling about her. She said slowly:

"Was she pregnant when you kicked her out?"

Abel flushed. "I don't know. She hadn't begun to show, so I couldn't have known. She made her choices. I did what I could, and picked up the result of her bastard children when she died. You should be thanking me."

Ruth clenched her fists. She was white with rage. Getting up she knocked her chair over, instinctively clutching the rock, preventing it falling, her movement triggering a panic reflex reaction from Abel who tumbled backwards to fall spread-eagled onto the floor. As she moved to lean over him, he drew himself into a ball, cowering from her, his arms together shielding his face. And this is how he remained until he heard the sitting room door slam shut, her footsteps in the hall, and finally the front door open and close.

It was a while before Ruth stopped shaking, so infused was she with her anger. Why could that man not have given her a lasting memory that she could have shared with her brother and carried to her grave? Now this hurt to add to her feelings of rejection, with no possibility of release.

Her squeezing grip on the rock had caused one of its razor-sharp edges to draw blood which would soak in and leave a surface stain for a future memory.

The ring was forgotten but not lost, to be rediscovered on the finger she had unconsciously slid it onto in the heat of the moment, by her other hand's absent-minded twiddling fingers.

When she had calmed down, she had become numb, and her heart filled with icicles of cold hate, hatred for her fellow humans, the weak, fickle, grasping and pathetic human beings who surrounded her, save for her brother, of course. Yes, she would protect her brother from this knowledge, and make up a story that would give him a sense of family history that he could share with his children. She would show him their mother's ring and tell him a story as to how it came to be in her possession, and would have him agree that she would be its caretaker, unless something happened to her, and that it would hang from her throat on a silver necklace that they would choose together.

The piece of dolostone with its inset crystal and the stain of her blood she would leave with her brother.

And as she brooded, she considered how she would do this, and how perhaps the Herkimer 'diamond' ring could help repair the rendered circle of their mother's love.

And so, it happened that she bought an engraved plaque for their birth mother and had it set close to the Coney Island Brooklyn Wall of Remembrance in the MCU Park, New York's first memorial to 9:11.

She did this so that the memory of Myriam, their tragic mother, would share the graceful and beautiful tribute to those who had innocently lost their lives on September 11th 2001.

She did this so that their mother would be included when families came, not just for grief, but for the comfort of shared sweet memories within the sound of children laughing as they played, or just to sit and listen to the quiet voice of the ocean.

She did this to try to erase the hurt of having missed her mother's loving time when it was most needed by her and her twin brother.

But for her she would never marry, never have children never give her private personal love to another.

No, never!

Chairman
18

The chairman was not what he seemed.

His impeccable credentials of professorship at a leading North American university, with degrees in the classics, languages and comparative religion, whilst publicly known as a benevolent atheist, hid a profound hatred of religion.

Jack Connelly was also a cousin to the President.

The reason for this hatred was a thwarted homosexual love affair with a young priest during a blissful holiday romance in Italy during his early student days.

He had met Giovanni when visiting the Sistine Chapel in the Vatican when he, as a young priest, was leading groups of tourists sightseeing the interest spots within Vatican City.

It was love at first sight for Jack. This beautiful tall young Italian with his brown curls, long eyelashes, dark eyes, full lips and perfect teeth instantly drew Jack to him, and magnetised Jack's footsteps to follow Giovanni until the tour ended and the tourist group had trickled away with their handshakes and appreciative thanks, leaving Jack self-consciously standing on his own alone with just Giovanni.

"I'm Jack," he said holding out his hand.

Giovanni shyly took his hand.

"*Ciao,*" he answered. "Are you here on holiday?" he went on haltingly.

Still holding his hand, Jack asked, "Are you free for coffee?"

Freeing his hand but smiling, Giovanni said, "I have things I need to do now," but seeing the look of disappointment on Jack's face he went on, "but I am free this evening if you want."

Jack was now grinning back. Taking back Giovanni's hand, he said, "I sure do. Where can we meet?"

Giovanni thought for a moment then mentioned a place.

"Time?" asked Jack.

"Eight o'clock if that's OK with you?" It was Giovanni's turn to grin.

"Sure is," said Jack laughing out loud.

"Sure is," Giovanni mimicked back, and raising his hand in farewell said, *"A presto,"* before disappearing from Jack's sight.

Giovanni was late, whilst Jack waited impatiently. At last he arrived with a shrug and an apology.

"Sono in ritardo, mi perdoni?"

"Sure, At least you came. I thought you might have changed your mind," said Jack. "I have bought a bottle of wine. Are you happy with this?" pointing out a bottle of Gaja Barbaresco Costa Russi 2013 on the table. He saw Giovanni raise his eyebrows in appreciation.

"I hope the description will not disappoint," Jack continued and read from a card.

"The Gaja Barbaresco has a glorious Nebbiolo nose of cascading damask roses straight from the garden after a heavy

rain. *On the palate, red plums and mulberry juice are perfumed with freshly turned earth. Of the crus, this is the most generous, with a looser structure and silky texture. 2013 is a cool vintage and the freshness of the finish is a testament to this. It is forthcoming and delicious."*

Giovanni laughed. "I am honoured with your choice. So much expense on our first..." He let the missing word with all its potential meaning lose itself before rushing on with, "Perhaps some water as well?"

Jack noted that Giovanni had shed his black habit and white collar for light blue T-shirt and grey slacks. The T-shirt had *Gesù mi ama* on the front.

Leaning across Jack touched Giovanni's arm before sitting back in his seat smiling, his eyes tracing Giovanni's features.

"I really am pleased to see you. I haven't been able to stop thinking about you." He watched the self-conscious expression on Giovanni.

As the silence between them grew Jack blurted out, "Tell me why you became a priest." He waited.

"My family is very religious you know," Giovanni said finally. Continuing, "There has always been someone in the church. I didn't know what to do with my life, so it seemed the right thing to do."

"And when did you discover you liked men?" Jack said, the words shocking him as much as they shocked Giovanni.

Giovanni half rose, flushing.

"*Non capisco,* I er don't understand what you mean."

Full of bravado Jack said, "Don't go. You must have a sense as to what I feel about you, but if I am wrong forgive me, but stay and have a meal with me anyway." Jack took a deep breath, and smiling held out his hands in a gesture of welcoming supplication.

"*Perfavore?*" he begged.

Full of confusion Giovanni sat back down. "This is so new to me, this…" He fell silent.

Jack's heart leapt. He could hardly contain his sense of victory.

"Let us eat and enjoy each other's company tonight, and let tomorrow take care of itself. What do you say, *che cosa ne pensi?*"

Giovanni was now smiling broadly and nodding his approval. Raising his eyebrows, he questioned, "*Carpe diem?*"

"*Carpe diem*," agreed Jack.

He poured two glasses of wine, and raising his glass repeated, "Yes, *Carpe diem!*"

19

Still basking in the afterglow of his Roman holiday the call, when it came, delivered not just a delayed shock that left him dumbfounded, incapable of absorbing the full meaning of the words falling about his ears, but the inability to have any reaction to them. His rigid muteness shocked his college roommate, who came upon him, the fallen mobile, a harbinger of the message lying useless on the floor, now just a speechless messenger of a murdered future.

His tutor was called, and having directed that Jack be placed in a comfortable chair and helped to take some sips of water, stayed with him holding his hand until, with the gentle coaxing of his name, Jack's eyes began to focus.

"Jack, Jack," the face that opened up before him repeated. "Jack, Jack what's happened?"

And then as understanding flooded into his head the awful realisation, Giovanni was gone, never to be seen again, never to be held and kissed and smelt, ever again. Never! Never! And then the dam broke, and from the deepest part of him came the wracking sobs, the heaving shoulders, the howls of anguish, and the shouts of, "No! No!"

The college physician was summoned and injected a sleeping drug. Jack was put to bed in his rooms. His mother contacted.

And all this time, no one was yet aware as to the cause of his collapse.

20

Jack feasted on the memories, their first meal, his brazen insinuations, the incredible mutual realisation of their feelings, the heightened sensation of the sight, and sound, and touch of each other, in their loveness. Oh, the pain of it, the ecstasy, the almost continuous need to eat and drink. How beautiful was the light, the buildings, the streets, the squares, the noise. And later, there was the visit to meet Giovanni's family as his new best friend. How shy Giovanni was in their introduction. How cocksure he was in their acceptance of him. How blind he was in seeing anyone other than Giovanni, and of his need to be with him, and how he had pressed Giovanni to take a break from his priestly duties, despite the cautions of his parents. How he ignored any hesitation from Giovanni, any reservation from them, any challenge of responsibilities to family tradition and to the church.

How they had proceeded to hire a car, and under Giovanni's direction travel the Italian countryside and coastline, staying in pensions, sharing rooms as two students, enjoying the tourist attractions, the local rustic meals, the fresh cooked food, and the wine. And of course, the lovemaking and afterwards the sleeping in each other's arms. How blissful was the time, and at the last when Jack had to return, how hard the parting, how sincere the promises made to meet again, when it would be Jack's turn to show Giovanni his America.

But the memory of the phone call could not be denied.

"*Scusami*," said the female voice. "Are you Mr Jack?"

"*Si*," said Jack, "*Chi è questo?*"

"I am a relation of Giovanni, *la zia*, an aunt. *Capisci?* Do you understand?"

"*Si*," said Jack again, impatient to understand why this woman was making the call, why it wasn't Giovanni. Vague alarm warnings fluttered in his brain.

"*Giovanni è morto*. He has died." A silence. "*Capisci?*"

As the phone fell from his hand the voice continued to repeat "*Capisci?*" until finally, after a long pause, also going dead.

It was a second call to Jack's mobile twenty-four hours later that would intense the agony, and later bring the anger, the rage, the unforgiving fury, and the hatred.

Jack's mother had answered the call.

"*Scusami*," said the male voice. "*Tu chi sei,* who are you?"

"This is my son Jack's phone." And then to be quite clear, "I am Jack's mother."

"I am the father of Giovanni," said the voice. "Can I speak with your son?"

"He is not well," Jack's mother replied. "Can I take a message?"

"This is very difficult for me," said the father, then after a delay. "My son has died. He killed himself."

There was a long pause, then, "Your son Jack is the reason."

Another pause as Jack's mother absorbed this.

"I don't understand," she said.

"Your son had an unnatural relationship with my son. It is forbidden by the church. My son confessed this, and because he thought he would be removed from the church he killed himself for the disgrace."

He repeated, "Your son Jack is the reason."

"How did he die?" Jack's mother said helplessly, as if knowing would make a difference.

"He threw himself from a tower in the Vatican," said the father.

"That's terrible, that's so terrible." Then after a hesitation, "What do you want from me, from my son?"

"*Niente,* nothing!" came the reply. I just want for your son to know that we have lost the prized jewel from our family, and that your son is the cause of our tragedy."

Before she could respond the call was over.

She sat for a time thinking how she could tell her son this dreadful news, and then how she could prevent this news becoming a scandal. She decided that she would wait and see what was published in the papers, in the social media. Perhaps Giovanni's family would seek to keep the matter private, as quiet as possible. Perhaps Jack's name would not be disclosed. Perhaps Jack did not need to know of this call.

Yes, she would wait and see how the land lay, and then decide.

It was not Jack's mother who conveyed the facts of the suicide to Jack. It was his roommate who had read the notice, and in whom Jack had confided the blissful details of his holiday with his Italian friend, details that described the delights of Italy and hinted at the intimacies of the relationship.

The notice was a small item in the *International New York Times*.

It said:

THE TRAGIC DEATH OF YOUNG ITALIAN PRIEST

The body of a young man was found at the base of the Vatican's infamous Borgia Tower. He had apparently jumped to his death. His family have asked for their privacy to be respected. No further statements would be made.

And so, it was when Jack spoke of this to his mother, and she admitted to her prior knowledge and then recounted the call she had taken from Giovanni's father holding Jack responsible, that Jack's hatred for a blind pitiless God began.

21

It was fortuitous for the revenge that was spawned from his hatred that he shared his rooms with Jonas Burden, a student in the chemistry of gases, and that this relationship would continue for the next twenty years until Jonas worked for a company that had access to the Rocky Mountain Arsenal or RMA, a United States chemical weapons manufacturing centre located in the Denver Metropolitan Area in Commerce City, Colorado, for both conventional and chemical munitions, including white phosphorus, napalm, mustard gas, lewisite and chlorine gas.

The RMA was also a site for the stockpile of sarin or GB, a heavy colourless, odourless liquid nerve agent, where death can occur within ten minutes after direct inhalation of a lethal dose of its gas due to suffocation from lung muscle paralysis, unless an antidote, typically atropine and an oxime, such as pralidoxime, was immediately given, the on-hand availability of which, of course, was unlikely if its use had been deliberate.

Good Times
22

The lives of David and Hannah became as one, their early days a heady mixture of discovery and sharing.

Their discovery of each other was all consuming, when it was impossible for either of them to get enough of the other, and not just the passion, but the need to find any excuse to seek each other out during the day, to brush against each other, to hold hands at mealtimes and social gatherings, to make inane talk when the sound of their words made only sense to them, to look at each other and smile and giggle and laugh at the very presence of the other, to push and shove and play as gambolling puppies.

Their delirious joy spilled out of them onto anyone in their proximity, infecting any casual observer with goodwill, causing a reaction of spontaneous grins in the shared feeling of happiness that distracted thoughts and transcended moods.

In a nutshell the fusing of these two perfectly matched halves changed the lives of all those kibbutzniks within the orbit of their kibbutz, and produced a chain reaction that spread amongst them making ordinary of daily life something special to look forward to, and then to enjoy.

The condition of access to the bedchamber required David to propose marriage, the reply to which of course was waiting to be eagerly answered by an impatient Hannah. Marriage because, despite the sexual freedoms of the kibbutz way of life, Hannah had insisted that access to her treasure would only be granted to the one she loved, and that the one she blessed must make a proposal of marriage, which in traditional Judaism was viewed as a contractual bond commanded by God when a man and a woman came together to fulfil God's commandment to have children. Then, and only then should procreation take place, and in so doing merge each other into the single beautiful soul of a child.

And so it came to pass that Hannah and David became engaged in Jewish law and within the Talmud, mutually promising to marry each other at some future time and on terms formalized in a document known as the *shtar tena'im* or the 'document of conditions', which having been read was bound by Hannah's best friend Rachel, a replacement for her deceased mother, and in the absence of David's mother Myriam, sealed by Ruth in the breaking of a plate.

Then on a selected Tuesday, to respect the absent chanting of the Torah, there followed the marriage ceremony, consisting of the two separate acts of the *kiddushin* or sanctification, the betrothal, and then under the *chupah* canopy, the wedding itself.

Two blessings were recited before the betrothal, a blessing over wine, and then the betrothal blessing with the wine tasted by the couple.

David gave Hannah a traditional plain wedding ring and recited the declaration, "Behold, you are consecrated to me with this ring according to the Law of Moses and Israel," before placing it on her right index finger.

Hannah presented an identical ring to David quoting from the Song of Songs, "I am my beloveds and my beloved is mine."

At the end of the ceremony David broke a glass, crushing it with his right foot, in a sign to temper joy.

Then all the guests shouted "Mazel tov!" dancing excitedly in front of the seated couple to express their joy in entertaining them.

When the wedding feast, with its copious food and wine, was well under way, David and Hannah slipped away to their waiting car, already packed with their suitcases, to drive to their honeymoon suite at Jerusalem's King David Hotel for four nights and then on to a Caesarea Beach Front Studio for ten nights, before driving back to their kibbutz via the Mount Carmel National Park.

And then there would be the longed-for lovemaking of committed adults.

23

They hardly spoke to each other on the journey to Jerusalem, holding hands and frequently smiling and glancing at each other as they drove, before arriving finally at the famous pink quartz King David Hotel.

The details of where they were to stay during their two weeks' honeymoon had been kept secret from them, only to be revealed from the envelope containing the reservation documents, when they had got into the car. Their excitement was intense with the sense of the unknown, so that when at last they were there, with the car door being opened, their bags being taken, the car removed for parking and they were being led to the reception desk for the signing in formalities, it was as if they could finally release a breath that had been held in suspension since the day had begun, and during which they had drifted barely aware of the organised details involved or of their contact with those that loved them and milled about them making sounds of pleasure and joy, this day when they were legally joined and celebrated. Then it was the giggly signing of Mr and Mrs, the quiet congratulations from the reception staff, and the request to follow the porter with the luggage into the ornate lift, down the fourth floor corridor to the Deluxe Old City Suite, the door held open for them, and then whilst David gave an extravagant tip, Hannah was pushing open the doors to the balcony calling over her shoulder, "You must come and see this!"

For there before her was a breath-taking view of the hotel gardens leading onwards to the Old City, divided into its four quarters of the Armenian, Christian, Jewish and Muslim faiths, each quarter with its incredibly rich history dating back thousands of years, and only a fifteen-minute walk away. But when he joined her, and she took his hand sweeping her other arm to encompass the sight before them, he only had eyes for her, this beautifully radiant young woman who shone before him, and gripped his heart in a vice of agonised love. Seeing him so transfixed she hesitated, becoming self-conscious, and with her colour rising reached out to hold both his hands and lean into him for their first married kiss. After what appeared an age they parted, and still holding hands re-entered their room to see the display of red roses, and the iced bucket of pink champagne with its two crystal glasses standing ready. Whilst she sought the scent of the flowers, he loosened the wire on the bottle, removed the foil and carefully levered out the cork, restraining it at the last, to say to her, "Come here. Stand by me." And as she did, holding the cork by her ear, he released it the last centimetre for her to hear its hiss, and as it came free, he moved the neck so that the visible spume emerged beneath her nose allowing her to inhale the essence of the vintage grape. Laughing at her surprise he poured wine, and as she took her glass, he raised his.

"To us," he said taking a sip, and then, "to you and all the beautiful babies that we will make together."

"Why, you!" she exclaimed. "Not so fast. We may need to practise a little first."

"No," he said, drawing out his reply, "we will have to practise a lot!"

And he took their glasses, putting them down before taking her in his arms to whisper into her hair, "You are my beauty, and I will love you always."

Pushing him away, just a bit, she looked up into his face and she knew that this was true.

"And I you," she replied, and then more business-like, "But now I must unpack, and while I do you must go and book a table for dinner. You can also take a look at the gardens and the swimming pool if you like. I do not want to see you now for at least an hour."

With that she pushed him into the corridor.

When he returned sixty-one minutes later, having knocked and finding the door ajar with its 'Do not disturb' notice hanging on the outer doorknob, he found her in one of the hotel robes, brushing her hair. As he came up behind her to lean over her and kiss her neck, she twisted around, and pointing towards the bathroom said, "It's time for your shower. I don't want a smelly man in my room! And make sure you shave and wash properly, because I shall be inspecting every little bit of you."

It was his turn to redden, and by the time he had shed his clothes and turned on the water he was fully aroused.

"Not so little," he said to himself looking in the mirror.

When he joined her, wearing his matching robe he saw that she had drawn the curtains, switched on the bedside lamps, turned down the bed, and still in her robe she was propped up on the pillows. They were now both red-faced, breathing heavily. The tension between them was palpable. As he stood awkwardly with his arousal straining his garment, she patted the space next to her.

"No touching," she said, "well, not until I say you can."

As he lay down beside her, she got off the bed. "You must now do everything I say. Do you promise?"

His tongue had stuck in his mouth, and he couldn't speak. He made a noise and nodded.

She let her robe fall to the floor.

He was now completely mesmerised, drinking in the lusciousness of her form, her full breasts with their erect nipples, her tapered stomach with its hollow navel leading to her swollen mound of Venus surrounded by dark brown curls, her generous thighs and calves, her soft arms that hung in supplication loosely by her side below her smiling face. He had forgotten how to breathe.

"Now," she said, "remember your promise to do as I say. No touching!"

With that she knelt at the foot of the bed, her knees apart straddling his legs. He was now powerless to move, just gazing up at her as she began to inch her way along his calves, her knees pushing aside his robe until she was positioned above his rigid member. And as her kneeling thighs griped his sides and her hands rested on his shoulders, she lowered herself so that the lips of her mons surrounded him, making him give an involuntary jerk as the wet heat of her covered his throbbing desire.

"Now," she said, "you may hold my hips, but nothing else."

And as he lay trembling beneath her, she began to slide herself up and down his length, his hips jerking their uncontrollable response.

"Stop!" she commanded. "You must learn to wait, to wait for me."

By now they were both breathing hard, their mouths making small gasping sounds that startled the air between them, their eyes wide open and locked together.

"I can't last," he pleaded, griping the soft cheeks of her bottom.

"You must!" she hissed at him, digging her nails into his chest, but she knew that the time had come.

With a movement that she had rehearsed many times in her mind, she raised her hips and taking hold of his rigid sword positioned it at the entrance to her treasure, lowering herself until she felt the resistance. With her knees gripping his hips, she tensed a moment longer then forced herself upon him.

"Now," she demanded. "Move now!" and as she plunged down he reared up until they were welded together, he straining for his release, she grinding herself against him, crying out small whimpering sounds as her sheath quivered and clutched at him and drew from him his groans and spurting seed, their bodies convulsing against each other for what seemed eternity, until with near unconsciousness she fell against him, her breasts pressing into his chest, her face burrowing into his neck, his face against her hair, each breathing their mingled scents of blissful loving.

As he folded his robe about them, they drifted into a sleep of profound satisfaction where all memories of the past and thoughts of the future were suspended, until the call of nature would drag them slowly back.

Later, as she rolled away and covered him with his robe, she said, "Careful, I must check for blood. Lie still while I tend to myself, and look at the sheet, and you. We don't want to give housekeeping any excuse to gossip."

Later still, having washed and dried him, she lay full length upon him within his arms, and whispered into his ear, "I am sorry to tell you, but you must now give me time to heal."

As he turned to face her, she saw his look of concern, and thinking it was for himself, quickly continued, "But that doesn't mean that I cannot still give you pleasure."

And as she said this, her hand reached down to grasp his member. Feeling his renewed arousal, she smiled and said, "So soon? You are such a naughty man. But you are my man."

And quoting again her wedding vow she repeated the Song of Songs. "I am my beloved's and my beloved is mine."

And with this she slipped over his body, her breasts softly brushing his thighs, and with her hand cradling his giver of life, her mouth commenced his thrilling spin towards a second and much more painful climax. But before he reached it, she stopped to look at him. As he raised his head to look desperately at her, she grinned and said, "Tell me when."

Nodding, he let his head fall back as she continued, and as the uncontrollable rush began, he shouted out, "I'm coming, I'm coming!" gasping and jerking as she received him on her tongue.

"Well," she said as she returned to lie within his arms again. "Will this do for my lord and master?"

"Oh yes," he said. "But only as a stop gap. I can't wait to be with you once more, and more, and more."

"And me with you." Then kissing him she said, "and now what shall we do next?"

"Well," he replied, "If you are not too full, perhaps we should eat. I am starving."

Laughing, she pushed him away. "I don't want to get dressed, so can we have room service?"

"Leave it to me," said David, and swinging his legs from the bed grabbed the hotel phone.

"How may I help you?" said the female voice.

"Um, this is the Deluxe Old City Suite. We are a little tired from our journey and wondered if we could cancel our dining room booking, and have something served in the room?"

"Of course," came the reply. "I will send the room service manager to your room with the menu and wine list."

"Thank you," said David. "Perhaps in twenty minutes to give us time to get ready?"

"Of course, I understand," came the reply again.

Hannah, who had her ear to the receiver gave David a playful push.

"Well that's given the game away," she said. "You are such an innocent," and made a dash to the bathroom.

When they came down for breakfast holding hands there was a noticeable change in their manner. They were more assured, more knowing. They had become adults. Hannah had already planned the day, and going to reception she announced:

"We will be walking to the Old City to see the attractions of the Dome of the Rock and al-Aqsa Mosque for Muslims, the Temple Mount and Western Wall for Jews and the Church of the Holy Sepulchre for Christians. Perhaps we will walk the

Via Dolorosa, the Way of Sorrows, from the Antonia Fortress to the Church of the Holy Sepulchre with its nine Stations of the Cross, and go inside the Church for the remaining five. Then we will come back for a swim."

As she stood proud of her knowledge, smiling at everyone that would listen to her, David just stood there grinning swinging her arm.

"You see how my wife is in charge? But as long as there is a beer in it for me, I will be following her anywhere she wants to go."

"Oh you!" she retorted and pulled him out of the hotel entrance leaving the attentive staff to give one another a wistful knowing look.

24

They drove to their Beach Front Studio in Caesarea through the Neve Ilan Forest, past the Latrun Monastery, Shemen, past Ben Gurion Airport and Ariel Sharon Park, onto the Kvish HaHof coast road past the towns and villages of Ne'ot Golda, Park Si'im, Ben Tsiyon, Gan Beracha, Ne'ot Hertsel, Bat Hen, Bitan Aharon, BeitYanai, Ein Hayam, Khofim, Heftsiba, finally turning left after the Caesarea Golf Club to Hahoresh and the Studio.

All the while, Hannah sat with the map on her lap reeling off the places and their reducing distances like a navigator to her rally driver. Except David was anything but, getting Hannah to repeat the names again and again to reassure him that he was still on the right road, so when they finally arrived, he was soaked through, desperate to get out and have a cold beer. But still Hannah would not be deflected from her role of know-all, insisting that he remain in the car whilst she read out to him the details to their waiting accommodation.

"The property is a five-minute walk from the Caesarea Beach. It's called the Beach Front Studio, and it features an outdoor pool and panoramic views of the Mediterranean Sea. It has a private balcony with outdoor seating. The air-conditioned studio includes a lounge area with satellite TV. It also has a dining table and a well-equipped kitchenette with oven, stovetop and microwave. It features wooden floors. Guests can relax in the swimming pool and garden. Free Wi-Fi access is available as well. The Caesarea Golf Club is just ten minutes' walk from the Beach Front Studio and Caesarea Antiquities Park and Harbour can be reached within a twenty-minute walk along the beach. The supermarket, restaurant and café bar are 200 metres away. Haifa Airport is twenty-eight miles."

And then she started to read the trusted reviews.

"Lovely garden cottage, beautiful view to aqueduct, easy access to the National Park, very kind hosts, I can't wait to go back again."

"And I can't wait to get there," came David's groan.

She stopped reading and looked sideways at him. He had now inclined his seat and was pretending to snore.

"Well!" she said. "So rude!" and pinched his arm as he started to laugh.

It was everything they could have wanted, and ten days later full of sun, sea, sand and sex, and comfortable in each other's company, they were on their way home via the Mount Carmel National Park, with Hannah again reading aloud.

"The Mount Carmel National Park is Israel's largest national park, extending over the Carmel mountain range containing over 10,000 hectares of pine, eucalyptus and cypress forest, with its Mediterranean ecosystem recognized by UNESCO as a biosphere reserve."

They had much less to say on this last leg of their journey to the kibbutz, and David drove with Hannah's hand resting on his thigh. Every so often he would catch her looking at him, and as he did, she would smile at him and her hand would squeeze him gently.

And as his heart turned over, he thought that if this was all there was to be for him in his life, he could never complain. But then he thought, what if she had to leave him, how could he bear to be parted from her? And he started to grieve, and suddenly a sob caught in his throat and tears flowed down his cheeks, and she was telling him to pull over, and then holding him tight in her arms as she too wept with him, instinctively knowing and sharing such sweet sorrow.

And then there was Hannah's pregnancy, the public noticing of her morning sickness, the kibbutz telegraph announcements of the good news, the daily enquiries after her health, the scrutiny of the swelling belly, the gossip bulletins of "she's blossoming," or "she looks a bit off colour," or "she had such and such for breakfast, lunch and supper," and "she's eating for two," or "she's doing too much," and "she mustn't lift such weights," and "the baby's low down at the back so it's a boy, or high up at the front so it will be a girl," and "only so many months, weeks and days to go," and finally, "it's coming, it's coming!"

25

David was in the cornfield when he got the call. He heard the sound of a woman's screeching voice before he understood the words, standing up and looking over the corn stalks with the other workers. Then as the words, "it's coming, it's coming," became clearer he became the focus of their attention, with their laughing whoops, cheers and shouts now joining in. "It's coming, hurry David, go to your wife, go to Hannah, take an ear of corn for your firstborn, take our best wishes," and other more ribald calls of, "you lucky dog, don't faint, don't get drunk, get your shekels out to wet the baby's head!"

Dropping his armful of cobs save for one, David started to run.

A car was waiting for him at the kibbutz main house, with a friend to drive him to the Lis Maternity and Women's Hospital, part of the Tel Aviv Sourasky Medical Center.

As he got into the car she said:

"You're not to worry. Because of her pre-existing high blood pressure and the risk of preeclampsia, when her waters broke, we thought it best to call an ambulance and get Hannah into hospital quickly, just as a precaution."

Gesturing with her eyes as she started the car, she said, "Take a look at the information on the hospital and preeclampsia I printed off for you."

David, who had yet to speak, nodded his head and picked up the papers from the back seat.

Mumbling his thanks, he read first about the hospital:

The Lis Maternity and Women's Hospital is at the leading edge of medical care, with advanced treatment approaches, expert clinicians, sophisticated technology, personal care, and comfortable, modern facilities, exactly what one would expect from a world-class hospital.

With its MommyLis maternity club, it provides special services including delivery unit introductory tours, childbirth courses, breastfeeding courses, personal breastfeeding consultation, training in newborn CPR and online forums.

He started to relax a little, and then he read about preeclampsia:

Preeclampsia can cause serious damage to your organs, including your brain and kidneys. Preeclampsia is also known as toxaemia or pregnancy-induced hypertension. Preeclampsia with seizures becomes eclampsia. This can be fatal.

"Oh fuck," he said looking at the driver. "Not again."

"What's that mean?" she asked.

"My mother died giving birth to me and my twin sister Ruth, a massive haemorrhage."

"I didn't know," she said, "but Hannah will be OK. She is in the best possible place."

He tumbled out of the car when she dropped him off at the entrance. He was burbling when he reached the reception.

"Hannah, my wife, she's having a baby. I must go to her. Where is she? Please hurry!"

The receptionist looked up at the wild-eyed, perspiring, dishevelled, handsome man that stood in front of her.

"Why, of course mister?" she said smiling at him. "Mister?" she repeated.

"Er, yes," stuttered David. "Er, Schiff."

"Let me look. Yes, here we are. Your wife Hannah, yes?" she asked to confirm. "She was checked in two hours ago. Now is there anyone who can be with you?"

"My friend Bayla, she is parking the car," said David.

"Well let's wait for her and then I will give you both the directions to get to the Delivery Suite."

When they arrived on the delivery ward they were taken to Hannah's room. They found her looking pale, but very pleased to see David. She held her hands out to them.

"Hullo Bayla, hullo David," she said, and seeing David's anxious look continued, "You are not to worry, but I have high blood pressure. They say that the best treatment for it is to deliver the baby, and that only if it is too slow will I need to have a caesarean section. So hold onto me my darling and I will look after you."

She squeezed his hand as the midwife came into the room.

"You must be David," she said. "Now mother is doing well, and with your help we are going to deliver you a beautiful baby."

As she talked, she took Hannah's blood pressure.

"How is it?" David asked.

"I see you are an expert," she answered. "Well, still a little high, but as long as mother does her stuff everything will be fine. Would you like your friend," looking at Bayla, "to get you a drink?"

David shook his head.

The frequency of the contractions gradually increased.

After one particularly painful contraction, when clutching David's hand Hannah had cried out, David said, "I wish I could suffer this for you. Tell me what it is like so that at least I can know what you are going through?"

As Hannah lay moaning and grunting, the midwife answered, "The pain of contractions has been described as a feeling similar to very strong menstrual cramps, broken glass churning around in one's tummy if you know what I mean, with the birth as an intense stretching and burning sensation. Does that help?"

Hannah was nodding furiously as the next contraction came.

"Oh dear," said David weakly, and then asked. "How long will it take?"

"Well," said the midwife, "the signs are good. Mother is four centimetres, so it will be a little while before we get to the second stage when she is fully dilated. After that, up to three hours before delivery, during which you can really help mother with the hard work of giving birth. Are you up to it?"

"Oh yes," said David. "I am, I will."

David and Hannah looked at each other.

"You are, aren't you?" said Hannah. "I want you here, to stay with me until we have our baby. But I don't want you at the business end watching. I don't want you to be remembering my private bits like this. I still want you to want me afterwards, do you hear?"

"I am, I won't, I will, I promise," and he hung onto her clutching hand as another gasping contraction followed.

"So," said the midwife. "Why don't you take a small break, have something to eat and drink, have a walk about, have a pee, and then you will be ready for the last lap. Bayla can stay and fetch you if you need to come back sooner. Oh, and don't forget to wash your hands."

Finally, with commands of "Push now!" and "it's coming, its coming!" came the crowning and then the glory, their firstborn joy to the world, with black hair, sightless eyes and wailing, flailing limbs akimbo all forlorn, arrived.

"She is so beautiful," said Hannah as she cradled her.

"But what of her nose, it's squashed flat?" asked David as he inserted a finger into the baby's clutching hand.

"Well dear," said the midwife. "Baby's bones are very soft and as long as her nose is given a little push each day with the help of a little plaster, her nose will become perfectly straight, just like her daddy's."

As for the newly picked corn cob, it would be allowed to dry out with its kernels hardening to a polished brown, and kept to remind any curious regard of the kernel that it was harvested on the day of their first born, their Avishag.

In time, there would be a second and then a third child.

Visit
26

When Ruth's flight touched down at Dublin Airport in Collinstown, County Fingal, Eire she was met by Shamus of G2. Her reputation as a highly skilled and efficient agent of Mossad, currently seconded to the CIA and with links into M16 preceded her, and so every facility was availed her in the finding and meeting of her father. Having spotted the noticeboard with her code name that awaited her at the departure gate, and made the perfunctory greeting, little was said between them on the car journey to her Dublin's Trinity City Hotel. As they drove, she was given an envelope with her instructions and told by Shamus that she would be contacted the following morning over breakfast. Until then, the time was hers.

Having checked in and perused the contents of the envelope, she decided to go on a walk about.

She enquired as to places of interest.

"Ever seen the Book of Kells?" she was asked at the enquiry desk.

"No," she replied.

"Well, it's worth a look. It's on display in the University Library of Trinity College, and is only a ten-minute walk away. There is still time before the library closes at five."

"Perhaps I will," she answered. "Do you have access to Google?"

Looking it up on Wikipedia she read:

The Book of Kells, also known as the Book of Columba, is an illuminated manuscript Gospel book in Latin, containing the four Gospels of the New Testament of Matthew, Mark, Luke and John, together with various prefatory texts and tables. It was created in a Columban monastery in Ireland, and may have had contributions from various Columban institutions from both Britain and Ireland. It is believed to have been created c. 800. The text of the Gospels is drawn from the Vulgate, a late fourth-century Latin translation of the Bible, largely the work of St. Jerome, who, in 382 AD, was commissioned by Pope Damasus I to revise the Vetus Latina collection of biblical texts then in use, that became, during the 16th century, the Catholic Church's officially promulgated Latin version of the Bible.

It is a masterwork of Western calligraphy representing the pinnacle of insular illumination regarded as Ireland's finest national treasure.

The manuscript takes its name from the Abbey of Kells, which was its home for centuries. Today, it is on permanent display at Trinity College University Library, Dublin. The Library usually displays two of the current four volumes at a time, one showing a major illustration and the other showing a typical text page.

When she had finished her visit and was strolling back to the hotel, she thought to herself, "How strange it is that our Catholic Irish father is connected to his Jewish children through this fine book."

Ruth was twenty-six, but exhilarated as any six-year-old at the prospect of meeting her father for the very first time. She had an early supper and, in spite of her excitement at the day to come, slept well.

Whilst she was at breakfast the following morning, she was joined by a man she didn't know, but thought she recognised. He didn't introduce himself, but sat down opposite and stared at her. While his hair was thinning and bleached blond, there was no disguising the eyes. They were green, the same colour green that Ruth saw in the mirror every day. And the shape of his jaw, cheekbones, nose and ears that shaped his head were a giveaway to the heritage of the twins.

She broke the silence between them. "Are you our father?" she asked. "The father of me and my twin brother David?" she continued as if clarification was needed.

"Yes," he said. "I had no idea that this day would come."

And then in an exaggerated Irish accent,

"And be gosh and begorrah here ye are, yer mamai's bar-a-gold."

Ruth didn't know how to respond to this familiar stranger. She wasn't sure if she was being teased. Her feelings were mixed, between excitement at being confronted by her father, and caution at his playfulness. She did what she was trained to do. She waited for things to develop, for more information, before she committed herself.

He waited for her response, and when it was clear that she was not going to speak, he spoke again. "Do you want to meet some more of your family and share some good craic? I have the time to take you."

"Craic?" asked Ruth.

"Gossip, some good Irish gossip," explained her father.

"I do, but I will need to check who you are first. Sorry, I want to trust you, but you do understand."

"To be sure, to be sure," her father said grinning. "Make your call, and then I will tell you how to improve your blather by kissing the Blarney Stone. And you don't need to be calling me Father if you prefer not to. I am happy with Patrick or Pat."

The call that she made from the hotel telephone kiosk to the number given and introduced with her code name, confirmed that her father was who he said he was, and that under his dyed bleached hair was a matching blond to hers.

She confirmed this much to her father, but not the aside comment, that despite a thorough initial interrogation there were still areas of his past criminal life within the Mafia that were open to further questioning. So, he kept secrets, and she needed to be circumspect about what he told her, and that she should stick to her intelligence cover story however much their relationship developed.

Above all she must remember that he was still under licence with his new life in Eire, and constrained with his movements and what he could say to her. So all she said, smiling at him was:

"I accept you are who you say you are."

27

As they drove south towards Cork, her father gave her a road map and started to describe the journey they would make.

"We shall be taking the scenic east coast route to Bray, the longest established seaside town in Ireland known as the Gateway to the Garden of Ireland, passing the Sugar Loaf, a mountain east of the Wicklow Mountains National Park; then Wicklow on the river Vartry ,where from the Bride's Head on a very clear day it is possible to see the Snowdonia mountain range in Wales, then Arklow, Gorey, Ferns, Enniscorthy and Wexford scene of a notorious massacre of local loyalists by the United Irishmen who executed them with pikes on Wexford bridge; then on to Waterford known for Waterford Crystal, a legacy of the city's former glass-making industry, then Dungarvan mentioned by the British Poet Laureate Sir John Betjeman, who lived in Ireland, in his poem *The Irish Unionist's Farewell to Greta Hellstrom* where each stanza closes with the line *"Dungarvan in the rain"* recounting the story of his unrequited love for a woman called *Greta Hellstrom*, and finally down to Glanmire, our destination, a small town situated nine kilometres outside Cork, Ireland's second largest city."

And then, to fill the initial awkward silence between them, he elaborated on the story of the Blarney Stone, and what the kissing ritual involved. "The Stone 'Cloch na Blarnan' is a block of limestone built into the battlements of Blarney Castle over 500 years ago in Blarney, about eight kilometres from Cork and a little more from Glanmire. According to legend, kissing the stone gives the kisser the gift of the gab, the bla in the blather. But to touch the stone with one's lips, as is required to receive the gift of the gab, the participant must climb to the castle's rampart then, lying on yer back, lean over backwards on the parapet's edge with the help of someone to hold yer legs to get into position. Although the parapet is now fitted with wrought-iron guide rails and protective crossbars, the ritual can still trigger attacks of acrophobia, and that before the safeguards, the kiss could be a kiss of death for anyone not properly held."

"Like the fatal kiss of Hades, after he abducts Persephone, the sweet daughter of Zeus and the harvest goddess Demeter, from the upper world she loves to reign with him as his queen in the dank depths below?" banters Ruth, showing off her Homer by teasing him.

"Well I don't know about that," her father responded a little perplexed, "but don't you worry my *cailín milis*, my sweet girl, I'll be there to hold on to you and save you from falling into the Underworld!"

"That's good gas," retorted Ruth with a grin, "and how many times have you kissed the stone?"

"I'll be, and already learning the Irish. You're not such an eijit." And her father looked at her admiringly. "Well daughter, I think we're going to get on grand. Perhaps we should take a break soon, enjoy some lunch and I can introduce you to the black stuff."

"Tell me about Glanmire, who I am going to meet, what you do for a living, and how you ended up here," probed Ruth.

"Oh, I will to be sure, but let's deal with your interrogation over food. I know a nice little place in Wicklow, which is not far."

He watched her take a sip of the dark stout from her glass, and saw her wrinkled nose with a smear of creamy froth on its tip.

"What do you think?" he asked.

"Well," she said, "it's a bit bitter with a sort of cheesy smell to it. It's different from any Guinness I've ever tasted."

"Take a swig," and he waited for her to do this. "Now do you see the ring of foam around the glass bowl? That's because its draught Guinness and every swig you take will leave another ring. Guinness is Dublin's name. In Cork we call ours Murphy's. Whatever, it's a dry stout or porter, a dark beer made from water, barley, roast malt extract, hops and brewer's yeast, with a portion of the barley roasted to give its dark colour and characteristic taste. By the time you go you'll have got to like it, I'm certain."

"I didn't say I disliked it," and with that Ruth took another swig. "I see what you mean about the rings," she said, and continued to drink until her glass was empty. "There, I've got five rings!" putting her glass down.

Her father downed his in one.

"You'll only leave one when you've got a thirst. Fancy another?"

"OK," said Ruth. "Hit me."

"Now that's yer American talking for another I'm thinking, me bonnie girl," and he went off to the bar.

Returning with two fresh pints, he raised his glass. "*Sláinte*" he said, "to the O'Briens!"

"*Sláinte*, that's 'cheers' yes?" she asked raising her glass. "I take it you now include me as an O'Brien?"

Later over their coffee she reminded him of her earlier questions.

He leaned over and took one of her hands that lay on the table. She let her hand rest in his, liking the contact, and suddenly aware of a new unfamiliar feeling that swept over her, the comfortable protected feeling, she supposed, that a child must have for a beloved parent.

"I never thought this day would come. I never thought that if you discovered where I was, that you would take the trouble to find me, but here you are, and how very pleased I am to see you, me darling girl, me bar-a-gold." Her father had become quite emotional.

She gently withdrew her hand, and sat back and waited with a faint smile masking her rapidly beating heart for him to continue.

"You want me to stop my blather, I'm guessing. Well you must know a little about my past from your friends in the service. Did they tell you I came over to the USA with my parents from Liverpool via Cork? I was about fifteen, and got a job in the Manhattan Fulton fish market. I was a quick learner and hard worker, and didn't mind a fight. Soon I got noticed by the Mafia," and here he hesitated, and, seeing no reaction from his daughter, went on, "they used me as a collector in the numbers game and in due course I became a lieutenant. My father died from a heart attack, and my mother returned to

Cork to be with his sister who had stayed there rather than go to the USA when we migrated. By this time, I was making enough money to look after myself, and in due course I met your mother. She was so beautiful, even with her wonky teeth, and had she not died having you I would have paid to get her new ones, and perhaps she would have become a top model. But she didn't survive the birthing, and knowing she was married to a Jewish moneylender, who I assumed was your true father, I didn't feel any claim to her twins. It was only later after he had given you to another Jewish couple and your looks became an issue with him, that I realised there could be a connection with me. But by then there was nothing I could do to change things, and anyway I reckoned you were better off where you were than with me."

Looking hard at her father Ruth said:

"You didn't try very hard, did you?" But she didn't want to spoil the moment, so she didn't press the point, and went on with, "What do you do now?"

Relieved with the change of subject he replied to her new question. "I run an independent charter boat out of Cobh for sightseeing and fishing trips, and with Cork airport being half an hour away, it is very convenient for my guests. So, I pretty much suit myself with my time."

Very convenient for a little smuggling, Ruth thought. Something that she should check out for her report back, a condition she had reluctantly accepted for the help, both monetary and informative, she had received from her intelligence chief.

"Do you own the boat?" Ruth asked.

"I sure do," her father answered, and then to pre-empt the next question went on with, "I had enough money from my New York savings to buy the *Mary Bell* outright."

"Lucky you," said Ruth, with a pull-the-other-one half smile.

"If you say so," her father retorted.

"Do you have any hobbies, you know any special interests?" asked Ruth, wanting to penetrate further into her father's private persona.

"Well, I play the taps," her father answered with a shy smile.

"Kitchen or bathroom?" Ruth responded thinking she would never keep up with her father's humour.

Hearing Ruth's smiling retort, and realising his daughter had no idea what he was talking about, he led her on a little, trying a jokey response. "I haven't thought of that, but it could be possible, and as you are my long-lost daughter, I will try for you. Would it be the sink or basin you had in mind?"

"I haven't a clue," said Ruth, now well and truly out of her depth.

"Well now, I'm thinking you need a little more information." Her father was grinning broadly. "What you need to know is that I was persuaded to join a New York drum and bugle group by a fellow worker in the fish market. He had heard me play the mouthpiece to my horn, which I used to practice on whenever I got the chance. 'Taps' is a bugle call played at dusk, during flag ceremonies and at military funerals, by the United States armed forces. The official military version is played by a single bugle or trumpet. A famous call is Day Is Done."

He moderated his voice to recite the first verse:

"Day is done, gone the sun,
From the lake, from the hills, from the sky,
All is well, safely rest,
God is nigh."

And then pursing his lips he mimicked the bugle call.

"That's lovely," said Ruth.

"Well there's more," continued her father who was enjoying his chance to impress his daughter. "The original set of lyrics that accompany the music was written by Horace Lorenzo Trim, and the melody of the taps is composed entirely from the written notes of the C-major triad, i.e. C, E and G, with the G used in the lower and higher octaves. This is because the bugle, for which it is written, can only play the notes in the harmonic series of the instrument's fundamental tone, so a B-flat bugle plays the notes B-flat, D and F. Taps uses the third, fourth, fifth and sixth partials. The word taps comes from the same source as tattoo, originating from the Dutch *taptoe*, meaning 'close the beer taps and send the troops back to camp, otherwise'," he paused

Ruth finished for him

"They'll get too drunk."

"That's the truth of it," her father laughingly agreed.

"And one final thing," he went on, "three single slow drumbeats are struck after the sounding of the tattoo. This is known as drum taps."

He stopped, feeling foolish, thinking he had talked too much, but then he saw his daughter's soft look and felt her hand cover his. "Perhaps you will play for me sometime?" she said.

"That would be grand," he beamed, little realising that the first time Ruth would hear taps would be just before her wedding breakfast.

"Now I think it's time for us to be on the move. My Aint Nóra is expecting us for tea, and I know she is baking buttermilk scones and her homemade apple cake to welcome you. And," he paused to emphasise the point, "she is making her special Irish stew with dumplings for supper, which are to die for."

With that he went to the bar to pay and joined her outside at the car.

When they had settled into the driving, Ruth said:

"So you better tell me about my Irish family and Glanmire. And you still haven't yet mentioned your mother, my grandmother."

"Your grandmother is dead. Sorry, I should have said. She died of cancer soon after she returned to Ireland," her father replied.

"And is there family on Aunt Norah's side?" asked Ruth.

"No, she is my maiden aunt. She never managed to find her true love, and because of her love for books spent her life as a librarian in Cork."

"So there are just the four of us O'Briens left?" queried Ruth.

Seeing her father's look, she elaborated, "You and Norah, me and David?"

"Yes," he nodded. He waited for her. She was difficult to read.

"Go on about Glanmire," she said.

"Not too much to say. It's a town in the parish of Rathcooney with a population of about fifteen thousand. It has

127

primary and secondary schools, two Catholic schools and a few hundred Irish-language speakers, which don't include me. In the 1800s it was a small village with woollen factories and mills lining the banks of the river Glashaboy. The stone bridge located in Riverstown is one of the oldest in Cork. Oh, and Sarah Curran who married Captain Henry Sturgeon in 1805 at the parish church located on a hill above the village, was the lover of the hanged Robert Emmet, the Robert Emmet whose speech from the dock before sentencing is remembered for its last statement, and which made him famous amongst executed Irish republicans.

"Let no man write my epitaph. For no man who knows my motives dare now vindicate them nor prejudice or ignorance asperse them."

Ruth turned and looked at her father. "For not a lot to say you seem to know a lot."

Shrugging his shoulders, he said, "I'm not a tick Irish bog man don't you know. I can use a computer and log into Google."

He lapsed into silence.

Not wanting to break it, Ruth looked out of her window at the passing countryside with its soft hills and gentle green fields and hedgerows bathed in the muted light of the northern latitude, so much different from Israel's harsh bright white light over its arid stony ground.

She thought:

"Who is this man, our father, and how does he fit into our world? I need to talk to David and tell him where I am and what's happening with me."

28

Ruth's briefing had confirmed that her instinctive judgement of her father was right when it came to how he earned his living, for he had indeed brought his Mafia ties with him. Those connections had been a necessary CIA requirement for him to secure his protected position with Eire's G2. With its responsibility for the safety and security of the Irish Defence Forces, G2 operated both domestic and foreign intelligence sections, providing intelligence concerning threats to state security to Eire's government from both internal and external sources.

So having an inside link to the Mafia with all its Irish contacts was valuable, and consequentially Patrick O'Brien came under the control of Shamus, the very same Shamus that met Ruth at Dublin Airport, and had helped Patrick establish his charter boat business based at Cobh, with its useful connection to Cork Airport and importantly by road through Dublin to Limerick and Galway in the west, and through Dundalk in the north to Northern Ireland's Belfast.

Patrick's charter boat developed into a successful business for sightseeing and fishing trips, but whilst this provided valuable income in the season, it also offered a front for its other purpose of being a hub for people and goods trafficking that needed to be kept off the radar. This undercover service allowed for the sensitive movement of secret agents and their special cargoes, entering and exiting Eire via the ports of Dublin and Belfast with their connections to the mainland British ports of Liverpool and Glasgow, as well as *Mary Bell*'s selected sea trips into and out of Cork between the Atlantic Coast countries of Denmark, the Netherlands, Belgium, France, Spain and Portugal, and the Mediterranean's coastlines of Spain, France, Italy, Croatia, Albania, Greece, Turkey, the Middle East and North Africa.

The *Mary Bell*, with its engineered deep-V hull and comprehensive fishing station with 360° visibility, was designed for fishing in safety and comfort in a variety of weather and sea conditions, with overnight cabin accommodation for up to six people. Built in 2017, the 3100kg, nine-metre-long, three-metre-wide, 0.6m draft boat was driven by a 500hp Mercury Verado petrol engine, and provided with GPS for precise navigation and VHF for secure communication. The cockpit had an exterior floodlight for night-time activities. Inside was a fully equipped galley. With both port and starboard walk-arounds, easy access was via the stern, where twin swim platforms included a ladder for access from the sea. Indeed, the *Mary Bell* was perfect for comfortable overnight fishing trips. With her large fuel tanks, she was also perfect for longer trips when transferring agents and illicit cargoes secretly into and out of Eire.

Patrick was well known to the Irish coastguard or IRCG, based at Crosshaven Cork, one of the fifty coastguard units located in coastal areas and inland waterways, and operated by volunteer crews who worked off pagers and answered calls twenty-four hours a day 365 days a year to help those in their local community.

With its mission to reduce the loss of life within the Irish Search and Rescue Region on rivers, lakes and waterways, to protect the quality of the marine environment within the Irish Pollution Responsibility Zone, Harbours and Maritime Local Authority areas, and to preserve property, the IRGC provided an essential support service to the *Mary Bell* whenever she put to sea, even when *Mary Bell* went on a clandestine trip under the guise of fishing.

Ruth's mobile call to her brother confirmed that Hannah and her first-born daughter, Avishag, were well, and that David was shortly to go on a missile launch programme refresher course.

"How long will you be away for?" she asked.

"A few days," he replied.

"Well I am in County Cork, Ireland with our father. He tells me that we are now O'Briens, at least honorary O'Briens. I will be taking some mobile photos for you when I am shown around. I don't know how long I will be staying, but perhaps a couple of weeks. See how things go with Dad. I will ring again when I have more to tell you. Love to Hannah, and a kiss for the Avishag."

She deliberately kept her call short so that she would not have to answer detailed questions about their father. It was not that David could not be trusted, but that her training made her naturally cautious of phone tapping. And anyway, there would be lots of time to give him a full description of the news of their mother and father in the USA and Ireland when she next saw him in Israel.

Quarry
29

Having been shown to her room in her father's cottage on the outskirts of Glanmire, unpacked her small case and freshened up, she joined her father for Norah's special tea in Norah's town house.

It was everything her father had promised.

"Wonderful apple cake," Ruth said to Norah.

"When you have had a walk around the village, and got your appetite back my Irish stew with dumplings will be waiting for you," said the delighted Norah.

As they wandered the streets, they ended up at St Joseph's parish church above the village, referred to by Patrick. Whilst they rested and took in the view Ruth asked, "By the look of your home, you seem to live a bachelor's life. Is there not someone else?"

"There have been some ladies in the past, but no one at present," and as if to forestall the question, "and no, there are no brothers and sisters waiting to meet you."

"You must get lonely then." Ruth said this as a matter of fact rather than to keep a conversation going.

"Well I do have Norah, and some business friends, and now I have you?" raising his eyebrows as if he wanted confirmation to a question.

"And David too, if you can make the journey out to see him," Ruth concluded.

"Yes, David too, if my masters will allow it," he nodded. "Now I hope you don't mind, but I have to be away for the next couple of days from tomorrow, and I have taken the liberty of setting you up with a friend of mine to show you round. His name is Michael Cochrane and he is a writer who spends his spare time exploring the countryside, and getting in some rock climbing if the weather's good and he can find someone to share a rope with. He's going to leave your visit to the Blarney Stone to me, but other than that he will know some lovely parts of the Emerald Isle for you to visit. He is very trustworthy. I think you will like him. Is that OK?"

"I suppose so." Ruth shrugged, not quite sure how to respond.

"As long as you are not frightened of heights, and can drink the black stuff you will get on famously," said her father. "Oh, and happy to ride a motorcycle. And now I don't know about you, but I'm ready for Norah's stew."

The following day she slept late and missed her father leaving. She was woken by Norah who, having let herself in to her father's house with her own key, was speaking to her through her bedroom door.

"Ruth dear, I hope you slept well. I'll be cooking your breakfast if that's all right, so if you want to get up I will have it on the table in about twenty minutes. Don't bother to take your shower until after."

She didn't wait for the answer.

When Ruth came downstairs in a dressing gown she found hanging up behind her door, she could smell and hear the sound of cooking bacon. As she entered the kitchen, she saw a table laid for her, with a loaf of soda bread and a block of Irish butter.

"I made the bread fresh this morning," said Norah, "the traditional way with flour, salt, baking soda and buttermilk. The butter is from a local farm. Can you eat bacon? I'm hoping you like bacon and eggs and black pudding. I need to know if it's tea or coffee?"

"Now that I am maybe both Catholic and Jewish, and with that amazing smell coming from the kitchen, I am ready to eat everything on my plate. And coffee will be fine," she answered.

"That's grand, coffee coming up. Help yourself to hot milk and sugar. Now how do you want the eggs?" asked Norah.

"Easy over," Ruth was smiling at so much attention.

"I'm thinking easy over is you wanting the eggs' top side to be cooked?" Norah turned to look at Ruth with her spatula raised to emphasise her query.

"That's right," said Ruth.

"Then I will do what I do for your father. I will baste them until the white has bubbled," smiled Norah.

Having served her niece, she sat down beside her and poured herself a cup of coffee, remaining silent as she watched Ruth eat.

"Are you not having anything?" Ruth asked with her mouth full.

"No dear. I had something earlier. And anyway, it will soon be time for lunch which I'm guessing you'll be missing today," pointing at the kitchen clock which showed that it was half past eleven.

As she put her knife and fork down Ruth said, "That was delicious."

"You're very welcome," replied Norah pouring them a second cup. "Now before you go up to shower, let me tell you about today, and then while you're waiting for your man Michael to come, me and you can share some craic and have great gas."

Sitting now freshly showered in the front room, Norah's great gas was a series of probing questions about Ruth's past, the answers to which she manoeuvred so that they were about her life with David in Israel.

Finally, when Ruth had just started to get in her own questions, asking for details on Michael, there was a knock on the front door. Ruth glanced at her watch. It was one o'clock.

"That'll be Michael," said Norah, getting up and going to the door to let him in.

30

Michael was nothing like anything she imagined, as she rose to greet him. First of all, he was like a grinning bear of a man, who ignored her hand and proceeded to gather her up in a bear hug that lifted her off the ground, before putting her down to examine her at arm's length. She guessed he was in his early forties.

"As beautiful as they said," he exclaimed. Turning to Norah he asked, "Any chance of a cup of tea?"

"Sure ting," replied Norah. "I will make a fresh pot."

Taking Ruth's arm Michael sat them down on the settee.

"Well now," he said facing her, "your papa has put me in charge of you for the next couple of days, if that's OK with you of course?"

Ruth hadn't quite got over the hug, but she was feeling a sense of security about this man, and she nodded back.

"Well then, first things first. Are you fit? Are you strong? Are you willing? Cause I think you are." His questions and assumptions followed on top of one another, giving her no time to answer or confirm each one as they came.

So she sat there with a puzzled look on her face and asked, "What for?"

"For the climbing of course," he replied. "Didn't your papa say? And you'll be needing proper shoes to start with. But don't worry I will take care of everything. So after our tea we will drop down into Cork, get you togged up, and then reconnoitre Dalkey Quarry on the outskirts of Dublin, for our climb tomorrow."

By now Ruth was gobsmacked, and as Norah came in with the tea, she looked up at her and lifted her palms up as if to say *What's going on here?*

To regain her composure, she turned to Michael and said:

"I didn't hear a motorbike. My father said to expect to ride on one."

"Ah well, it's true I have one but it's in for a service, so it will be a car instead. Are you disappointed?" Michael queried.

"Well, I am rather," answered Ruth.

"So now I know I will make sure next time I have it with me," said Michael, nodding mock seriously.

"How do you know there will be a next time?" Ruth challenged smiling.

"Aren't you the awkward one? I guess I will just have to wait and see. But I'll be hoping." Michael smiled back.

Two and a half hours later, having been fitted out with new boots, socks, padded trousers, sweater, waterproof top and helmet, with the rest of the equipment needed coming from Michael himself they were driving into the quarry car park.

Their conversation on route had been taken up with Michael asking whether Ruth had any previous experience of climbing, a head for heights, what other sports she was involved in, raising his eyebrows when she mentioned Sambo.

"What's Sambo?" he asked, making a silly face at her. "It sounds like a South American dance."

"I'll show you when we get out of the car," she answered haughtily.

"I can't wait," he said.

He then filled in the time with a narrative on the wonders of rock climbing, the correct etiquette for following the lead rope connected climber, safety calls, safety belays, secure positions for each pitch of the climb, running belays, the periodical fail safe attachments to the face that not only allows for the rope to pass through, but also reduces the fall distance of the lead climber to twice the distance to the last belay, the technique of three point connected to the rock climbing movement with one hand and two toes, or one toe and two hands whenever possible, bridging, straddling or walking the space between two rock faces, laybacking or lying sideways against the face with both hands in a sideways crack holding the weight of the body braced by the feet pressing against an opposing left or right hand angled shift of the face, jamming various combinations of curled fingers and thumbs and whole fists into various-sized cracks in the rock face to support the body's weight against feet braced on either side of the crack when there are no footholds to give support, abseiling or using the rope to descend the rock face when climbing down is impossible "because the eyes and hands are on the wrong end of the body, unless of course one was to hang upside down, which would be impossible without going into a nose dive with embarrassing consequences, ha ha", rope work and knots, artificial work when climbing sheer faces that need a hammer for securing iron pegs into the face to hold slings until she shouted:

"Stop! Enough!"

In the silence that followed she looked across at him, and seeing his flushed face realised that all his talk covered up his shyness towards her. So she rushed to add:

"No, that's not what I meant to say. I am really interested, and I am excited at doing this. Perhaps when I am involved you can tell me more, starting with explaining about what gear is. Perhaps now you can tell me more about you," and she reached across and touched his arm.

"Of course, of course, how stupid of me but I would rather know more about you. Are you attached? How long are you going to be here? Will you marry me?" He was grinning now.

Ruth laughed.

"Well I'll be and all this on our first date." And this time she turned to look at him, seeing him as if for the first time, his craggy good looks, and feeling a twinge in her stomach, wondering what it would be liked to be kissed by him.

When they had parked and were both out of the car Ruth beckoned to him. As he got near to her, she closed with him and he suddenly found himself flat on his back with her arms trapping and locking together his leg and neck.

"There you are," she said as she held him in his helpless state before releasing him to lie back, feeling his powerlessness in her presence. "*Sambo* is a Soviet *martial art* and combat sport. The word SAMBO is an acronym for *SAMozashchita Bez Oruzhiya*. That was a wrap-around strike and scissor take down from a distance, which could have led to me making a strike to your throat. Impressed?"

He sat up feeling a little embarrassed, casting around to see if they had been observed. "Well," he said, "I had better be really careful not to upset you."

But secretly he was pleased with her prowess, and excited by her close physical contact.

They spent the next hour walking the levels of the quarry, during which Michael pointed out some of the routes on the various slabs of rock, and explaining the degrees of difficulty of the climbs, starting with Difficult, Very Difficult, Severe, Very Severe, and then Extremely and Exceptionally Severe also graded between E1 to E11.

"You mean to say that the lowest grade is Difficult. Do I like the sound of that? What happened to Easy?" Ruth asked.

"Easy is scrambling without a rope," he elaborated. "Difficult requires a rope for safety reasons, either technical or due to the exposure, that's all. I am confident you can start with a Very Difficult climb."

"What's exposure?" Ruth asked nervously.

"Well that's all about the gradient of the rock, and how far you would fall if you did. But then you will be at the end of my rope, making one-pitch climbs up to one hundred feet, and in due course you will learn how climbers protect themselves however difficult and however high the climb may be. Because—" he paused for effect "—all climbers want to get to the top of their climb without falling. Nobody wants to die."

"I am very pleased to hear that!" exclaimed Ruth and, to give her time to adjust to the implied danger, asked, "What was your most difficult climb?"

"The two hundred feet vertical Cemetery Gates on Dinas Cromlech, a striking rock outcrop in the Llanberis Pass, Snowdonia in Wales, first climbed in 1951 by Joe Brown with Don Whillans, both legendary rock climbers, using one hundred foot ropes, and only slings, karabiners and chock stones for running belay safety," he said.

"Choc stones? Chocolate stones?" she questioned hopelessly, fearful of his reply.

"Ah, chock stones with a K, blocking stones," he said ignoring the implied joke. "Well, you're talking over seventy-five years ago, when the gear was limited to various-sized pegs which could not always be hammered securely into a crack, and so instead a choice from various-sized stones found at the base of the climb would be carried in one's pocket, to be jammed into the crack with a sling looped around the secured stone and attached to the lead rope by a karabiner as a running belay, to be removed by the following climber when it was his or her turn to make the climb. Not always reliable with the stones sometime popping out, one after another, if a fall took place. But then there was little choice if the really hard climbs were to be attempted with minimum risk."

"Perhaps now is the time to explain what gear is all about, briefly that is, and then tell me more about Cemetery Gates. The name sounds a death wish to me, so plenty of exposure I'm guessing?" Ruth asked.

Michael grinned at her. "Gear is everything needed to make a climb. Is that short enough?" He waited for her to nod and then continued. "As I said, Cemetery Gates' face is vertical. In fact, it has a one-degree overhang, and it's at the top end of free climbing difficulty, OK?" he said to bring talk about climbing to a temporary close. "So if you've seen enough, and don't want to ask any more questions, I suggest we pop into Dublin and have a jar and something to eat. How say you?" Michael stood looking at her, feasting on her ruddy cheeks and windswept hair.

Glad for a rest from all the new knowledge that was being poured over her, and self-conscious of his stare, Ruth shyly smiled at him. "I'm guessing a jar is a drink of some sort, and if so, that's sounds great. So yes, I am all yours."

"*Oh, I hope so,*" Michael thought, and then, "I will give Norah a ring and tell her our plan for this evening, so she won't be worrying."

He took her possessively by the arm and steered her to the car.

31

Having parked behind Dublin's St Stephen's Green they made their way to O'Donoghues Bar.

Michael talked as they walked:

"It's a place I use whenever I am up in town, and the live music is grand. And the grub's not bad either. When I was at Trinity, I had digs on the Green with a fierce Belfast landlady who always used to glare at me suspiciously whenever she saw me, and O'Donoghues was one of my haunts. Now I am a respectable writer and behave myself, and they give me a room if they have one. So here's de ting. Either only one of us drinks, or we stay overnight and get rooms. Do you want me to enquire?"

"You did say rooms?" Ruth asked grinning at him, knowing full well what he hoped for.

"What else could it be, me being a virgin and all?" Michael knew he was treading a fine line with the daughter of his friend, but his blood was up, and his head well and truly turned by this lovely young woman.

Michael, who was remembered behind the bar, enquired after the rooms, and having found them a seat ordered two glasses of draught and two chasers of Bushmills Irish whisky.

And so the evening progressed as they ate the kitchen special, listened to the music and, bending their heads close together to be heard, swapped life stories, hers an edited version of boring backroom intelligence work, still single and likely to stay so, and his a Geography degree at Trinity, followed by lecture work to become a professor there, where the term times allowed him to indulge in his passions for mountaineering, poetry and writing, and although there had been relationships with some broken heartedness, there had not been the one, at least not yet.

"I've seen the Book of Kells," interrupted Ruth, "on the afternoon of my first day in Ireland. Is this Irish providence now that I know that we both must have stood in the same place to see this historical beauty?"

"Why, what a delightful way to store such a memory and now to share it with me. I would love to show you more of Trinity, more of my country." And Michael's eyes gleamed at her across the table.

And as time and drink flowed and they let a contented silence, surrounded by the noise of chatter and singing, engulf them there passed a look of unspoken wanting to be alone together, wanting to share the intimacy of each other.

Taking her hand, he asked:

"Are you ready?"

She answered by getting to her feet and following him, first to the bar to collect their keys, two glasses and a bottle of Jameson Redbreast ten year single malt whiskey, and then upstairs to their rooms.

Noting where his room was, she said, "Give me a few moments and I will join you."

He could hardly bear the anticipation, shedding his clothes, jumping into the shower, finger rubbing his teeth with the complimentary toothpaste and then, with a towel around his waist, pull back the bedclothes on the king-sized bed, group the pillows together and with the bottle now open on the bedside table pour two measures, and wait.

She deliberately made him wait. Part was due to her indecision over whether she should be flinging herself at him at all, and part that she needed to exercise some sort of control over what was inevitably going to happen, and so tease his patience to make him suffer the doubt of not appearing. But it was useless to pretend. She had started to want him the moment he picked her up in that bear hug. There was something so assured about him, the presence of a yearned for father's warmth and smell, and dare she think it, a father's consideration and his love. Other men in her life had never satisfied her for long, and as time passed leaving her certain that the unconditional love of soulmates would never come for her, that the 'fathers' in her life had poisoned her chances to give and to receive that fulfilment. But perhaps, she said to herself, perhaps this man may be the one. *Oh, how I long for him to be the one*, she thought. And with this hope flooding through her, she knocked gently on his door.

As she entered, she noticed his bare chest and legs as he propped himself up on one elbow. He noticed her jumper and slacks, and gestured for her to join him by patting the space beside him. Suddenly she was overcome with shyness, and sat instead on the side of the bed looking away from him. Without hesitation he came up kneeling behind her, putting his arms around her shoulders resting his head next to hers, breathing deep the sweet soap scent of her skin.

He spoke softly, "I was worried that you wouldn't come, that I had presumed too much, that I had lost you as soon as I had found you. But you are here, and you must know that I will never demand from you that which you are not prepared to give, and that if I had to, I would make this moment last a lifetime."

She turned her head towards him until their mouths were close and then leaned in to press her lips to his, parting them enough to let her warm breath fill his nostrils and then receive his urgent kiss, to take in his probing tongue and welcome it with hers. Then his hands were pulling free her sweater, pressing her back onto the bed and, still kneeling, bending over her kissing her again, pausing a moment to notice the ring on the silver chain that rested in her cleft before his hands were stroking down towards her breasts, then cupping them as her arms went round his neck pulling him onto her open mouth.

The kiss seemed to last forever, filling her with warm bliss, and when he moved to end it, she hung on tighter, her teeth grasping onto his swollen lips. But break it he did, and as she lay mourning the loss of him, he was now kneeling on the floor pulling down her slacks and her panties, admiring the muscle tone of her athletic body. Now he was caressing her legs, lifting them by her ankles until they were folded back onto the bed and she was opened to him allowing him to lean forward and rub his cheeks along her inner thighs. As she felt his breath on her skin, she raised her head and shook her head. He immediately released her ankles and said:

"Please forgive me. I can't help wanting to know you intimately, to feast at your well, to pleasure you and show you that I adore you."

But as he made to move away her legs scissored about his head, trapping his lips upon her labia majora, and with her hands pulling him against her and his tongue now doing its work her head fell back gasping aloud the climax she craved, and which overwhelmed her for the very first time. And now he was lifting her onto the bed and covering her body with his, his legs insinuating themselves between hers. Now, as he commenced to press himself into her willingness and her legs wrapped themselves about his hips, locking them both together again, she felt the strength of him inside, and called out to him,

"I am yours, I am yours!" watching his face contort and his neck arch back as he shuddered his climax into her.

But it was in the aftermath, as they lay wrapped up together, their heart beats slowing, seeing each other afresh, that the wonder of that moment was revealed. For when he smiled at her, he said:

"I love you. I love you with every fibre of my being."

Later, in the dark, with his hand resting on the exquisite silkiness of her inner thigh, close to the tender moist warmth of her core, he awoke to find her hand on him, pulling him whispering:

"Come, come here, come now."

And as he rolled sideways towards her, her hand still clutching him she kept repeating, "Come, come now," and "Please do it now, I want you now."

And as he leaned towards her, his mouth taking and sucking a breast, his hand cupping her sex, his fingers probing, she dragged him over her, biting his shoulder and raking his flanks.

Now her pleading was urgent with, "Please," and "don't stop," and "deeper," and "wait," and "yes," and "move," and "harder," and "faster," until he lost all control, thrusting wildly at her, grinding their pelvic bones together until, arching her back, she convulsed moaning and crying and sighing, "thank you, oh thank you."

"Now," he said, "it's my turn," and putting his hands beneath her buttocks, he pulled her tight towards him, disgorging his seed with a series of grunting, sounds.

"Will it ever be as good again?" she gasped when calm arrived.

"As long as you say 'please' and 'thank you' I don't see why not," and within a few seconds he was fast asleep.

When he awoke and found her missing, he panicked, throwing back the bedclothes to stand by the bed, and then hearing the cistern flush fell back with relief and anticipation flooding over him. Then he heard the door open and close and felt her satin body slither over him.

Whispering into his ear she said:

"Say it again. Say what you said last night."

"What was that?" he teased.

"You know, what you said." She bit the lobe of his ear gently.

"About our climb today, was that it?" He pretended stupidly.

"Well, if you didn't mean it. If all I am to you is a forgettable lay," and she pulled away from him.

Dragging her back, he said:

"No, you can't go, you must never go.

"Say it!" she hissed.

He gathered her up onto his chest and holding her as close as he could he whispered harshly,

"I love you. I love you with every fibre of my being!"

She wriggled free laughing. "And I love you too, more than I can ever say. But I smell a little fishy and I must get up and wash."

"Those are my little fishes. Do you think one made it to be our first born?" he asked.

"You will have to wait and see, and now I'm starving and need a big Irish breakfast for my first climb." With that she pulled on her clothes, opened the door and slipped away to her room.

But the thought of a child with this man remained with her, both frightening and delighting.

32

On their drive to the Quarry they sat in silence, except for the one question that nagged Michael. What was the story behind the ring on the silver necklace? She answered him, telling him of the circumstance of their birth, how their mother had lost her life delivering them, and that the 'diamond' was all they had of her. She told him that she had researched Herkimer 'diamonds', learned all she could about them, that the fact that they were not real diamonds, but quartz crystals of exceptional clarity made their mother's crystal more real because of its destructibility, and the need for it to be protected and kept safe and sound and valued as life itself.

"One day," said Ruth, "I want to go to the Mohawk River Valley, a possible site of our Herkimer diamond, and imagine that I could run with Hawkeye, Chingachgook the last of the Mohicans and his son Uncas, in the New York forests as they flee from Magua of the Hurons." She glanced across at Michael and asked, "Have you read the book by James Fenimore Cooper? It is a favourite of mine."

"Yes," he said. "Believe it or not, I was given it as an end of term star prize at my preparatory school when I was thirteen and it has always been a favourite of mine too. It seems we have much in common." He reached across and took her hand and brought it to his lips. "I hope I shall be there to run with you and Natty Bumppo, your Hawkeye."

They did two routes, Paradise Lost on the West Valley Rocks, a very popular first-time climb, and Arrow Head on the Upper Cliffs, another VD with good exposure and when the top was achieved, gave great views over Dublin Bay. Ruth tried not to be disconcerted by Michael's nonchalant amble up the first climb with a pipe stuck casually in the corner of his mouth as she played out the rope, and ended up climbing Paradise Lost twice, the first time on a tight rope with a great deal of scrabbling and puffing and coaxing, and the second time, after her first abseil back down, much faster, so fast that when she appeared at the top, Michael had yet to fully reel in her rope as she reached him at the belay. On Arrow Head she suffered one moment of freezing on the final slab arête with the greatest exposure, experiencing her first uncontrollable leg shake as she hesitated in making her move, calling up to him, "Hold onto to me," and hearing his reply, "You're quite safe, I will never let you go," before she overcame her fright and continued on to join him at the top and stand looking out at the magnificent view over the Bay, flushed with the adrenalin of her achievement.

As they walked back to the car, she held his hand and talked nonstop of her satisfaction at her achievement.

At the car, he said:

"You have done very well for your first time out. You are strong and move easily and with confidence on the rock. Will you be wanting to do this again?" He waited desperately hoping.

She turned to him reaching up to him and kissed him.

"As long as…" she said into his mouth.

"As long as what?" he begged, savouring their kiss.

"As long as," and here she pulled his head down and whispered into his ear, "you make love to me afterwards."

When they arrived back at her father's house they agreed to meet at Norah's in an hour, having showered and changed.

When Michael appeared, he found Ruth looking stern-faced over a cup of tea.

"What's up?" he asked.

"Norah had a message for me to call in. It said it was not urgent and that I was not to worry."

"So why the long face?" he asked again.

"It's code to mean that something serious is up, and that when I ring back, I must expect to return to base as soon as possible," she explained.

"Have you rung back?" Michael could feel the dread in his stomach.

"No, not yet," she replied. "But I must first thing tomorrow."

He reached across the table and took her hands in his,

"Then we have tonight," he said.

Capture
33

The capture of Israeli soldiers by Hamas had occurred before. The first was of Sergeant Nachshon Wachsman.

At home on leave, Wachsman was instructed by the military to attend a one-day training course in northern Israel. He left on Saturday night after Shabbat, telling his parents he would return on Sunday night. Israeli intelligence learned that Wachsman had entered a car in which there were Hamas militants.

Nachshon Wachsman was kidnapped by Palestinian Hamas at the Bnai Atarot junction in central Israel on 9 October 1994, and held hostage for six days, ending in a failed Israeli rescue attempt, during which Wachsman was killed by his captors. Three captors and an Israeli officer were also killed.

Sergeant Nachshon Mordechai Wachsman was born 3 April 1975. He was the third of seven sons born to Yehuda and Esther Wachsman. His father was Israeli-born, while his mother, born in a German displaced persons' camp, emigrated to Israel from Brooklyn New York. As a dual citizen of Israel and the US, Wachsman was raised in Jerusalem. He was a soldier of the Israel Defence Forces, volunteering for an elite commando unit of the Golani Brigade.

On 11 October 1994, a videotape was broadcast showing Wachsman, with his hands and feet bound, before a keffiyeh-covered militant who was displaying Wachsman's identity card. After the militant recited the hostage's home address and identity number, Wachsman spoke, with the armed militant behind him, saying, "The group from Hamas kidnapped me. They are demanding the release of Sheikh Ahmed Yassin and another 200 Israeli prisoners. If their demands are not met, they will execute me on Friday at eight p.m."

Nachshon's parents appealed to Prime Minister Yitzhak Rabin, President Bill Clinton, and Muslim religious leaders, for support.

On 14 October 1994, with time running out until the ultimatum, prayer vigils were held with over 100,000 people representing religious, political and social segments of the Israeli population gathered at the Western Wall. Responding to a request by Esther Wachsman, Nachshon's mother, women lit an extra Sabbath candle for her son.

Meanwhile the Israeli military had captured Jihad Yarmur, the driver of the car that had picked up Wachsman. Interrogating Yarmur, they learned that Wachsman was being held in the village of Bir Nabala, a place under Israeli control located ten minutes away from Wachsman's home in the Ramot neighbourhood of Jerusalem.

Prime Minister Rabin authorized a military rescue attempt.

Coincidently, also on Friday 14 October 1994, Yitzhak Rabin, Shimon Peres, and Yasser Arafat announced that they had won the Nobel Peace Prize. When Peres was asked his opinion on the 'peace' that he had achieved in Oslo in light of Hamas' impending deadline, he responded that the peace process involves 'calculated risks'.

At eight p.m., on 14 October 1994 the hour of the ultimatum, elite IDF commandos from the Sayeret Matkal Special Forces unit carried out an operation to free Wachsman. It was thought that Wachsman was being held behind an iron-covered door, but in fact it was a solid steel door, and the first explosion only dented the door. The commandos immediately lost the element of surprise, giving Wachsman's captors inside time to shoot him dead and position themselves for the impending firefight. A second explosive charge was prepared and the door was finally blasted open a minute later, and after a heavy exchange of gunfire with gunmen waiting on the stairwell the commandos reached a second door, but had to wait another four minutes for the charges to be set. During this time, the commandos shouted to the gunmen inside to surrender, while the gunmen replied that Waschsman was already dead and that they preferred to die. After the team broke through the door, another exchange of gunfire took place before the room was finally secured. Wachsman was found dead in the room. His body was slumped in a chair, wearing a keffiyeh and civilian clothes. He had been shot in the throat and chest at close range. In total, three gunmen were killed and two taken prisoner, while the leader of the commandos, Captain Nir Poraz was killed and nine commandos wounded.

The Wachsman family were informed of his death personally by General Yoram Yair.

The second capture was of Corporal Gilad Shalit.

On 25 June 2006, Palestinian militants from the Izz ad-Din al-Qassam Brigades, Popular Resistance Committees, and Army of Islam crossed into Israel from Gaza through an underground tunnel near Kerem Shalom, attacked an IDF post and captured Gilad Shalit. Two Israeli soldiers were killed and another two, apart from Shalit, wounded. Two of the attacking Palestinian militants were also killed. Shalit suffered a broken left hand and a light shoulder wound, and was taken via a tunnel back into Gaza to be held by Hamas as a hostage at an unknown location in the Gaza Strip until his release on 18 October 2011, five years later, as part of a prisoner exchange deal.

Corporal Gilad Shalit was born 28 August 1986, and was a former soldier in the Israel Defence Forces Armor Corps when captured. Shalit's Hamas captors issued a statement the following day, offering information on Shalit if Israel were to agree to release all female Palestinian prisoners and all Palestinian prisoners under eighteen, as well as Marwan Barghouti.

These were not met.

During his captivity, Hamas turned down requests from the International Committee of the Red Cross to be allowed to visit Shalit, claiming that any such visit could betray his location. Multiple human rights organizations criticized this stance, claiming that the conditions of Shalit's confinement were contrary to international humanitarian law. The Red Cross insisted "The Shalit family have the right under international humanitarian law to be in contact with their son".

The only communication in the early months came through an intermediary, who claimed that a low-ranking Hamas official, Ghazi Hamad, asked him to convey to Shalit's parents assurance that Shalit 'was alive and being treated according to Islam's laws regarding prisoners of war'. The only contact between Shalit and the outside world were three letters, an audio tape and a DVD in return for releasing twenty female Palestinian prisoners.

The United Nations Fact Finding Mission on the Gaza Conflict called for Shalit's release.

In August 2009 the high-ranking Hamas commander Abu Jibril Shimali, whom Israel considered responsible for masterminding Shalit's capture, was killed during the violent clashes between Hamas and the al-Qaida-affiliated Jund Ansar Allah organization in Gaza.

On 18 October 2011, Shalit was released in a deal that secured his freedom after more than five years in isolation and captivity, in exchange for 1,027 Palestinian prisoners, including some convicted of multiple murders, and carrying out attacks against Israeli civilians. According to Israeli government sources, the prisoners released were responsible for 569 Israeli deaths.

Shalit became an Israeli sports columnist.

34

The capture of David Schiff by Hamas militants for a prisoner exchange deal was dissimilar to that of Sergeant Nachshon Wachsman, in that there was no deadline with threat of execution. The similarity was with Gilad Shalit, in that he held the same rank of corporal in the Israel Defence Force's Armour Corps and that he was captured in a cross-border raid via an underground tunnel near the Israeli border.

But it was similar save for one essential difference and which, as such, changed the intended response to his capture, and the consequences that flowed from this difference.

For whilst the fate of Gilad was negotiated and his release eventually successful, David would be reported lost as a result of an unforeseen and unintended accident with the outcome exacerbated, because his apparent death was then deliberately kept secret, until it was too late to prevent the ratcheting up of the violent responses that followed.

Hamas' goal for their latest plan was to kidnap a soldier of the Israel Defence Force without bloodshed to either Israeli soldiers or civilians. In doing this Hamas would demonstrate a new non-violent behaviour during the kidnapping, whilst outwitting the Israelis at the same time.

This plan was to follow the unsuccessful attempt in 2014, when two squads of armed Palestinian militants had crossed the Israeli border through a tunnel near the Kibbutz Nir Am, by repeating it.

This surprise re-entry into Israel at the same place was based on the premise that, for the Jews, lightning wouldn't strike twice. Furthermore the entry would be achieved, despite Israeli's work on building a deep underground wall equipped with sensors along its thirty-seven-mile border with Gaza to thwart Hamas' infiltration through tunnels, by Hamas sufficiently lowering the tunnel and jamming the sensors to nullify the effect of the Israeli defences.

And as a distraction, a small explosion would be set off at the Western, or Wailing Wall, before the kidnapping took place, big enough to attract and infuriate Jewish attention but not dangerous enough to cause loss of life.

And all of this, as with the previous kidnappings, in order to continue to focus world opinion on Hamas' legitimate demands.

Unfortunately, although the distraction and kidnapping were achieved without casualties, and the kidnapped Israeli soldier successfully spirited into the tunnel en route to Gaza, the charge to block off the tunnel to the pursuing Israeli forces exploded prematurely, completely burying the leading Palestinian soldiers, but leaving the last to enter, the Israeli David Schiff and his attending Hamas guard, partially buried but alive, trapped with only a limited supply of air.

So instead of a crowing victorious video showing David alive and unharmed, and a statement that emphasised the non-violent kidnapping result where no one was seriously hurt, and where David would be kept safe and well until a resolution had been achieved with the return of the 'illegally' held Palestinians, the return to the Palestinian people of their rightful land in Israel, and the suffering and dire plight of the1.8 million Palestinian people trapped in the enclave of Gaza to be heard in the court of worldwide human justice, there was now silence. A silence that would be filled by a furious Israel and a perplexed world public opinion that was unable to understand the point to the kidnapping.

And the longer the silence grew, the louder Israel shouted its demand for David Schiff to be returned unharmed, and the angrier Israel threatened retaliation if this was not forthcoming within a deadline. Finally, losing its patience, a revenge plan of action was put in motion that would demonstrate finally how sick and tired Israel was of the disrespect the Arabs had for the Jews in their public denial of the Jewish State of Israel, and of the rights of the Jews to their homeland and to practice their faith.

35

Katsas agent Myriam, proficient in Arabic, expert in the art of subterfuge including disguise, had been summoned to contact her Mossad handler.

Peter answered his secure scrambler phone.

"Thanks, Myriam, for the call back. I need you to return to me as soon as possible. A serious situation has developed concerning your brother, which has yet to break, but which when it does will move fast and have far-reaching consequences. Let me know your earliest possible arrival time, and I will book your passage from this end. I await your call."

The phone went dead.

Forty-eight hours later Myriam was sitting facing Peter.

The extent of the information that she had been able to gather on route from news channels was that a group of Hamas soldiers had breached the Gaza Strip border with Israel and, having abducted a part-time Israeli soldier from a kibbutz, had retreated back through their tunnel of entry blowing it up behind them. No known demands had been made by Hamas, and no visible reaction had come from Israel.

"Do we know what David's condition is?" was Myriam's first question to Peter.

"No," he answered. "There is a complete silence on this. What we do know is that, following the distraction of a small explosion at the Wailing Wall, David was captured at his kibbutz without difficulty and without injury or loss of life, and taken out of Israel into Gaza through a tunnel that we had failed to detect, and which was then blown up to prevent our pursuit. None of our usual contacts have heard anything. We need to send someone into Gaza to find out what's going on, and as you have been out of the area for some time and not currently high on Hamas' radar, and suitably qualified, we want you to carry out this investigative mission."

"Of course, but I would like to contact David's family before I go," replied Myriam. "And will you also contact Michael for me, tell him I will be out of circulation for a bit, and give him a number to ring in an emergency?" As with everything in her life Ruth, briefed her handler with only the essential need to know information on her private activity.

"Yes, to the second. I assume it's serious with Michael?" He gave her a quizzical look as he answered. "As for David's family you've got twenty-four hours with Hannah, but you must not disclose your involvement. I assume she knows you have been away, so use your university work cover story to explain why you can't stay with her longer, but that you will keep in contact with her as more facts become known,"

Ruth went straight away to see Hannah and her two children, the first born daughter Avishag meaning 'her father's joy' "*who appears in the Bible attending to King David in his old age as she will for me*" remarked her father, and then nine months later almost to the day, because David could not keep his hands off Hannah, a son, Aryeh or Ari meaning 'a lion', "*a selfish provider, just like his Dad*".

Ruth remembered remarking that both names began with the letter A.

"David has always been in a hurry with his decisions," said Hannah, "and if he could solve the naming choice of our children in the As, why would he need to continue into the Bs?"

As Ruth picked the children up when they ran to greet her, she couldn't help smiling at her brother's typical thinking, and then as she embraced the pregnant Hannah her concern for her brother took over as she listened to Hannah's desperate plea,

"I haven't had any news of David. I know they took him because we were together when they entered the kibbutz, and I witnessed David's immediate reaction, which was to approach them with his hands raised and tell them to take him and leave without harming anyone else, which they agreed, having got an assurance from us that they would be given time to escape. It was all over so quickly." And as she started to weep in Ruth's arms she wailed, "I miss him so much. What am I going to do without him?"

Holding her close Ruth said softly, "Have faith, dear Hannah. Be calm. Israel will do everything to find him. He will return. He is too important to all of us, particularly now your third child is on the way," and she squeezed Hannah tightly until her sobbing subsided.

But Ruth knew the history of kidnappings, and how fraught the negotiations could be, and how risky the outcome. Reaching behind her she unhooked the silver necklace with her mother's Herkimer diamond, pulling it free to place it around Hannah's neck.

"The ring belonged to our mother. Now it will be in your safekeeping until David is returned safely, when you can then hang it around his neck."

36

Myriam entered Gaza on the Tuesday from the Egyptian side, heavily disguised as a dark-skinned man dressed in a Palestinian *thobe*, keffiyeh dress and headscarf, with fake passport and ID papers under the name of Abdallah. The scar cross on her forehead had been covered with suitably coloured make-up.

The problem in overcoming her female voice was for her to have an electrolarynx, or a 'throat back' device, used to produce speech by those who had lost their voice box, usually due to cancer of the larynx. Hers was about the size of a small handheld battery-operated electric razor, which was held under the lower jaw to produce the vibrations for synthesised speech.

The voice box also had another purpose. This was, when placed in a clear signal position on the target, to act as a homing device for a programmed incoming missile.

The overt reason for Abdallah's visit was to meet with a builder and discuss the urgent supply of cement needed for Gaza's continuous reconstruction programme. So it followed that upon receipt of Abdallah's letter of introduction, the builder would grant Abdallah the hospitality of his house as a matter of honour and sacred duty, with all its ingrained custom of generosity shown regardless of personal cost. And provided Abdallah's disguise was not uncovered, he would have a secure place to stay until it was time to react to the reality of David's situation, whatever that was.

The builder, who was a double agent for both Hamas and Mossad and therefore expected to provide the information requested from the coded demands within Abdallah's letter, had also followed his instruction to send his family away to allow for maximum secrecy during the days of Abdallah's visit.

"*Ahlan wa sahlan.* Welcome," said the builder as he poured the strong Arabic coffee from the Dallah into the small handless coffee cups, and then offered with a plate of fresh dates. "*Kayfa hālak?* How are you? I see you have a problem with your throat. I trust this does not make difficulties for you. How may I help you at this time?"

"*As-salāmu alaykum.* Thank you for your concern but I manage well," croaked Abdallah with a smile. "Azizi, my friend, you will have understood from the letter that I am seeking information. This information is to do with the health of a friend that has recently and reluctantly visited this fine country, and of whom there is no news. I would therefore be most grateful if you could make enquiries on my behalf, and provide me with the answers. I must also emphasise that this matter is extremely urgent, and that a failure to find him will have the most serious of consequences."

"I understand what you say, and I will make the necessary enquiries," said Azizi. "While you wait my house is your house, and I will prepare a room for you to rest."

"*Shukran*. I am tired now and I would like to rest. May I also impose on you to grant me the private use of a bathroom, in order that I may treat my condition, and that my meals may be sent to my room?" asked Abdallah.

"Most certainly," replied Azizi. "If you will follow me, I will take you to our finest guest suite."

As Myriam rested with a fresh robe and the protective headscarf that covered her throat, she reflected back on her visit to see Hannah and the two children. It had been a fraught time, Hannah with her drawn face and eyes red from weeping.

"I know so little. Only that he has been taken and there is no news. Why did they take him, such a beautiful human being who never intends anyone harm, is loved by so many and gave such love to me? Why, oh why? Tell me please!" And Hannah had commenced to weep again clinging to Ruth.

Ruth raged at her ignorance of any facts, her helplessness to provide any comfort. And not just for David's wife and children, but for herself, who loved her brother above all else, even Michael who had so recently shaken up her life and disturbed her feelings so completely. Even the possible child that may this moment be growing inside her. And as the rage cooled to the tempered steel of revenge, she vowed that she would do anything to find him and bring him back, and if a hair of his head was hurt, avenge his loss.

And it was with this in mind that her mission had been planned. Find out what had happened, and when she knew, play her part in the negotiations to free him, or in Israel's retaliation if the worst outcome was to be the result.

Later, when she had eaten and lay on the edge of sleep, her thoughts drifted back over her early life with her brother, her dear, sweet, innocent brother, her best friend, who had turned to her as a mother for his comfort and protection, but who also delighted her with his silly jokes and generous hugging nature, and fulfilled her sense of purpose with his intimate thoughts, hopes and fears, all the days of their growing up together, since the time of the incident.

And frowning to herself she remembered how she had saved him then, been completely ruthless in doing what she knew was necessary, never hesitating for a moment once she had decided what must be done.

With their stepmother drugged asleep, David, with his promise of pleasure as bait had tempted the drunken Asher onto the roof. As he had stepped through the door to see the smiling David waiting there, he had failed to see the hidden form of Ruth with the raised baseball bat come at him until it was too late.

How all the rage dissolved from her with the blow, how shocked and trembling David had become, how calm she had remained as she commanded his obedience in dragging Asher's unconscious form to the rail, and then between them somehow lifting Asher's shoulders to lie over them, and then be joined sideways by his trunk and legs before he was rolled over to fall away down into the basement yard. How in the empty silence she grabbed the bat and David's hand and hustled him inside to the bathroom, washed the bat and their hands, and having replaced the bat, pulled him into their bedroom and onto his bed, covering their spooning bodies with the bedclothes, her arms wrapped about him whispering into his ear,

"There, there, my brother, it's over, he will never hurt you again, and I will look after you and keep you safe. And as long as we say that we know nothing and that we spent this night together here in our beds, no one can prove otherwise. Trust me and everything will be alright."

She had held him until she felt his body relax, and sensing his sleeping she had tucked him up securely, and got into her own bed without any feelings of remorse.

37

It was the following afternoon that the builder knocked on Abdallah's door.

"*Masā' al-khayr*. May we take tea together, so that I can give you my report?"

"*Shukran*. Give me a few moments and I will join you," answered Abdallah.

As they sat together Abdallah said, "I see you are gifted in the making of Maghrebi mint tea. I find it very soothing for my condition. Now tell me what you have been able to discover about our friend?"

"The news is not good," said Azizi. "There is talk of an accident in one of the tunnels, and some deaths. There is no talk of the good health of our mutual friend, as there would be if that friend had arrived without harm. I may know more details tomorrow. It is very dangerous for me to rush to discover all the information at once. Can I beg your patience until then to learn more?"

"Of course, but it must be tomorrow," replied Abdallah and returned to his room.

They met again at midday.

"*Masā' al-khayr,*" said the builder, and then went on quickly, "the story is that due to the premature detonation of the explosives the tunnel collapsed upon our friend and his companions who were then accidentally killed. This was never intended to happen, only that our friend was to be held without harm as ransom for exchanges. Now that the plan has backfired," and here he gave an apologetic smile, "there is panic and indecision as to what can be said to explain the situation, and therefore a delay with the broadcasting of any news. There is even the view that it might be better never to admit the failure of the mission and just let it become a mystery that is never solved."

He paused to get Abdallah's reaction.

Despite the shock, grief and anger that flowed through Myriam, she managed to keep the reaction from her face.

"I hear what you say, that this was an unintended accident. But I must report back to my people. Will you therefore arrange for me to make a secure satellite call? I will wait in my room until this can be done."

Two hours later the satellite phone was brought to Abdallah's room. Myriam dialled the number which was routed through several secure links.

"Yes," said a voice that eventually answered.

"This is Abdallah. I have some news," said Myriam. "There has been an accident. The outcome is disappointing and there is little to be done. Perhaps you would indicate your reaction."

Myriam waited whilst a muffled conversation took place at the other end of his line. After several minutes the reply came.

"Tell your friend not to worry, and then proceed to the special place of interest according to *halakha* before sunset, and leave your gift."

The phone went dead.

The phone was collected by Azizi who was anxious to know how Abdallah's people had reacted.

"There is obviously concern," answered Abdallah. "But there is also understanding. I am to return at the weekend, having rested further and perhaps taking some exercise tomorrow. May I ask that you suffer my presence till then?"

"Of course," said the builder. "You only have to ask."

"My people will be very grateful for the courtesies that you have extended to me. Perhaps we may share an evening meal together, and I may be granted the honour to present you with a gift for your wife."

During their meal together, and following the presentation of the Palestinian full-length *thobe* with its decorated *qabbeh* chest pane and *libas* pants, an *araqiyyeh* close-fitting head-cap, and a *shambar* veil big enough to wrap across the lower face and hang down the front and back of the shoulders, Abdallah, now feigning difficulty with his voicebox, on which he blamed the failing battery, asked the builder,

"Tomorrow would you accompany me for my walk and a visit to the Great Mosque of Gaza, after which I will retire in preparation for leaving early the following morning?"

"I would be pleased to do so, just indicate the time," replied Azizi.

Knowing that the builder might wish to join the faithful at prayer, Abdallah timed his walk to the Great Mosque so that he could say to him,

"I must rest. Let me stay here whilst you attend the Adhan, and then we can return together."

He watched the builder enter with the other worshipers, and then walked slowly to find a suitably unobserved place to secure the transmitter with its own self-destruct explosive, which would detonate destroying the voice box when the missile exploded.

Retracing his route to the builder's house, Abdallah waited outside until the explosion happened, and then under cover of the shocked reaction that brought householders onto the street, he re-entered the house, and settled down to wait for the early morning when he would change into a woman dressed in the gift he had presented for Azizi's wife. The travelling bag would be turned inside out, its secret panel space, freed of the gift of woman's clothes and a passport for Myriam's new female role, ready to take Abdallah's clothes as another gift if discovered. Abdallah's passport was burned and the ashes disposed of in a toilet.

Now, as a woman, she would leave Gaza. If questioned, she would blame her leaving to join concerned relatives living in Egypt, on the turmoil caused by the attack.

In the event her escape was unnoticed as she joined an exodus of panicked fleeing and frightened people massing at the exit point, desperate to leave Gaza for fear of the Palestinian and Israeli tit for tat violence that would most certainly follow.

Plot
38

It was during the 2021 World Combat Sambo Championships, fighting in the sixty-four kilogramme weight class in Tashkent, Uzbekistan, representing Israel, that Ruth first met Vasili Oshchepkov.

Vasili Oshchepkov happened to share the same name with one of the pioneers of Sambo, who had lived for several years in Japan training in judo under its founder Jigoro Kano, only to die in prison after being accused of being a Japanese spy during the 1936 to 1938 Great Purge, when hundreds of thousands of people died at the hands of the Soviet government.

And as if the coincidence of the name wasn't enough the connection to being a spy was also real. For Vasili Oshchepkov, who was the Russian Sambo team coach, was also an ex member of the Foreign Intelligence Service of the Russian Federation, the successor of the First Chief Directorate or PGU of the KGB, of whom a former director of the SVR RF Sergei Lebedev had stated, *"There has not been any place on the planet where a KGB officer has not been"*.

Vasili Oshchepkov, always seeking to improve the collection as well as the dissemination of foreign intelligence, was on the lookout for fresh sources, and Ruth fell under his scouting eye. This, of course, happened to suit Ruth as she had also been encouraged by her handler to be 'available' to any foreign country's approach with a view to the opportunities of double agency. That was not to say that her proficiency in Combat Sambo, as a losing finalist to a Russian champion, was any the less important in the representation of her country Israel; just that her sharp intelligence, quick wits, stubborn courage and fluency in Russian made her the perfect candidate to undertake such a role were it to come about, which now it did.

So it was Ruth's contact with Vasili Oshchepkov and the relationship that developed that would connect her to Jack Connelly, and cast her into an intelligence role of critical importance to world peace.

39

The routine Russian surveillance of emails linked to the White House led to those between Jack Connelly and his college friend Jonas Burden being seen by a sharp-eyed Russian hacker, and brought to the attention of Vasili's SVR RF handler who in turn summoned Vasili to a review meeting.

"These fall into your scope of interest," he said. "We need to discuss them and decide if any of your contacts can help to understand them."

From: Jack Connelly [mailto:jackconnelly@xmail.com]
Sent: 29 December 2027 17:29
To: Jonas Burden
Subject: Re: Cold Cuts

Hi J,

How's it going? Arrangements for me to meet the Roman group we spoke about are going ahead, and so it will soon be time for me to serve up the cold cuts with pickled raisins without a single pip, please! They need to be packed in airtight plastic for preservation, freshness and easy for me to carry. Text me when you're ready and I'll confirm the T&P.

Your buddy,
Jack.

From: Jonas Burden [mailto:jonasburden@yahoo.com]
Sent: 30 December 2027 10:15
To: Jack Connelly
Subject: Re: Cold Cuts

Jack,

Are you sure? Are you really, really sure? Ring me.

Jonas.

It was in the New Year that Ruth received a phone call from Vasili.

He spoke in English:

"Follow the news. We need to meet as soon as possible. Suggest Rome at the usual place. Confirm earliest arrival."

She immediately arranged a meeting with Peter.

"I've had a call from our Russian friends. They want to meet with me in Rome. Says it's to do with the news. What does that mean to you?"

Peter googled latest news, and it was full of the escalation of missile activity between the Israelis and the Palestinians, the bitter exchanges brewing between the US and Russia and the attempt to involve the different religious faiths in a gathering in Rome to encourage a peaceful solution.

"It's got to be about this," said Peter, "so you better go and find out."

Ruth and Vasili met at the eighteenth-century Antico Caffè Greco just across the Ponte Cavour Bridge on the west side of the River Tiber, with its marble tables and where it was known that Keats and Byron had drunk coffee.

When they had ordered theirs and got through the formalities Vasili said, speaking in English:

"Look, we both know that our relationship is a two-way street, and that we keep it going for that one important situation when the need is great. Well now it's here. There is a situation going down which we have had our eye on for a little while. I leave you to guess how, but it is to do with the developing Middle East crisis that is interesting our masters, and in particular a meeting of religious leaders being set up here in Rome to encourage a peaceful outcome that could be seriously fucked if something is not done to prevent it being sabotaged."

Myriam continued to listen.

"Some time ago the relationship between a Jack Connelly and a Jonas Burden came to our attention. They shared rooms at university. Firstly, we took an interest in Jonas who was taking a Chemistry degree, as we monitor all exceptional students who follow specialty science courses. Well we all do it, don't we?" and he looked over at Myriam, who raised her eyebrows and shrugged with a half-smile, but kept silent. Nodding, Vasili went on, "Well, we hacked his emails to see who he talked to, and slowly built a picture of a developing friendship, perhaps more on his side, between him and this Jack, who happens to be a cousin to the US President. It seems that Jack had a tragic relationship with an Italian priest, who took a dive off a tower in the Vatican, and was comforted by Jonas, who appears to be of the same persuasion as Jack. Whilst Jack's heart was elsewhere breaking apart and not really focused on Jonas, he was still happy to accept the comfort offered by him; for Jonas this was the big thing. For Jonas this was the first love torch that he would carry, and so become susceptible to the mind of Jack and his stated hatred of the Catholic Church, and slowly, bit by bit become insinuated into Jack's desire for revenge against all religion. Well, in the normal event, so what? But then there is Jack's connection to the President, which leads to our friend Jack being appointed to chair the meeting of the religious leaders here in Rome, and which in turn, leads us to this recent cryptic email from Jack."

At which point he took out of his inside pocket Jack's email and Jonas' reply, and held it across to Myriam.

Myriam read it several times and said, "So it's about 'serving up the cold cuts with pickled raisins without a single pip puzzle', is that it?"

Vasili smiled as he took the paper back. "I always knew you were sharp. Have you memorized it?" he asked. Myriam nodded. "Well can you tell me what it means?"

"How long have I got?" she asked.

"How long do you need?" he replied.

"Let's have another coffee and something to eat," said Myriam. "You order while I have a think," and looking at the menu pointed to the *torta margherita*, and its description which she translated to herself from the Italian:

Torta Margherita, or as Pellegrino Artusi, the godfather of Italian cuisine, wrote in his 1891 cookbook masterpiece La Scienza in Cucina e L'arte di Mangiare Bene, is a light and fluffy cake adorned simply with a dusting of icing sugar. The slices of pure white coated cake are said to resemble the white petals of a daisy, lending the cake its Italian's name of margherita.

As they waited, Myriam started to make some notes on her paper serviette. She continued to say nothing until after she had finished her *torta*, a delightfully light and simple cake of flour, eggs, sugar and butter with, she noted, some lemon zest for its slightly tangy flavour.

"I see you like your cake," teased Vasili as he watched her, enjoying the chance to study her beautiful features. It would always be difficult for him to hide his feelings and keep the relationship professional.

"Four hundred calories, which I will have to burn off later," she retorted. "It's your fault for bringing me to this place of exquisite Italian confectionery."

She felt his gaze until finally he was forced to say,

"Well, have you got anything for me?"

Taking her time, she said:

"Have you already worked it out? Perhaps not as you are asking or perhaps you are just testing me. Anyway, before I do say what I think, I need to know why you have chosen to involve me, and if you will share everything that you are thinking?"

"We chose you because," and here he smiled sheepishly, "we are aware of your links into the CIA. And we are involving you because we rate you, I rate you, and that yes, we will hold nothing back as this is too important to play games."

"OK," replied Myriam. "I think 'cold cuts' is about revenge, pickled is another way of saying anagram, an anagram for raisins, and without a single pip excludes one of the Is."

"Which leads to?" he asked.

"Sarin," Myriam said. "Really nasty stuff."

"Yes, we thought it was to do with Jonas' link to the Rocky Mountain Arsenal, the RMA, and what is stocked there. But we needed your American head to confirm this, and you have." Vasili reached across the table and taking one of her hands in his, and looking deeply into her incredible green eyes as if they were the lovers—he was pretending and wishing they were—went on, "We cannot be involved without uncovering our position. So it has to be down to you to take this on and neutralize this threat with your American friends. Do you understand?"

"And what happens if I fail?" Myriam asked.

"A lot of 'Good' men are going to die, and there are going to be billions of very unhappy religious followers," Vasili answered.

"I better get on with it, then," Ruth said. Gesturing with her hand, "On you, yes? My treat next time then? Ciao!"

"If there is one," Vasili said with a mocking grin, then as she got up to leave, he called out, "Wait!"

Smiling now he said, "*A thing of beauty is a joy forever.*"

Sitting back down Ruth frowned, before asking:

"Keats?"

"You could be sitting where he sat," said Vasili continuing, "*Beauty is truth, truth beauty.*"

"Is this a pass?" asked Ruth. "Because if it is, remember, *"Nothing ever becomes real till it is experienced.*"

Vasili made a sad face, and blew a kiss at her as she left.

40

When Ruth returned to Jerusalem and met with her handler, things started to move very quickly. First, she briefed Peter, and then an emergency meeting was arranged with Israel's National Security Council, Israel's central body for coordination, integration, analysis and monitoring in the field of national security, and the staff forum on national security for the Israeli Prime Minister and Government.

Drawing its authority from the government and operating according to guidelines from the Prime Minister, the National Security Council, or NSC, was established in 1999 by the office of Prime Minister Binyamin Netanyahu following Government Resolution 4889, in the framework of lessons drawn from the Yom Kippur War. Its responsibilities were anchored in law, starting in July 2008 partly as a response to the Second Lebanon War.

The NSC is a closed circle of power, being part of the Prime Minister's Office, reporting to him directly and receiving commands from him on issues related to national security. It comprises of the Security and Foreign Policy section, the Counter-Terrorism Bureau, and two advisors covering legal and economic issues. Since December 2006, the office of the head of the NSC and the staff of the Foreign Policy Division, the Security Division and the Legal Advisor, have been located in the Prime Minister's building in Jerusalem. Having been the de facto capital of Israel as the touchstone of prophecy, still contested by Palestine as their capital, Jerusalem had been the city for modern-day Jewish practical administration purposes since 1948 and was convenient and suitable for decision making and, as the Council's work was considered secret, able to be done outside of the public eye. So whilst the Council's work authority might be vague and the Prime Minister not necessarily inclined to accept its recommendations, decisions on how to react to a security problem could be reached quickly by him.

The Prime Minister spoke. "Let me recap," he said. "In hindsight our missile attack on the Great Mosque of Gaza was launched prematurely as a knee-jerk reaction to the provocation of Hamas' bungled hostage taking, and before we were aware of the facts regarding our captured citizen. Nevertheless it has happened, and we were forced to retaliate to the bizarre Palestinian response with their secretly acquired long-range missile on the site of the Second Temple, our Jewish Holy Temple depicted by the Magdala stone, which now, with great irony, is the site of the Islamic shrine, the Dome of the Rock.

"Our response, as you and the world well know, was our strike on Mount Sinai, a strike necessary to indicate Israel's deep sense of frustration at the continuing Palestinian attacks on our country and a demonstration of Israel's potential might in defending its territory against any and all belligerent aggressors.

"Now the nuclear might of America and Russia have squared off against each other, with the world holding its breath and seeking to de-escalate tensions through a gathering of the world's religious leaders, and I quote from their invitation:

"To present a unified message to the World's Leaders, calling for them to restrain from mutual destruction."

He broke off to ensure he had kept his audience's attention. "Whilst this could be a coded message for the Jews and the Arabs to behave themselves, we have become aware that these invitations to the religious representatives attending the Convocation for Peace at the Vatican in Rome have become an invitation to an unforeseen danger at this meeting, the danger of a serious threat to assassinate all those that attend." He paused. "Of course, this must be prevented at all costs. But there is a problem. Whilst we know about the threat, we cannot reveal how we came upon our information, and because Israel is now considered persona non grata, our lines of communication to those who can respond cannot be direct, cannot reveal our source or lead back to us. We need a messenger, and luckily we have one, here in this room."

And motioning with his hand he turned to look at Peter and Ruth, who sat side by side.

41

That evening a prototype two-seater Lavi single-engine fourth-generation multirole jet fighter, developed by Israel Aircraft Industries in Israel in the 1980s, and now fitted with long-range fuel tanks was on its way to Cork Airport. Planned to be the mainstay of the Israeli Air Force with considerable export sales forecast however, the Lavi was cancelled in 1987 due to competition with American jets, leaving two prototypes that had been preserved and were available for service. With their unique design in being small, aerodynamic, highly manoeuvrable jets, with sophisticated software-rich systems, low-armed drag and ability to carry a large payload at high speed over a long distance, they were ideal for this off-plan emergency high speed flight to southern Ireland.

In the second seat sat Ruth.

Now streaking across the night sky, Ruth reflected on the rapid events.

How quickly the decision had been reached to use her father Patrick as the conduit, who, having received the briefing from her would get the information to the Americans, allowing her to make her own way separately to the United States and be ready in place to be invited into the CIA channels communicating with Israel, without any admission of Israel's prior knowledge.

How the decision to use the Lavi to get to Cork as fast as possible, getting the Lavi prepared, selecting the pilot, planning the route, getting the landing clearances, and suiting her up for the high-altitude flight, had been achieved.

But then of course the commands had come direct from the very top, from the Prime Minister of Israel himself.

She also had time to think of her brother. The fact that she would never see him again, that it would have been better if she had died and he had lived. Perhaps not now of course, now that she was carrying Michael's child. But again, she agonised, David would not be there to see her child and take part in its life, as she would in the lives of his children. Oh, how cruel fate was. How angry and confused it made her. Would she ever be free of these feelings?

And then her thoughts shifted back to Michael, reminding her of what might be possible for her. She could be seeing him very soon, if only for a brief period before she continued on to the US.

Ruth's next day pre-booked onward journey from Dublin to New York's JFK airport was on an Air Lingus seven-and-a-half-hour flight, with its four-hour backward time slip.

In the hours between landing and departing, her father had been there to meet her at Cork Airport, and whisk her away to his house, where Michael was waiting. It was a wonderfully surprised moment to see him, her father giving them a few precious hours to hold each other and exchange their intimate voices of pleasure and longing, before Michael had to leave them alone for Patrick's briefing, and the discussion as to what was expected of her father and what he felt he could achieve.

"How do I explain receiving this information?" asked her father when she had finished her brief.

"Well you don't," answered Ruth and now she had to admit to the scope of her knowledge. "The Americans know about your Mafia past and your present G2 links into the intelligence agencies of UK, Europe and Russia, and so by refusing to give your source you force them to deduce the possible options open to you. In the meantime, Israel's secret intelligence service will have leaked the information to MI6 so that the CIA will be able to corroborate the facts from them. After that, they will be too busy tracing Jack and Jonas. And that's where I will be invited in. The CIA will want to know if you have said anything to me, and in confirming this allow me to offer the CIA my neutral services in helping to make contact with JC, without having to involve another CIA asset."

"Well I'll be," her father said wistfully, slowly nodding his head. "I don't suppose there's time for the Blarney Stone? There has been so little time for us, what with Michael and you rushing about, and now this. When do I see you again?"

"Soon, I promise, soon. And you will be top of the list." She reached out and took his hands in hers,

"All right," he replied, "but I will be holding you to your promise. Now what about something to eat? I can book a table for the three of us," and he started to rise. Still holding his hands, Ruth squeezed them hard forcing him back into his seat.

"Wait," she said. "There's something else I need to tell you, which is going to hurt you. So you must prepare yourself."

"Oh dear, I thought everything was going swimmingly," he said.

"Well, you now know the kidnapping events in Israel that have led to the nuclear standoff, the peace meeting of the religious leaders, and the threat to them. What I have yet to tell you," and here she paused, looking into his eyes and gripping his hands tightly, "is that the captured Israeli soldier at the centre of this is your son and my brother, David."

She felt him stiffen.

"But you are going to get him back, aren't you?" he asked. "That's what Israel is so good at, rescuing people from impossible situations?"

She sighed.

"No. It's too late for that. He is not coming back."

And now the dam broke, and all the feelings of loss and grief that she had held back flowed from her, and as her father stood up with the shock of it, she flung herself into his arms wracked with sobbing gasps of:

"I miss him so much," and, "I don't know how I am going to live without him."

When she finally regained control and pulled back from him she was shocked to see the grey pallor of his face, the devastation in his eyes. And then there was his howl of anguish, his agonised tormented words:

"But I will never have the chance to know him now, my boy, my son that I have failed." And he too began to weep, but silently, his shoulders shaking within her grasp as it was now her turn to try to console him.

Later, when calls had been made to Norah to fetch over a loaf of soda bread, butter, a block of vintage Irish cheddar and if possible a sweet pie and she had said, "Of course dear, but the pie will have to be what's in the cupboard," and to Michael for him to come over with a bottle of the best Irish malt he could find, the three of them sat and ate, and drank the toasts of David who could not share this bounty, but would never be forgotten. Only when the last crumb and last drop were finished did they fall asleep, emotionally drained, on the sofa in front of the banked up open fire, with Ruth between the two men, a hand of hers in each of theirs.

Norah, who knew better than ask her questions, let them be, waiting in the kitchen just in case she was needed. She would be told in due course, but already knew enough to know that death was in the air. Her second sight had known of the impending death of her sister, and that the secret love of her life would never leave his family for her and that she must lead a spinster's life.

But her gift had not always visited her to foretell doom and gloom and so, despite the high drama in the adjacent room, she couldn't but feel a sense of optimism and hope that settled on her as she waited overseeing her substitute children, her *leanaí*, with a smile hovering on her face.

42

With only days before the much-publicised Convocation of the world's religions, its Chairman Jack Connelly gave an extensive interview to NBC News. The questioner immediately got to the point.

"You are a cousin to the President. So besides this special relationship, what qualifies you to chair this sensitive meeting of the world's religious leaders, the outcome of which must be to achieve a de-escalation of tensions between Russia and the USA?"

Jack Connelly felt confident in his answer.

"You know my record of academia, and my particular interest in comparative religions. You know that I am an atheist, and so will not be influenced by any superstition behind the different beliefs in God. Therefore, in my opinion, my knowledge and my neutrality make me the ideal candidate to lead discussions that will achieve consensus. I would also like to suggest that my personal relationship with the President is a benefit to my contribution to the meeting, in that, with the trust and understanding between us, I have the best level of communication to this country's first great office."

The questioner prodded.

"Nevertheless, I understand that you will be on your own at the meeting, and so a great deal of trust is being given to you to by the President to achieve a successful outcome. So could you describe the process of bringing together such different interpretations of faith and their individual beliefs in their own unique descriptions of God, to produce a common point and consensus in formulating an agreed message to the leaders of the world?"

Jack Connelly waited a moment before answering.

"The invitation, when it was sent, expected to have the approval of each of the country's political leadership represented. It was addressed to the most senior title within each religious denomination. It said," and he read,

"In the knowledge that a nuclear bomb has been detonated on Mount Sinai, and that the American and Russian nuclear weapons have been placed on a high state of readiness, you are invited to attend a meeting of religious leaders to present a unified message to world leaders calling for them to restrain from mutual destruction. To underline unity, you are asked to consider presenting a common definition of the meaning of 'God' that is centred in the English meaning of goodness. Implicit in the definition of goodness is 'that which does no harm'. This focus on goodness is to replace all partisan forms of prayer with a simple human entreaty, from one human being to another, to make peace and to use the communication channels of each faith, from its leadership to its followers, to do so."

The questioner prompted:

"I understand that the title 'The Good Year' has been given to the meeting of religious leaders. Whose idea was this and why was it chosen?"

"Although the meeting itself was jointly considered between the USA and Russia, the formatting is mine," said Jack. "The title, 'The Good Year' has been taken from a suggested code word used by two eminent persons, who wish to remain anonymous, and chosen by me to describe an outcome that focuses attention to this meeting being a positive moment in time, and of this year of 2028 being a good year."

"You know secrets whet the appetite of journalists to know more?" enquired the questioner hopefully.

"Sorry, I cannot be drawn. There is so much at stake," answered Jack.

"All right, perhaps we should not jinx the outcome, but history may wish to know the source of this hope when all is said and done." The questioner made a wry face. "So reluctantly, I will move on. You haven't much time to get consensus, and an agreement on the message to be broadcast. Have you got a strategy to deal with such disparate representations of the truth?"

Jack sat back with a half-smile. "Why of course," he replied. "They will each have a turn to make their individual contributions, to say their piece to aid peace. I am gambling on my neutrality and determination to reach a conclusion that satisfies everyone."

The questioner gave Jack a quizzical look. "With so many different interpretations on the meaning of God, and the vested interests in the practice of the different religions, that will be some feat."

"I am confident that I can succeed," said Jack.

"And if you don't?" challenged the questioner. "What then?"

"Don't worry. I guarantee that there will be a conclusive outcome," answered Jack with a determined look.

"Such confidence, such arrogance," retorted the questioner. "And how will you present the agreed message so that the world's press will receive it and release it at the same time?"

Jack replied, "On the morning of the third day the message, having been printed and signed by every representative, will be posted onto whiteboards, so that when the doors are opened, the invited press will be allowed to enter, take photographs of the message to forward to their editors and for news desks to broadcast the message to the world."

"I see you are hoping for a sensational outcome," said the broadcaster.

"Indeed, I am," answered Jack.

Getting up to shake Jack's hand the questioner said, "Thank you for talking to me, and on behalf of the world may I wish you the good outcome you aspire to achieve."

Convocation
43

Ruth's arrival at New York's JFK airport coincided with Jack Connelly's NBC interview, and so it was with this breaking story that she found her CIA contact waiting at the airport to meet her.

She was taken to a private room and briefed on the crisis.

Having absorbed it, but without giving her position away, she asked:

"Why have you chosen me?"

"Because of Five Eyes," said the CIA operative, Tim Reach. "This is very hot, and we have to get involved fast. So listen up."

He continued impatiently. "We have got some serious concerns on Jack Connelly, but we don't know how much good it will do us now that NBC is interviewing him, making it impossible to touch him. This bastard cousin to the President has made his position impregnable, with his interview being specifically approved by the President's office. We can't admit to the hacking information I've shown you, as we don't know the source, and we can't point the finger without it. With the NBC interview, Jack Connelly will now become a celebrity and be pursued by the world's press, making it impossible to take him out quietly if we need to. All we can do is to keep an eye on him and his buddy Jonas, and make sure the pickled raisins don't get taken from the store, or passed about if they are already in circulation."

He glared at Ruth as if it was all her fault.

"Well, what do you want me to do?" she asked.

"What you are trained to do. Make contact with him and stick to him until the meeting of the holy rollers is over and they are all safely back in their snug little prayer homes or whatever." He continued to glare.

"How do I do that?" Ruth asked. "You said that he is of the other persuasion, so a romantic play is not going to work. He has to need to have me around."

Tim sighed shaking his head.

"I know that's a tough one," he said. They sat in silence.

Tim Reach was an experienced operative with the CIA, due for early retirement if he didn't spoil his record now with a failure, and this case had all the earmarks of a potential fucking disaster.

"OK," he said at last. "We will get the President to give a directive that, as JC has become a star attraction in the media circus, he will need to have close protection. So when I get the instruction I'll give you the nod. It's got to be you, because the fewer who are in the know the better it is, and we can't afford any possible leak about the dodgy emails getting out."

"You will also need to get the Chief to speak to his cousin about it, so that when I turn up on the scene it won't be a surprise," said Ruth.

"Good thinking," responded Tim, and Ruth could see from his relaxing shoulders and grudging smile that he was

195

getting more comfortable with the situation. "Now let me know how I can contact you when everything is set up, so we can go over the details of you making your introduction to JC, and how we can then keep in touch with the dedicated smart phone we will be giving you."

44

Vatican City, *Città del Vaticano,* is officially the State of Vatican City, a country located within the city of Rome. With an area of approximately forty-four hectares and a population of 1,000, it is the smallest state in the world by both area and population. However, formally it is not sovereign with sovereignty being held by the Holy See, the only entity of public international law that has diplomatic relations with almost every country in the world. It is a sacerdotal-monarchical state, a type of theocracy ruled by the Bishop of Rome, the Pope. The highest state functionaries are all Catholic clergy of various national origins.

Since the return of the popes from Avignon in 1377, they have generally resided at the Apostolic Palace within what is now Vatican City, although at times residing in the Quirinal Palace, *Palazzo del Quirinale,* a historic building in Rome, located on the Quirinal Hill, the highest of the seven hills of Rome.

Vatican City is distinct from the Holy See, which dates back to early Christianity and is the main episcopal see of 1.2 billion Latin and Eastern Catholic adherents around the world. Its independence was granted in 1929 by the Lateran

Treaty between the Holy See and Italy. But according to the terms of the treaty, the Holy See has full ownership, exclusive dominion, and sovereign authority and jurisdiction over the city-state.

Within Vatican City are religious and cultural sites such as St Peter's Basilica, the Sistine Chapel and the Vatican museums, featuring some of the world's most famous paintings and sculptures.

The Vatican Obelisk, a seventy-five-foot high four-sided, narrow tapering monument which ends in a pyramid-like shape at the top, originally taken by Caligula from Heliopolis in Egypt to decorate the *spina* of Caligula's circus, is the circus' last visible remnant.

This area became the site of martyrdom of many Christians after the Great Fire of Rome in AD 64. Ancient tradition holds that it was in this circus that Saint Peter was crucified upside-down, this form of crucifixion requested by him as he felt he was unworthy to be crucified upright in the same manner as Jesus. As a result, Catholics use this cross as a symbol of humility and unworthiness in comparison to Jesus.

The unique economy of Vatican City is supported financially by contributions known as Peter's Pence, from Roman Catholics throughout the world and from the sale of postage stamps and tourist mementos, fees for admission to museums and the sale of its publications. Vatican City issues its own coins and stamps. There is a Vatican Pharmacy carrying top-brand beauty-care products and perfume at prices for many items lower than those in nearby Italian drugstores. The pharmacy does not carry products which are contrary to Catholic social teaching, such as contraceptives, abortifacients, sildenafil (Viagra) or medical marijuana.

The religious leaders started to arrive the day before the meeting, although it would be truer to say religious representatives. For many reasons, faith leaders declined to be the face of their faith. Perhaps there were good reasons amongst them, but the fear of appearing to compromise individual faiths to their faithful played a part, and the excuses of age, health and other urgent work reasons were well used. But as long as the religious representative was endorsed by their leader, and could speak good English, that would have to do.

Some did attend in person, including the Pope and the Archbishop of Canterbury, as their representations covered the two principal protagonists of the USA and Russia. They were also hosts with their Catholic and Anglican administrations to the invited guests, and as such needed to be on hand to greet the arrival of all the representatives, whoever did in fact come.

Soon the guests were settled into their rooms, allocated their guide and mentor and were congregating for their first meal, during which they would receive their briefing of the timetable of events to come.

Ruth had successfully introduced herself to Jack Connelly, and had got him to accept her close but unobtrusive presence. Her reports back to Tim were full of detail, but with nothing to suggest any collusion of JC with Jonas Burden. The examination of stock records at the RMA and the separate watch on Jonas revealed nothing untoward. The tone of conversations between Ruth and Tim began to suggest the possibility that the emails with their interpreted messages were perhaps not the prelude to mass murder, but maybe just scare talk. Nonetheless Ruth's vigilance of Jack Connelly continued and now, with the security checks of the Vatican Police, a sense of confidence in the successful outcome of the Convocation began to form. Furthermore, the demeanour of Jack Connelly was very relaxed, even to the extent at having his luggage and quarters thoroughly checked, and submitting himself to the polite body searches that all the delegates were required to have as they moved from one secure area to another.

45

The first day of the Convocation arrived. Following a fitting out, the delegates were dressed in their golden-coloured gowns. Giving their names to Ruth they were checked against the master list of recorded names, individual photos taken and iris scans made, and one by one let into the swept and secure meeting room. Last to enter was Jack Connelly, who was dressed in black to separately identify him and who, having taken up a position at the head of the table, called the delegates to attention and asked them to take a random seat.

Rapping his knuckles on the table to get attention, he said:

"Welcome to this important Convocation. I do hope you are satisfied with your accommodation, and with the information given to you at the introductory briefing." Jack smiled into the room, and then taking his time went round the table focusing on each delegate, endeavouring to meet their eyes. "Now before we get to the business of the day, I would like to talk about water." He was pleased to see their surprised interest. "You will see that unopened bottles of natural spring water have been set before each place. It may interest you to note that today's water, San Pellegrino, is produced in the San Pellegrino Terme, a *comune* in the province of Bergamo,

Lombardy, Italy. The water will have originated from a layer of rock four hundred metres below the surface, where it is mineralized from contact with limestone and volcanic rocks. It emerges from three deep springs at a temperature of about twenty-two degrees Celsius. The springs are located at the foot of a dolomite mountain wall which favours the formation and replenishment of a mineral water basin. The water then seeps to depths of over seven hundred metres and flows underground to a distant aquifer. San Pellegrino mineral water has been produced for over six hundred years. In 1395, the town borders of Mathusanash Pellegrino were drawn, marking the start of its water industry. Leonardo da Vinci is said to have visited the town in 1509 to sample and examine the town's 'miraculous' water. Analysis shows that the water is strikingly similar to the samples taken in 1782, the first year such analysis took place. Tomorrow there will be different natural spring water, Acqua Panna from the region of Tuscany dating back to the Romans, and on the third day San Benedetto, water bottled near Venice known for its low mineral content, will be offered. With over two hundred and fifty brands of Italian mineral we have made a lucky dip choice. Now please check the top to your bottle before you, and do not drink from it if the seal it is already broken. This is not said to worry you as to the purity of the water offered, but rather to emphasise the care and attention that is being taken for your secure well-being."

He allowed time for the delegates to examine their water bottles before he continued.

"Perhaps you will open your bottles and fill your glasses." He let them help themselves. "Now I would like to use water integrity to highlight its vital significance for all known forms of life, as water is indeed the elixir of life."

Turning to the whiteboards he unveiled the prescribed messages written on them.

"You will each be familiar to the importance of water in your individual faiths. But it may also interest you to know something of other faiths' water values." And here he pointed to the whiteboards, and read out:

"Indigenous people honour and respect water as sacred.

"To Hindus, bathing in a river causes the forgiveness of sins.

"For Buddhists, water symbolizes purity, clarity and calmness.

"In Judaism, water is important in ritual cleansing.

"In Christianity, water is associated with baptism.

"For Islam, water is life, and a gift from God.

"The Baha'i's use of water reflects unity between all people.

"In Taoism, water is the essence of nature."

Pausing to smile at the assembled, he said:

"So perhaps our common value of water is a good place for us to start to find consensus."

Feeling he was now in control he then asked generally:

"Are you all comfortable?" Nodding, he went on. "Now may I remind you of the following important points. Once we are gathered at this meeting table, the doors will be locked on the outside, and the key kept with our security co-ordinator Ruth, to whom you have already been introduced. The language to be used in this room is English, and I am assuming that each of you speaks for all the countries that come within the reach of the faith you represent."

He allowed a moment's reflection to receive any dissension to this. There was none, and so he continued:

"To achieve equivalence all of you will wear the similar golden-coloured gowns whilst you attend these meetings. I am wearing black to highlight my presence.

"There are no identification badges, but of course you may identify yourself to whoever you choose to.

"Passing amongst you, you will draw from my bag of numbered balls the sequence number for your turn to speak, if you wish, placing your ball in the bowl on the meeting table before each of you.

"The meeting will be chaired by me, an atheist. My credentials were in your welcome pack. I hope you have read them, but I am happy to answer any further questions you might have. I will play no part other than to advise you on the order of speakers, your time taken, and when the proposed breaks are suggested.

"There is a telephone for emergency purposes, and which I will use to advise the reception desk, situated in the outside hallway, to unlock the door when we have concluded our day's business.

"No mobiles are allowed. It is vital that our business conducted in this room, stays in this room. Obviously, the world wants to know what is being said here, but that must wait until we have consensus on the third day about the message we wish to give to the world.

"The time allocated is approximately five minutes per speaker, progressing from one speaker to the next in a continuum.

"When it is clear that there is nothing further required to be said by anyone, the meeting will stop.

"To ensure confidentiality and allow each of you to speak without constraint, no notes may be taken.

"Any posting onto the whiteboards, behind me, will require your agreement, and will be done by me.

"At the end of each day the whiteboards will be wiped clean by me before I ring through and ask Ruth to unlock the doors.

"The suggested discussion today, the first day, will include the meaning of God as it appears to each of you.

"The second day will be to hear representations on the form of words to be considered for the broadcasted message, which I will post onto the white boards.

"The final morning, I will produce the agreed text as a written proclamation for signing by each of you.

"I will also post the agreed proclamation on the whiteboards.

"When we are ready on the third day, the doors will be opened to the invited press, for them to photograph us and your agreed message shown on the whiteboards, and then to forward their copy to be broadcast to the world.

"Finally, there is a medical team on standby if required.

"Are there any questions?"

Because of the secrecy of each day's meeting, the individual responses to the meaning of God on the first day were only ever to be known by the delegates and the chairman. They were however essential in the putting of Jack's plan into effect, as the different descriptions would have to be woven into a single message for the third day. So it was that he wrote on the whiteboard a title summation of each delegate's statement, which included those below, but not posted in any order of importance.

Goodness, Kaumaram, the Great Breath, Supreme Being, Omniscience, Omnipresence, Divine Simplicity, All Loving, Incorporeal, Creator, Sustainer of the Universe, He Who Is, Allah, Yahweh, I Am that I Am, The Trinity, Elohim, Adonai, Tawhid, Progenitor of the Universe, Brahman, Baha,

Waheguru, Jehovah, Ahura Mazda, Omnitheism, Pandeism, Oneness, Henotheism, Pandeism, Panendeism, Pantheism, Elyon, the Grand Design, Krishna, El Shaddai, Al-Rahman, Supreme Soul, Vaishnavism, Absolute Truth, Bath Kol.

This diversity of description of 'God' was what Jack thought would happen, and so would help him to demonstrate the difficulty of selecting a single descriptive title that could be used to represent everyone in the group.

"For us to achieve a consensus," Jack said, "we need to find a word that means the same to all of us, and also to all the faithful within every faith, a word that represents the very best of our common humanity. Let us therefore consider a different approach by separating our diverse divine differences from our common human condition. Let us consider death, our individual deaths when the measurement of the value of our individual lives can be seen in the extent of the selflessness of our lives at the time of our passing."

The word 'goodness' had caught Jack's eye. Pointing to it on the whiteboard he said, "I would like to suggest the word 'goodness', for surely, we wish to be remembered for our 'goodness' rather than for our 'badness'."

If Ruth had been in the room, she would have been shaken at the way Jack Connelly spoke the word 'badness'. It was how he paused after 'our', before spitting out the 'bad' of the word and then hissing the 'ness'. But of course, Ruth wasn't there, and so she did not see the way Jack's eyes narrowed or how his mouth twisted into a sardonic grin.

46

Ruth's report to Tim on the evening of the second day confirmed that there had been no cause for alarm.

"I have followed him everywhere. I eat with him, do almost everything but sleep with him. I am there when he is frisked before entering the meeting room. I am outside the locked door of the meeting room during the meeting and there when he comes out. The meeting room is guarded, inspected, scanned and sealed between sessions. His bedroom is checked over when he is in session. The alarm on his bedroom door has not been trigged after he turns in, and the CCTV of his bedroom corridor, the lifts, staircases and front and back hotel entrances, checked by my team, has shown up nothing suspicious. The delegates pretty much keep to themselves, and there have been no absentees at the meals or at the meetings. JC's relaxed. I would say he is enjoying himself. It feels more and more as if the emails were just frustrated wishes rather than deadly demands."

"Only one more day to go, so keep it tight," said Tim. "Speak to me after the great reveal tomorrow," and he was gone.

In Jack Connelly's daily debrief to the White House on each day's progress, he reported that everything was going to plan. The Convocation would be ready to invite the press in at eleven a.m. on the final morning, with the Chairman using the internal phone to trigger the unlocking of the door. Ruth, who was the keyholder during the sessions, was with a picked group of the Vatican Police and Five Eye intelligence officers, to contain the movement of the press, and control their entry into the meeting room when the doors were opened.

For Ruth the tension of checking and double checking the delegates' movement, meals and security arrangements, left its toll. But she was supremely fit, disciplined and chose the right food to eat, so that despite a lack of proper sleep she stayed on top of her communication with her security team, and maintained the high level of alert vigilance required. She just had to get through the day and then she could relax her responsibilities to her precious human cargo.

47

Eleven o'clock on the third day came and went. The call to open the doors had yet to come. The tension of the waiting group, already high, continued to mount.

Focused on Ruth, who stood by the door with the key in her hand, press comments were being made.

"I thought eleven o'clock was the magic hour."

"What's the hold-up?"

"Can't we ring in and find out?"

Ruth, who could feel the pressure said:

"There is a protocol for this. We wait ten minutes, and then we ring. Don't worry. They are just getting ready, and we must give them enough time."

At eleven ten Ruth nodded to the reception desk.

"Make the call."

At eleven fifteen, the reception clerk called over:

"There is no answer. Do you want me to try again?"

"Yes," said Ruth.

After a five-minute ring:

"Still no answer," came back the reply.

It was now eleven twenty.

Comments were coming at her from all sides to open the door.

"Try once more," said Ruth.

Eleven twenty-five. And again, the reply came back, "Still no answer."

Ruth called the Vatican Police and Five Eyes detail to stand with her.

Speaking in Italian and then English she said:

"*Rimani con me e seguire le mie istruzioni.* Stay with me and follow my instructions."

She proceeded to unlock and open the door.

As the press group pushed their way into the room they were met with an incredible sight. Around the oval table the delegates in their golden gowns were slumped across their place settings on the table. The chairman in his black gown was also slumped at the head. Everyone froze, and then a frenzy of camera-shutter work started. It took a moment for Ruth to get the attention of her police detail.

"*Attenzione dettaglio!*" she shouted, "*Ottenere la stampa fuori di qui!* Attention detail, get the press out of here."

And as they joined with her in a line, with their batons drawn across their chests corralling and pushing them back out of the door, the press were still shooting their automatic cameras. Finally, they were outside the room. Ruth swung the doors closed and locked them, leaving her still in the room. As she turned to face the table of inert bodies, she saw the signed declaration that lay on the centre of the table, of the repeated message on the whiteboards:

We are prepared to sacrifice our lives for the goodness of the world

Outside pandemonium had broken out, and it would be a matter of just a few minutes before the images of the room, with its slumped delegates and the stark message was being beamed across the world. The telephones of the world leaders were alive with the hot traffic of furious questions and dumbfounded answers.

Inside the internal phone would still not be answered.

The time was now eleven forty-five.

Climb
48

The sense of relief now that the truth was out spurred Ruth on to see Michael as soon as possible. She had been quite specific in her demand to him.

"I can't face anyone, including my father. I must get away, somewhere, anywhere that I cannot be reached. Can you arrange something and let me know where to meet you? And please, no newspapers!"

Within an hour, he returned the call.

"I've booked us into a small hideaway hotel, the Bry Tyrch Inn just outside Capel Curig, in the Mymbyr Valley, Snowdonia, North Wales, near to Plas y Brenin the National Mountain Centre for the United Kingdom. I've been promised a room with a huge double bed and the best breakfast Wales has to offer. The centre is an ideal base for climbing and canoeing, if you have got any strength left for outdoor activities after I have finished with you. Don't worry about sports gear. There's a Joe Brown sports shop for anything we need. Just bring yourself and get to Manchester Airport. I will pick you up there in a hired car. Confirm your plane details and arrival time. I can't wait to see you!"

Then, after yesterday's frenzy of lovemaking, exhausted sleep, and a famished appetite for breakfast, with a packed lunch, climbing gear and ropes, they made some practice climbs; first on the Tryfan mountain in the Ogwen Valley, jumping between the rocks of Adam and Eve on the summit, and then onto the near vertical Idwal Slabs, used as a training ground for the Mount Everest conqueror Edmund Hillary, for some hand and feet friction only climbing experience, before returning to the guest house for a long soak in a hot bath, more slow loving and snoozing, and a delicious steak supper, and bottle of strong red wine with its bottle-shaped poem* that Michael had handwritten to celebrate their togetherness, and finally sleep, glorious sleep.

As she drifted into oblivion, the last thing she remembered was Michael whispering into her ear:

"Let it all go. Tomorrow is a new day, and you will need all your strength to cope with what I have in mind for you," and his body moulding itself tightly behind her, his forearm under hers, his hand sliding down to cup, the luscious form of her breast, his face against the soft part of her under arm, scenting her female smell tinged with the lingering perfume of Blue Grass eau de toilette by Elizabeth Arden that he had given her.

*First lovingly
remove the
bottle from
its waiting
place & safely
rest it to blood
temperature.*
*Then choose a place and time as
carefully as stillness, where the three
become an undisturbed ménage à trois.
When ready and relaxed, start the process
of companionship, companionship with each
other and companionship with this fine bottle.
Slowly, together, hold the bottle, and study it's
shape and description. Slowly, together, remove
the neck foil, and then the bedded cork. Smell the
cork, and put aside for memories' sake. Now, into
a pair of shiny fat bodied crystal glasses pour each
a half glass and let the moment pause. Then cradling
the glass gaze full the colour... breathe deep the scent
and slowly sip the first rich taste, the first moment when
past and present can meet, and know the truth of union.
Hold back the swallow until the very last and then, and
only then when thirsty satisfaction cannot be denied.
Rest and praise the sigh, remembering well all our
stories that have led to now.*

49

Now they were sitting on the Girdle Ledge belay point of the Cemetery Gates climb on Dinas Cromlech in Llanberis Pass, their legs touching and dangling over the 200-foot drop, looking across the valley to the climbs on Dinas Mot's rocky outcrop, before Michael stood up on the narrow ledge and said:

"Take in my slack," and then questioning, "Ready?" before unhooking himself from the belay, and with Ruth paying out his rope made the final step right around the arête to follow the fifty-foot incut to the top and the out of sight tree belay. Left alone and feeling vulnerable she waited for her rope slack to be taken up, and his "Ready!" confirmation call for her to follow, when she would unhook herself from the belay and, hanging the sling and attached karabiner around her neck, stand up on the narrow ledge and make ready to follow him, before calling out:

"Climbing!"

At last she was beside him once again.

She could not believe it. Her body was still buzzing with the adrenalin, her mind spinning with the achievement, her hands bloody with the effort. It had taken all her courage, particularly as she finger jammed her way up the crack of the vertical crux pitch, calling out to him "For fuck's sake, take in the slack!" as she used every last bit of her strength to make it, before hauling herself trembling onto the backside width of the ledge.

Michael had given her no time to think when he woke her with a cup of tea. It had been:

"How do you feel today? Are you comfortable in your climbing kit? Are you ready for a challenge? Do you trust me to look after you?"

She had just looked at him nodding, not knowing what to expect.

She loved the open Welsh countryside, its mountains, valleys and lakes, and the thrill of the climb. She couldn't get enough of the views, the air and the smell of the rock in her clothes. And she loved his company, watching him move through the rocks, so sure footed. She would go anywhere he asked, do anything he wanted. She was completely his slave.

"Today," he said, "while you still feel brave, we will do Cemetery Gates. Do you remember I told you about it? The Llanberis Valley is quite spectacular, running from Pen-y-Pass to Nant Peris, between the Snowdon Massif and Glyder Fawr. The climb is one of the three E1s on the Dinas Cromlech crag. You will need all your courage and strength to do it. Trust me, I know you can do it, and of course I will be on hand to give you a little help if you need it."

Since he had collected her at the airport, she had not wanted to talk, to tell him what had happened to her. In fact, she wasn't sure how much she would tell him, letting him into her secret world. She desperately needed to change the subject in her head, and he, sensing her need to be free of the recent past, let her be.

And so it was not until a week had passed and they had climbed Snowdon and made the 'knife-edged' arête traverse of Crib Goch that forms part of the Snowdon Horseshoe, and done some canoeing on the thirty foot deep, three quarter mile long Llynnau Mymbyr lakes fed by the Nantygwryd river, in the Dyffryn Mymbyr valley that runs from Capel Curig's Plas y Brenin to the Pen-y-Gwryd hotel, that she allowed the memories to seep back as she again hot tub soaked away her aches and pains, about how it had started with Jack Connelly, and where it had all ended.

50

Having been briefed to expect her, her initiated introduction did not surprise Jack Connelly when it came, other than that she was a woman. He studied her CIA badge carefully when she proffered it and said to him,

"I am your close personal protection officer. I will need to be in your daylight line of sight at all times. I have the bedroom close to yours, and can come to your aid at night if needed. I am prepared to put myself between you and harm, so treat me as a beloved sister who would sacrifice herself for her brother's well-being." She smiled to herself when she said this, thinking *These words I would only ever mean for my David, my Michael. For you I would let you take the hit.*

As he handed her badge back, he studied her, and saw a somewhat slight figure standing poised like a ballerina, looking back at him with her incredibly green eyes in a lovely face, framed by short blonde hair. He noticed the faded cross-shaped mark. He wondered how much she knew about him. Pretty much everything, he thought, but not his secret hatred. Only Jonas knew, and Jonas loved him too much to divulge it. But he would be careful, and find out how she felt about him, and whether she was sympathetic to his belief, or more accurately non-belief.

"If we are going to be so close perhaps, we could eat together and get to know each other better?" He was smiling now, exercising his considerable charm.

"Of course," she replied smiling back. "I am yours to command."

During dinner that evening he started off their conversation by asking:

"How much do you know about me?"

"I know that you are a professor at a leading university, that you are a cousin to the President, that you are an atheist, and that because of your connection to the White House and your belief or non-belief, you are well qualified to chair the gathering of religious leaders in Rome," she answered.

"Nothing else?" he probed.

Taking her time, she said:

"I am as safe with you as you are with me."

He glanced at her sideways.

"Diplomatically put," he replied, and half smiling went on, "Let me ask about you?"

"Sure," said Ruth, "but I have to tell you that anything about my past life or my current job is off limits. Sorry."

"That doesn't leave much," Jack said. "But OK. So can you tell me what you think about the job I have been given?"

"I think it is right that an atheist should chair the meeting," answered Ruth. "I am happy to accept that the people who chose you know what they are doing. Only you can know whether you can do a good job."

"I think I can do a good job, if you will help me," Jack replied.

"Help you? Help you how?" Ruth questioned, surprised.

"First I need to know about your faith," Jack said.

"Let's finish the meal, and then go somewhere quiet for coffee, and then we can talk more openly," Ruth replied.

When they had been served, and were sitting comfortably in a secluded corner, Ruth gave him her answer.

"I was born a Jew, but like you, I'm an atheist. But I do believe that there is good intention in people, and although I have taken tough decisions in my line of work against the enemies of my country and those that would hurt my family and friends, I would never knowingly go out of my way to hurt the good people."

"So what if I was to tell you that what I plan to do in the meeting with the religious leaders is for the good of the world, would you be prepared to help me?" asked Jack.

"You will have to tell me first, and I will see if I will," answered Ruth.

What he said next astonished her, and she could not but admire his brazen idea. And after all it fitted so well with her privately held views, how the world could be a really shitty place. But it was extreme, and she would have to think if she would, or indeed could help him. Or, of course neutralise him if she had to.

The ending, when it came, worked like clockwork. There had been enough time to get the story, the pictures and the message out to their editors, and then for them to commit their release to the world.

Now there was no going back. She stood with her back to the locked door, silently viewing the slumped delegates, prolonging the moment before she needed to act, needed to reconnect with the ignorant world outside the room, and bring it down upon her head

Lyssa, daughter of Nyx who sprung from the blood of Ouranos' wound following his castration by Cronus, Lyssa the spirit of mad rage and frenzy and rabies.

She took deep breaths as she steadied herself savouring the moment. After all this was the pinnacle of her working life so far, and if it didn't produce the reaction it intended, nothing would.

51

"Have you gone to sleep? Can I join you?" Michael's presence broke her reverie, as he carefully stepped into the bath, both feet pushing her legs apart to give him the space to lower his bottom between them, and then lean back on her breasts, his hands resting on her knees, her arms now around his waist, her hands reaching down to grip his manhood, and giggle into his neck as she felt him harden.

"You are a dirty boy, and it is my duty to make you clean," she said, and taking the soap she started to lather him.

Later, as she remonstrated with him over the damp patches on the bed where he had lain her dripping body and without so much as 'please' impatiently thrust into her, bringing her to another gasping climax, she said:

"I have something to tell you."

"Is it good or bad?" he asked.

"That depends," she answered. "It depends how much you want it."

"Tell me," he implored.

"Well, as I'm not sure you want it enough you will have to wait now until we get home," she teased.

"If that's the way it is, I'm going to tickle it out of you," and with that he proceeded to sit astride her hips and stroke the soles of her feet as she shrieked and writhed below him.

"Stop!" she laughed out loud, "everyone will hear us."

But she still didn't tell him.

From Capel Curig they took the A5 to Bangor and then the A55 to Holyhead in Anglesey to catch the afternoon ferry to Dublin.

There was one slightly unnerving incident on the boat. As they sat on the deck a young boy came and stood looking at them, or rather at Ruth. After a prolonged stare Ruth said:

"Have you seen enough to know me next time?"

At which he ran off shouting to his parents,

"It's her. Mum, Dad it's her, it's her!"

Ruth grabbed hold of the surprised Michael and hurried him to a people-free area, where she continued to stubbornly refuse to give any explanation despite his hard look of enquiry.

Finally, it was too much for Michael. He had been patient long enough. "Is this how it is going to be, silence until we dock? Surely, I of all people have a right to know?"

"I will tell you when I am ready," she retorted, but she knew she was being unreasonable.

He reddened. A hot rage swept through him. He spun her round to face him, his fingers digging painfully into her arms.

"Well fuck you!" he snarled, and then roughly pushing her away he strode off to complete the boat trip on his own until they were forced to meet up again when they embarked.

The car journey home was an icy affair.

By eight p.m. they were in Michael's house, and she still had not told him. All she had said to his repeated questions of,

"Well?" was "Not yet." Finally, as they entered the kitchen, she flung herself at him, hugging him and pulling his head down to her lips breathing out, "I'm sorry, I'm sorry. I can be such an ornery bitch," and then he was hugging her back, kissing her sorry mouth, all the anger draining out, a tide of joyous pleasure sweeping in. God how he loved her, how he loved the inside and the outside of her, the wanting when she was there, the hurting when she was not.

"Was that our first row?" she was laughing sharing in the joy, and then feeling his arousal grasped hold of him. "Yes, me too, but first things first, and I promise you will not have long to wait."

Ruth rang her father to say they were back.

"I need to come round," he said immediately.

"Good," she said, "and bring a bottle of the hard stuff."

The first thing he did when they let him in was to turn on the TV and tune it to the news channel.

"You've some explaining to do," he said, as he poured a shot into three glasses. They stood there watching the screen where the images of Ruth and Jack Connelly filled the screen.

The newscaster was speaking, "There is still no trace of the vanished security woman, who with the Chairman Jack Connelly, now in custody, appear to have pulled off a gigantic hoax on the world. The widely reported 'deaths' of the religious leaders in their Vatican meeting room with their message *We are prepared to sacrifice our lives for the goodness of the world* is now being seen as a stunt to bring the world leaders to their senses, as news of the terrible shock of their deaths followed by the huge relief of their rising from the dead, has created a worldwide emotional turmoil of grief followed by relief, with all the mixed emotions of joy, anger and laughter. And now a recent sighting of her on a ferry bound for Dublin Port has been made, and the Gardaí, the Irish police, are actively searching for her..."

Ruth bent down and turned the TV off.

"Do you think they will trace me here?" she asked the room.

"Unless they have this address, perhaps not," said the astonished Michael.

"But they do know about me, and my link to my daughter," said Patrick, "and so it must be just a matter of time."

"Time is what I need," interrupted Ruth. "Can we buy some, so that I can tell you both about it, and prepare myself for the hot glare of publicity when it comes?"

"I will do my best," said Patrick. "You and Michael will have to stay here out of sight. I will garage the car, and remove all traces of you being here before returning to my home. I will go and see Norah, tell her you are back but that your presence is to be kept secret. I will get her to bring you something for supper tonight. You can then get a good night's sleep. In the morning I will slip back and you can tell us about it. If the Gardai or press come knocking at my door, I will tell them that I know you have been climbing in Snowdonia, but that you are not using your mobiles, and that I have no idea when or if you will return here. OK?"

After a supper of lightly curried smoked haddock kedgeree that Norah had left for them, with instruction for Ruth to warm up and mix the cooked long-grain rice, hard-boiled eggs, sultanas and fish with plenty of melting butter, a recipe that Norah had been given by a Sikh gentleman that she had got to know briefly if rather too well whilst she was a

225

librarian, they lay in each other's arms ready for sleep. Michael asked:

"Well? Was this what you have been holding back from me?"

"Not quite," Ruth answered snuggling into his warmth. "What you really need to know, and what I really want you to want," and here she deliberately paused to get the maximum effect, "is our baby."

Michael sat bolt upright, throwing the bedclothes aside as he fumbled for the light. Now, looking down on her as she tried grinning sheepishly to cover herself up, he shouted out:

"What? You mean pregnant!?" And responding to her hushing, more softly, "and you let me take our firstborn up an E1 grade climb? What sort of woman are you?" And he gathered her up and started to kiss her, her eyes, her nose, her mouth, her throat, her breasts, her belly and her mound, "And you let me make love to you again and again? How could you?" he was now weeping with the joy of it.

"Well," she said as he calmed down. "Firstly, our baby didn't climb Cemetery Gates. I did. He or she just came along for the ride. Secondly, I have to keep making love because it is good for me, and what is good for me is good for our baby. And thirdly," she paused "I have to keep making love or I might get rusty." And with this she pushed him onto his back, pulled his pyjama bottoms down, and started to slowly suck the head of his expanding member until, satisfied that it was sufficiently hard, pulled up her nightdress to straddle him and begin the thrilling corkscrew piston motion that would bring them both to their jerking, twitching, gasping climax.

"Do you see," Ruth said as they again lay in each other's arms, "that this is not only good for me, but it is good for you too."

"Oh yes," whispered Michael. "I too never want to suffer from rust."

Ruth got up when she heard Norah downstairs, and went to meet her.

"No need to get up yet," Norah said. "I have put the shopping away, and tided up a bit. The kettle has boiled if you want to take up a cuppa. Now just give me your dirty clothes for washing and I'll leave you alone. I know your da will be around later, so tell him if you want anything else from the store, and I'll bring it round later."

Giving Ruth a big hug and a knowing wink she continued, "I know you have lots to talk about!"

Ruth gently shook Michael awake.

"Norah's been. There's a cup of tea on the side table. I'm going to have a bath so take a pee first if you need to."

Michael had his pee and sat back cross-legged in the bed sipping tea. He had decided. When she finished her bath, he would ask her.

"Now," said Ruth as she returned in her robe drying her hair, "it's your turn," and went to pull the clothes off him.

"In a minute," he replied taking her hands and pulling her to sit in front of him.

"Now look here," she remonstrated, "there will be time for this later," and moved to get off the bed.

"No wait," said Michael. "It's a pressing matter. I need to ask you something, something important."

Ruth relaxed back, "I don't see why it can't wait till Dad's here. I did say I would tell you both about it then."

She saw the determined look on his face and said, "OK, shoot."

Suddenly he was kneeling before her taking her hands in his. "I can't wait any longer. Will you marry me? Will you be my wife to love and to cherish forever and ever?"

The colour rose hot in her cheeks. She saw his grey serious face and questioning look. Her tears started to stream down her face, and then she was sitting astride his knees laughing and crying at the same time.

"Yes," she replied. "Oh yes, yes, yes!"

And then he was crying and laughing too.

"You realise that there will have to be two weddings," Ruth said, "a Catholic one and a Jewish one?"

"Whatever you want," replied Michael, the smiling soon to be husband to the most beautiful woman in the world, and father of the most loved baby of all time.

52

Patrick had slipped back into Michael's house unobserved, and the three of them were sitting around the dining table drinking their tea.

"Let me bring you up to date with the local activity," he said and, looking at his daughter, went on, "you better prepare yourself. The press are camped outside my door. I've told them you are in Wales, and that I don't know when you will be back, but I doubt that they believed me. It seems that the small boy that saw you on the ferry has become a national celebrity, and that from what he has said you must now be hiding somewhere in Eire. They have still to know about Michael, but it can't be too long before that cat is out of the bag, and then with the addition of a romance the whole thing is going to go bonkers. So we have little time to try to work out what can be done, if anything, to protect your privacy. But as a starting point here's what I suggest. You fill us in on your part in this sensational story, and then we decide."

Ruth poured another cup. "I will tell you everything I can."

Beginning with her assimilation into the CIA when she arrived into the US, she described her assignment to close protect Jack Connelly and how she came to introduce herself to him and what had been said when he had asked what her faith was.

"I said, I was born a Jew, but like you, I'm an atheist. But I do believe that there is good intention in people. And although I have to take tough decisions in my line of work, I never knowingly go out of my way to hurt the good people."

"He replied, So what if I was to tell you what I plan to do in the meeting with the religious leaders is for the good of the world, would you be prepared to help me?"

And I replied, "You will have to tell me first, and I will see if I will."

"So what did he tell you then," asked Michael and Patrick together.

"What he told me was an outrageous plan to hoax the world," answered Ruth.

Looking at her father she went on, "I thought he was going to tell me that he wanted to slaughter the religious leaders with some sort of gas, and thinking back I think he was quite capable of doing this. But he had obviously realised how difficult it would be to carry this out and survive the outcome, and because he is a very intelligent man he came up with the alternative plan, just as effective but without the bloodshed. His only problem was that he needed someone to help him. And what better person than me, his close personal security officer, who would be with him night and day to discuss details, and who could take an active part in carrying out the hoax. The most difficult part was having enough time to get the story out without any possibility of stopping it. I don't regret my part. The world has gone mad with the different faith nations fighting each other, and prepared to sacrifice their innocent people who just want to live a peaceful life with enough bread to eat, clean water to drink and a safe home to raise a family," and looking at them both, "that's what I want, anyway."

Then, before either of them could interrupt, and catching her father's eye, Ruth said to him directly:

"I have just got to tell someone, and you should be the first to know. Michael has asked me and I have said yes. We are going to be married, to be married twice."

She would not tempt faith and tell him about the baby, not yet.

Her father was pumping Michael's hand and coming round the table to take her into a massive hug.

"That's so grand," he said beaming at them both. "Now what's to do? I'm thinking that, with so many involved in this religious caper, no one is going to be charged with a crime. I'm thinking that the trick here is to get the story out the way we want it. And as the world loves a happy ending, I am thinking I know how to tell this one. But first a drink of the little green men's nectar, you know who I mean; our very own leprechauns who wear green coats and hats, spend their time making and mending shoes and who have a hidden pot of gold at the end of the rainbow, or in this case a bottle of the ancient hard stuff. And it just so happens I have a little drop with me. And then tomorrow I will tell you of my plan. So there is nothing left for you to worry about. Your father and father-in-law will take care of everything."

With that he produced another bottle of Tullamore and three glasses.

They were shaken awake at six the following morning by Norah.

"I have your father downstairs, and he said I am to tell you to get ready for the grand reveal, whatever that means. He says you are to dress fancy casual, and after your breakfast, which he is preparing, escape with him to the Castle where you will meet the press. He is using me, God forbid, to get the word out, 'the where and the when of it'. He says he wants it to be an Irish scoop. And as long as the main Irish papers and broadcasters are there, that should be enough to tell the world. So even if I can't be there, I get to light the touch-paper to set the hounds onto the trail of the two of you, a dirty dog fox and a brazen vixen hussy if ever I saw one."

When they arrived at the breakfast table, Patrick was in a state of flushed excitement, sitting down with them whilst Norah bustled about serving eggs and bacon and black pudding, the soda bread and the coffee.

"Eat," he said, "because it is going to be a long day for you. But I swear on the head of my departed mammy it will pass and you will get a break from the press's attention, for a bit anyway."

Ruth and Michael just looked at each other, and sat, mute, as they ate. After they had finished, Norah cleared the table and joined them. Patrick held out his hands to be held, nodding at the others to follow suit, until they ringed the table. Smiling he said, "So here's the plan. With the local Gardai to accompany us, and who I happen to know rather well, perhaps rather too well, I am going to take you to Blarney Castle, and then when you have both kissed the stone you will meet the press in the gardens. I will make a little speech, and control the questions put to you. After that heavens knows, but I am guessing that at some point they will need to get their stories out, and may then leave you alone. When you have had enough of the spotlight, I will take you to a friend's house to think about what you want to do next."

He waited for them to take this in and then continued, "We will be going in your car Michael, so get ready now, and whilst Norah goes to my house to get us an hour's head start, we will slip out the back and make our way to the Castle. Are you up for it? Of course, you are."

He could hardly contain himself.

53

The hour was not enough, with some of the press guessing that the Blarney Stone would likely feature; they were there to get their shots of Michael helping Ruth to kiss the stone. And of course, with tourists recognising Ruth as well, a crowd of well-wishing onlookers developed that followed the feted couple, now being shepherded by the police to a gathering point in the Castle grounds that Patrick had selected, and had a protected back and a congregating space in the front.

Finally, when the press and television had settled themselves, and the background voices and camera shutter noise had calmed a little, Patrick raised his hands for hush.

"My friends," he said. "You all know why you have come, but perhaps not why Blarney Castle has been chosen for this special moment. So," spreading his arms to encompass the castle and its grounds, "let me tell you. For over 200 years, world statesmen, literary giants and legends of the silver screen have joined the millions of pilgrims climbing the steps to kiss the Blarney Stone and gain the gift of eloquence, the gift of Irish blather. I myself have been so blessed, and now, so has my darling daughter Ruth with the help of her lovely man Michael."

He beamed at them both. "Some say the stone was Jacob's Pillow, brought to Ireland by the prophet Jeremiah. Here it became the Lia Fail or 'Fatal Stone', used as an oracular throne of Irish kings. It was also said to be the deathbed pillow of St Columba, our very own Colm Cille, our Church Dove, who lived from 521 to 597, founded the important abbey on Iona, and was the Irish abbot and missionary credited with spreading Christianity into what is today Scotland. On his father's side, St Columba was also the great-great-grandson of Niall of the Nine Hostages, an Irish high king of the fifth century. He was highly regarded by both the Gaels of Dál Riata and the Picts, and is remembered today as a Christian saint and one of the Twelve Apostles of Ireland. He is also the patron saint of Derry."

He paused looking about him to ensure he still had everyone's attention. "Are you with me? Well I'll go on. Legend says the Stone was removed to Scotland, where it served as the prophetic power of royal succession, the Stone of Destiny, and when Cormac MacCarthy, King of Munster sent five thousand men to support Robert the Bruce in his defeat of the English at Bannockburn in 1314, and a portion of the Stone was given back by the Scots in gratitude, and returned to Ireland. Now others say that it was brought back to Ireland from the Crusades as the Stone of Ezel, behind which David hid on Jonathan's advice when he fled from his enemy Saul. A few even have claimed that it was the stone that gushed water when struck by Moses. Whatever the truth, we Irish believe a witch saved from drowning revealed its power to the MacCarthys, whose Dermot McCarthy, King of Munster, built the third castle in 1446, of which this keep, that still remains standing, holds the blessed blather stone. And am I not proof of its power? So while I take a rest you will be wanting to ask your questions. Who will go first? Perhaps you of the *Irish Times*?"

And the questions came.

"Who planned the hoax? How did Ruth become involved? How were the religious leaders persuaded to be part of the hoax? Did Ruth think that the hoax had been worth it? Did Ruth have any regrets? Is the green emerald on Ruth's engagement finger signifying her engagement to Michael? Is the green stone to represent her Irish blood or her green eyes? When will the marriage take place? Where will the marriage take place? Will the first marriage be in Eire or Israel? Does Ruth plan to have a family? Will the Cochranes be living in Ireland?"

Raising his hands for the second time Patrick called out:

"I think that's enough. You have got lots to get on with. All requests for future interviews must now come through me, and I am in the book. So my friends let us call it a day. Best wishes to you all!

"*Beirigí uile bua agus beannacht, gach dea-ghuí oraibh!*"

54

In a top-secret place known only to Israel's Prime Minister, his Cabinet and Israel's need-to-know security intelligence, two men were being held in a state of induced coma. They were David Schiff and a Palestinian soldier by the name of Ibrahim Abu-Assad, whose name was memorable as it was similar to the Hany Abu-Assad born in Nazareth in 1961, and recorded in the list of people identified as Palestinians since the creation of Mandatory Palestine, in 1920.

The reason for the secrecy was that Israel did not want to broadcast the rescue of David Schiff, because that would entail acknowledging Israel's excavation of the tunnel to retrieve David's body, albeit alive if unconscious, and then to find with him the alive but unconscious Palestinian. They also did not want Gaza to find the evidence of this rescue by attempting to retrieve their dead Palestinian soldiers from their Gaza side, and then discover that the bodies of one of their soldiers and the hostage were missing. And there was the premature Israeli missile fired at the Gaza mosque to be explained.

So the tunnel was also blown up for a second time, to ensure that any evidence was properly buried, and that the tunnel could not be reused.

Therefore, until the future condition of the two men was established (and vital signs were encouraging) and a strategy had been devised to cope with the various possible outcomes if they recovered, it was decided to say nothing. After all if they died, a respectful burial could take place, and nothing said until the time was right, whenever that was, whilst if one or both recovered that could be turned to some future advantage, whatever that might be. But at this very moment there was no need to rush to precipitate an unknown worldwide reaction to the premature release of news on any recovery.

In the meantime, both David and Ibrahim would receive the very best attention that the medical services in Israel could provide, whilst the debate over what to say and who should be informed rumbled on.

And within the need to know, very careful consideration was being given to when David's wife Hannah and his sister Ruth could be told.

As for the dead Palestinian soldiers, they were removed from the tunnel by the Israelis and respectfully preserved for future release and burial, at such a time as they could be repatriated to Gaza without fuss.

And yet to be discovered there was also a hidden key in Ibrahim, hidden within the Palestinian soldier's sleeping memory of Haney's art juxtaposed against his knowledge of Palestinian intifadas, waiting to be unlocked, waiting to influence the unconscious Ibrahim with its balancing power to turn rage into peace.

For Ibrahim was a film addict and knew the work of his namesake.

Hany Abu-Assad became a Palestinian film director who received two Best Foreign Language Film Academy Award nominations.

The first was in 2006, for his film 'Paradise Now', about two Palestinian men preparing for a suicide attack in Israel, of which he said:

"The film is an artistic point of view of that political issue. The politicians want to see it as black and white, good and evil, and art wants to see it as a human thing."

The second was in 2013, for his film 'Omar', about a Palestinian baker who frequently climbs the West Bank barrier to visit his lover Nadia, a high-school girl whom he intends to marry.

A review said:

"Abu-Assad doesn't skimp on showing the brutality of the Israeli military but many of the most shocking acts of violence here are perpetrated by the Palestinians."

And Ibrahim also knew of the three intifadas and had participated in the third.

The term 'intifada' properly translated as 'shaking off', is a good description of the first two uprisings in 1987–1993 and 2000-2003 that failed to achieve the goal of Palestinian autonomy or eventual independence.

The first intifada was known as the war of the stones for the constant scenes of Palestinians throwing rocks against the Israeli army and police in daily clashes. For a time, the confrontation threatened to overwhelm the Israeli response. Senior Jewish leaders viewed the burden of the occupation as harmful to Israel's strategic interests and pursued a negotiated settlement with the Palestinian Liberation Organisation's leadership.

239

The second intifada, ignited after Ariel Sharon's visit to the al-Aqsa mosque in Jerusalem in 2000, was different in character involving many more pitched gun battles, suicide bombing and terrorist activities. It led to the establishment of extensive security barriers to insulate the Israeli population from Palestinian infiltration and attack.

The third intifada in 2014, also referred to as the Silent Intifada, Urban Intifada, Firecracker Intifada, Car Intifada and Jerusalem Intifada, when Hamas and the Palestinian Authority repeatedly called for 'a day of rage' against Israel, followed the kidnapping and murder of Mohammed Abu Khdeir, which occurred early on the morning of 2nd July 2014, a day after the burial of three murdered Israeli teens. Khdeir, a sixteen-year-old Palestinian, was forced into a car by Israeli settlers on an East Jerusalem street. His family immediately reported the fact to Israeli Police who located his charred body a few hours later at Givat Shaul in the Jerusalem Forest. Preliminary results from the autopsy suggested that he was beaten and burnt while still alive.

Weddings
55

From the toss of Patrick's lucky Irish ten-pence coin, with a salmon on one side given to represent Israel, and a harp on the other to represent Eire, the father of the bride spun it before Ruth and Michael and with Norah, to witness there was no cheating.

The coin landed harp up.

So the second wedding, to be mentioned first as is the Irish way, would therefore be in Israel, organised by David's wife Hannah as the maid of honour in the kibbutz, and conducted by the rabbi to the kibbutz, with Avishag as Ruth's bridesmaid and Ari as her pageboy, reprising their Irish roles at the wedding in Cork's Saint Fin Barre's Cathedral two months earlier, conducted by the Bishop of Cork.

The Jewish wedding would follow a similar pattern to that which David and Hannah had enjoyed at their marriage, which Michael found both enlightening and delightful, and where he got to understand the strong bonds of the kibbutz life, and the debt of gratitude that Ruth felt to Israel, for all that had been given to her and her brother David. But whilst Ruth and Michael would spend holidays exploring Israel with Hannah, and Hannah and David's children, Eire would become the base for their married life.

Ruth's baby boy, Patrick Michael, would be at both weddings. He was a Christmas day baby, born under the sign of Capricorn, paired with Earth, ruled by Saturn, father of Jupiter, who was king of the gods. He arrived into the world without complications, but screaming to be noticed. He was the apple of his parents' eyes; in particular, the Ard Cairn Russet Dessert, a dry, firm, sweet, creamy fleshed, conical shaped, golden yellow flushed with carmine-skinned apple of Cork, all of which perfectly described Patrick Michael after a warm bath.

On both occasions Ruth's father would give her away, and David would act as the best man to Michael. Relatives, who would be invited to both weddings, would only be expected to offer one set of wedding gifts, and these included the presence and the goodwill of the invited.

To ensure that the joy of David's miraculous presence was fully appreciated it was decided that there would be enlarged photographs of him at both weddings, to look over the proceedings and at the happy celebrating people there.

56

For the Irish wedding, Norah insisted that Irish traditions had to be followed. She made out a list to be discussed with Ruth, and having finally got a promise of uninterrupted time with her began the checking off her carefully prepared 'must dos'.

"The date of your shindig should be the Sunday closest to St Patrick's Day on the 17th of March," Norah began.

"Shindig?" asked Ruth.

"Why, everyone knows a shindig. It comes from the Gaelic *sinteag* to jump and leap. You know, to dance and be happy," said Norah.

"Ah like the Jewish dancing after everyone shouts *Mazel tov*," said Ruth. "But is shindig not Scottish?" asked Ruth again.

"Why the Scots must have taken it from the Irish, and the Irish would have had the *Mazel tov* idea before the Jews," said Norah defiantly. "Now you must stop interrupting, or we shall never finish.

"The ring must be the *claddagh* ring representing love, friendship and loyalty which may be passed from mother to daughter, or daughter-in-law, if there is a son first. Michael must buy it for you now, and as an engaged lady you must wear it on your left-hand engagement finger, with the point of the heart facing your fingertips. The ring must then be turned around on your wedding day so its heart faces your heart."

"Will you describe it to me?" asked Ruth.

"Of course, dear," said Norah. "The bezel forms two clasped hands symbolizing plighted troth and friendship, clasping a heart meaning love surmounted by a crown meaning loyalty. In the ancient tradition of Celtic handfasting, yours and Michael's hands are to be tied together during the ceremony, the tying of the knot to symbolize the joining of husband and wife. And I have composed a poem, the first verse of which I will have embroidered in the ribbon used to join you. Would you like me to read it to you?"

Ruth, who was quite entranced by Norah's words, smiled and nodded.

"So I shall," said Norah:

> *"Oh, to tie a knot that may never come undone,*
> *"And hold you fast together in all weather days to come.*
> *"Oh, to tie a knot in rope with happiness spun,*
> *"That will give you space together for joy and care and fun.*
> *"Oh, to tie a knot with lives that fuse as one,*
> *"And in health grow old together to the setting of the sun.*
> *"Oh, to tie a knot in time that must be run,*
> *"But will let you keep forever the love you have begun."*

Ruth clapped and hugged Norah. "That's lovely," she said.

"Now, to be serious," Norah continued. "To signify the importance of knowing hunger, potato soup must be included in the wedding feast."

"What?" exclaimed Ruth, "you must be joking?"

"Well my dear," answered Norah frostily, "I see I need to educate you regarding some important Irish history. The Great Famine or the Great Hunger was a period of starvation, disease and emigration in Ireland between 1845 and 1852. It was also referred to as the Irish Potato Famine, because two-fifths of the population were solely reliant on potatoes. During the famine, one million people died and a further million emigrated from Ireland, causing the island's population to fall by a quarter. So, you see, to be forgetting the potato would not do at all. Would it now dear? And anyway, I have a particularly good recipe which includes a combination of butter, onions, leeks and potatoes, with salt and pepper to season, and my secret ingredient, that when liquidised and mixed with the cream makes a delicious soup, hot or cold!"

"Cold potato soup? Secret ingredient?" mumbled Ruth quietly.

Norah's gimlet eyes bored into Ruth as if to say 'not another word', leaving Ruth with her mouth shut and a finger in front of her lips. When she felt she had properly made her point, Norah went on with her list.

"You may choose the main course and the dessert."

She waited for Ruth.

"May we have salmon and trifle?" asked Ruth hesitantly.

"Well of course," said Norah. "Irish salmon is the best in the world, but I'm not sure that trifle, whatever that is, is Irish."

"May we have the salmon whole on the bone, dressed with cucumber slices, with fresh mayonnaise and minted new potatoes?" said Ruth, "and I have always dreamed of trifle ever since I saw a picture of it in a cooking magazine with its description of sherry-soaked sponge fingers coated with raspberry jam, layered with fruit jelly and custard, with thick cream sprinkled with toasted almonds and hundreds and thousands on the top."

"From a book you say? What a fine memory you have, to be sure. But as long as the cream is Irish, I suppose you may, because as you know," and here Ruth chorused with her, "Irish cream is the best in the world."

"Well!" exclaimed Norah with a flush. "Now we really must be continuing. The drinks must include Murphy's, Irish cream liqueur, and Irish whiskey. And an Irish proverb must be read before the first drink is taken. And I have one for you.

"An Irishman is never drunk as long as he can hold onto one blade of grass and not fall off the face of the earth."

"I don't understand," said Ruth. "If he is holding a blade of grass, is his face not already close to the earth, and so if he lets go will he not just fall flat on it, unless of course he overcomes gravity and floats away?"

Norah knew she was being taken the Mick, ignored the tease and went on as if nothing had been said.

"And good luck must be given to the wedding day with a horseshoe, remembering to keep the horseshoe upright resembling a U otherwise the luck will run out. You might also consider adding a horseshoe into your bouquet, wear a horseshoe necklace, or sew a small porcelain version inside your gown."

Ruth couldn't resist a small joke.

"With all these horseshoes will I not be in danger of falling over?"

She looked at Norah to see how she took it.

"Well my dear that would indeed be unlucky, unless of course," and now her eyes twinkled, "the real reason was that you had let go of your blade of grass."

They both laughed out loud.

"Are there any more wedding requirements?" asked Ruth.

"Well my dear, since you are asking, if we can find them you must carry the Bells of Ireland and wear a wildflower wreath instead of a veil. And before you ask, it is a stem of tiny white flowers surrounded by apple green cups representing luck and," she said trumpeting, "they are also the flowers of Israel!"

"Well then of course we must have them," said Ruth weakly.

Norah was again in full flow.

"Plat a braid in your hair as a symbol of power and luck, and your guests should wear something blue to bring good luck to you on your wedding day.

"Have an Irish wedding cake, which I will make for you with fruit and honey, soaked in Irish whiskey, with a sweet white glaze topped with green-coloured marzipan shamrocks, which as you should know are the three leaf sprigs of young clover, the symbol for Saint Patrick, Ireland's patron saint who is said to have used it to represent the Christian Holy Trinity, or if a little cheating is allowed, mixed with four-leaf clovers which as you should also know are very rare, because each leaf represents something special; the first faith, the second hope, the third love, and the fourth luck.

"So much luck needed!" said Ruth.

Norah ignored her.

"You must carry a sprig of lavender to symbolize your love, devotion and fidelity to Michael.

247

"With the harp being the national emblem of Ireland, you must have a harpist play traditional Irish music before the ceremony, and uilleann pipes to play the exit to the wedding.

"And at the wedding meal your father Patrick will be wanting to start the meal by offering an Irish blessing. I have one. Shall I read it?"

Knowing she had more hope of stopping night falling, Ruth nodded.

"*May your mornings bring joy and your evenings bring peace*

"*May your troubles grow few as your blessings increase*

"*May your worst days to come be the best of your past*

"*May your hands clasp forever a loving friendship to last.*

"And when he raises his glass to toast the bride and groom everyone must answer with the Irish *sláinte.*"

"Now, wedding bells are to be given out to your wedding guests which they must chime to keep the evil spirits away.

"You and Michael must ring a bell together after reciting your vows.

"You must keep that wedding bell in a safe place in your home, and when there is a bit of a to-do, either of you must ring the bell to remind you of your wedding vows.

"You can use mini bells as place card holders.

"The groom must wear a kilt."

"I thought kilts were a Scottish dress?" queried Ruth mischievously.

"That may or may not be," said Norah, "but one thing for sure is that the Irish kilt is superior! And did you never hear of Riverdance performed during the 1994 Eurovision Song Contest by our very own Irish dancing champions Jean Butler and Michael Flatley to the wonderful music written by our

248

very own Irish composer Bill Whelan? Well, they danced in the Irish kilt! And I shall be arranging a group of Irish dancing girls and boys from our very own Cork Dance School to jig for you."

Norah's eyes were blazing,

"And the last thing. Your honeymoon must be in the Blarney Castle Hotel, so that I can keep an eye on you and your shenanigans. And don't forget, in Gaelic honeymoon is *mi na meala,* meaning 'the month of honey'. So you must drink the wine made of fermented honey, to boost your virility and fertility and make babies to be born nine months later. Do you hear?"

"How can I ever forget?" gasped out Ruth, as she hugged her thanks.

Resolutions
57

Shortly after the General Nuclear Response stand down for America and Russia that followed the exposure of the hoax, the code word Goodyear was exchanged between the Pope and the Archbishop of Canterbury, and a second secret meeting arranged.

This time it was the Pope who started the conversation.

"The Convocation of religious leaders was an extraordinary experience, with the need to convene it, the responses of the religious leaders during it, the formulation of the final message, the influence that it had on the outcome for world peace and the way the atheist chairman achieved consensus. I noted it was you that included the word 'goodness' amongst the definition of words for 'God', and that we both agreed that it should be included in the final message:

"We are prepared to sacrifice our lives for the goodness of the world."

"Yes, it struck me that 'goodness' was a better word than 'good' for describing God, as 'good' is absolute in its meaning, whereas 'goodness' contains 'good' but in infinite abundance," interjected the Archbishop. "But please continue."

"Thank you, I will," continued the Pope. "So now that the word 'goodness' has currency, it would be amiss of us not to spend it in ways that bring good returns to the message of Jesus in attracting greater membership for Christianity. So I propose that we start by considering including the word 'goodness' in our daily order of service, perhaps during the Little Hours, the fixed daytime hours of prayer in the Divine Office of Christians in both Western Christianity and the Eastern Orthodox Church, and as you know called 'little' due to their shorter and simpler structure compared to the Night Hours. I think it interesting that these traditional times of prayer for prime, the first hour at six a.m., terce the third hour at nine a.m., sext the sixth hour at noontime, and nones the ninth hour at three p.m., come from ancient Jewish practice mentioned in the Acts of the Apostles, with prayers consisting mainly of psalms. As you know the structure of all of the Little Hours is the same including, the usual beginning, three psalms fixed for the particular hour and do not vary from day to day, Troparia once or twice depending upon the day, a Theotokion that is proper to the hour, a brief psalm verse, Trisagion and the Lord's Prayer, Kontakion, Lord have mercy Prayer of the Hours, Concluding prayers, and Dismissal by the Priest. With the reformed structure of the Little Hours, the introductory prayer, hymn, psalms perhaps with antiphons, a reading, a versicle, and a closing prayer, could include the word 'goodness' in a new versicle. This could, purely as an example you understand, include:

"O: May God become 'goodness' in our hearts.

"P: And may our 'goodness' serve our fellow man.

"And perhaps also within the Lord's Prayer:

"Father let 'goodness' be your name."

The Archbishop couldn't help smiling at the Pope, and wondering at how difficult it must have been for him to even consider any change. "I see you have put some careful thought into this, and I am indeed humbled by the consideration that you have given to this idea. I like the use of the Little Hours to establish 'goodness' into the hearts and minds of people. It now also occurs to me that 'goodness' may also be included into Jesus' great commandment:

"You must love 'goodness' with all your heart, all your soul, all your strength, all your mind, and with 'goodness' your neighbour as yourself."

Pausing, he said, "May we now consider the means by which these ideas may be introduced, and if you will forgive my business speak, how they may be marketed to our congregations, and then, at a suitable time, meet again to discuss this further?"

"Certamente," said the Pope. "Now," he emphasised the word, "would you consider that this year has been a good year?"

"Any year in which goodness manifests itself must be a good year," replied the Archbishop, "but it takes the continual act of renewal for the tree of life to flower and be pollinated, and then bear the sweet fruit of 'goodness' for the people of the world to savour."

"I will pray for this," said the Pope, "and that your idea of 'The Practical Philosophy of Incremental Goodness', which I have given some thought to, could become a beatitude exhorting *'Blessed are those that do good'* and will enter the consciousness of all people, perhaps transforming the phenomenon of social media into becoming 'The Well of Goodness'."

"Amen to that," agreed the Archbishop.

58

A news clipping arrived in an anonymous brown envelope addressed to Ruth Schiff. It was a dated item from a local US newspaper. It read:

The cause of death of Jonas Burden, reported three weeks ago, has now been given as resulting from an accidental spill of a poisonous gas at the US Rocky Mountain Arsenal chemical weapons manufacturing center near Denver. Because of the secret nature of the RMA and its sensitive work, no further details are available.'

An unsigned handwritten note had been added:

Thought this might be of interest to you. Wish there had been a better outcome from our get together though.

Ruth looked at the news item date, calculated the weeks back and put that into the perspective of her first meeting with Jack Connelly. She paled as she realised that the clever Mr Connelly's plan to her, had had to be, in all probability, a second improvised plan, and not the original one he had intended. If it had been the latter, she and the religious leaders would now be dead and the world a very different and very dangerous place.

And as she pondered this, she also wondered whatever had happened to the resourceful JC.

59

Ruth's father Patrick died. They said that he had drowned at sea, the explanation that he had fallen overboard during a night storm. What he was doing on the deck in the first place was difficult to understand, since his place was in *Mary Bell's* cockpit. The story from the mate was that he had gone out to secure a hatch, lost his footing during a sudden roll of the boat and had gone over the side. Why he was not secured to the safety line was not explained.

"I thought he had secured himself," said the mate. "I was too busy with the wheel to watch him. One second he was there the next he was gone. It was impossible to look for him. All I could do was to put out a mayday call."

The hatch was examined, and there was no indication that it had been unfastened. There was no water in the bulk head to indicate this, and the fastening was in good order.

The Irish coastguard that came to the aid of the *Mary Belle,* having conducted their investigation, were also unable to provide further information, leaving a record of 'missing presumed lost at sea'.

No one noticed the arrival of *Mary Bell's* secret guest, as he stepped off the boat in his fisherman's garb, no one except for Shamus, who had been told to greet him with Patrick, when the *Mary Bell* docked. His name was Peter Chorack.

Peter's arrival in Cork followed a creeping realisation that, with the rescue and recovery of David and Hany, the retirement of Ruth from her intelligence work, and his continued single status that showed no sign of changing any time soon, his commitment to the role of a Mossad *katsa* based in Israel no longer held him. But more than any of this was the pull of Ruth, his private greatest love. So when an opportunity to check out Patrick's clandestine work in Eire beckoned, it had not been difficult for him to get approval to investigate this intelligence back channel, and then see if he needed to spend time on a more permanent basis supporting Patrick with his intelligence gathering for G2.

Now hidden in the secret cabin space, he was completely unaware of the events leading to tragic loss overboard of Patrick, until docking had taken place, and which the light knock on his hiding space had warned him was about to happen.

A memorial service was held for Patrick O'Brien at Saint Fin Barre's Cathedral, in Cork city within the ecclesiastical province of Dublin. Begun in 1863, the cathedral was the first major work of the Victorian architect, William Burges. It was now one of the three cathedrals in the Diocese of Cork, Cloyne and Ross. Its organ, built in 1870 by William Hill & Sons with three manuals and forty stops was expanded in 2010 by the organ builder Trevor Crowe to eighty-eight speaking stops, to become the largest organ in Eire. And it was to this organ that Patrick's favourite hymn *Abide with Me*, a Christian hymn by Scottish Anglican Henry Francis Lyte, written as a poem in 1847 and sung to the English composer William Henry

Monk's tune entitled *Eventide*, was sung by the choir and the 200 guests that attended.

Oh, how Patrick loved its first verse that he would sing to himself whenever he set out on one of his sea trips:

Abide with me, fast falls the eventide,
As darkness deepens Lord with me abide.
When other helpers fail and comforts flee,
Help of the helpless, oh abide with me.

As his coffin was released to the crematorium's furnace and the final words of the funeral service spoken:

We have but a short time to live
Like a flower we blossom and wither
Like a shadow we flee and never stay
Earth to earth, ashes to ashes, dust to dust...

An Irish Defence Forces bugler played the Last Post.

It was the closest Ruth would get to the New York Drum and Bugle Group playing the taps.

With his death, Patrick was only able to enjoy his grandson Patrick Michael for little more than four years. Ruth had been quite insistent in his naming.

"He must be called Patrick Michael. For if anything was to happen to either of you, I will need the comfort of speaking these names whenever I talk to my son."

Patrick O'Brien left his house to his daughter, and the rest of his estate to his son, David.

Michael sold his house and moved, with Ruth, into her father's house.

The death of her father focused Ruth's thoughts on the short time she had had to get to know him, replaying the vivid memories of their shared time together. Short and sweet, but never dull. She had been fortunate. She could not complain, grieving her sad happy sorrow.

She remembered her wedding, the fine speech her father had made and what a grand affair it had been under the capable hands of Norah. She could still feel the excitement of the day and how her heart had turned over when she saw Michael resplendent in his kilt, standing at the altar waiting for her to reach him on the arm of her father and then saying her vow to him

"I take you, in the presence of God and before these witnesses, and I promise to be loving, faithful and loyal.

"By the power of Christ, mayst thou love me. As the sun follows its course, mayst thou follow me. As light to the eye, as bread to the hungry, as joy to the heart, may thy presence be with me, oh one that I love, til death comes to part us asunder."

To be followed by their Vow of Unity

"We swear by peace and love to stand, heart to heart, hand in hand. Mark O Spirit, hear us now, confirming this, our Sacred Vow."

Then the exchange of rings, with the traditional Claddagh rings as Norah had described them, the circular band of two hands holding a heart with a crown on top, to signify a bond of love, loyalty, friendship and lasting fidelity between them, and the saying of the Claddagh:

"With these hands I give my heart crowned with my love."

Then, after the sipping of sacramental wine together from the Loving Cup, they resumed:

"Drink to the love that you've shared in the past, drink to a love that forever will last."

And then the traditional Irish blessing:

"May the road rise to greet you the wind in your hair,
May the sun warm your face and the rain fall elsewhere
May you live for your children and their children to see
And be poor in misfortune but rose rich in Tralee.
May the sun fall on home friend's hand give you love
May green grass soften steps under blue skies above
May that joy will surround the true hearts that are found
And drink from the well of happiness that abounds."

She had treasured her father's wedding speech notes that she had taken from him, and which she kept taped to the back the wedding photograph of her and Michael as bride and groom. She remembered how his words had finally released her love for her father, which up to that moment had been restrained by his past reluctance to accept his place in the lives of his two children. She remembered how the speech had begun, how the first words had hardly been uttered when he broke down sobbing, but holding his hands out to the assembled group, as if to stay their vocal and physical reaction to his outpouring, until, with a loud blowing of his nose on a serviette that caused embarrassed laugh, he was able to continue.

She remembered clearly those opening words.

"This is the happiest day of my life. For today, as I rejoice in greeting the new man in my darling daughter's life, I also rejoice in the returning from the dead of my son, my daughter's brother, husband to Hannah and father to Avishag and Ari, my David, who is here to share this joyous moment."

How the words that followed with his typical Irish Liverpudlian wit and all his heartfelt wishes were lost as she watched his face smiling and laughing and looking at her and Michael, and that when it was over he came to her place at the top table between Michael and David, and she had risen with them to their feet, to be engulfed in her father's arms.

She remembered the honeymoon. How, having gone to the Blarney Castle Hotel for their first night, she had been woken early the following morning by her father playing reveille on his horn outside her bedroom window, and the fully dressed Michael shaking her awake with a kiss, and the instructions to get dressed in her first day married outfit hanging in her wardrobe, to leave everything in the bedroom for Norah to take care of and meet him for breakfast.

How Norah had suddenly appeared to help her get dressed, as she had with her wedding dress, and said to her:

"Now you are to leave everything to me, and not to worry about Patrick Michael, who I will be loving and caring for as if he was my very own *babai macushla*. You will only be a call away to speak to him whenever you feel the urge coming on."

And how after breakfast Michael had blindfolded her and taken her outside, and when he had positioned her just right, he removed it to leave her staring at his clean gleaming motorcycle.

"This," said Michael proudly, "is your chariot Mare, a name I have chosen from the Song of Songs *I have likened you, my darling, to a mare in Pharaoh's chariots*, on which I am going to spirit you off to a secret hideaway. This chariot is our Triumph Trophy with…"

At 'with', Ruth knew that a glowing description of the motorcycle was coming, and she was rolling her eyes and sighing, and turning to face him trying to kiss him to stop all the detail about his incredible machine that he was quite determined she would hear.

Finally, she was able to say:

"Does this mean I am your stud mare, to be ridden at your pleasure? Now please tell me where we are going."

"Well," he said nodding, and then started to describe the rout in detail.

"But where to?" she begged desperately cutting him off.

"You will just have to wait to find out," was all he would say.

And it was everything she could have wished for. Dressed in her new motorcycling outfit and with their clothes packed away in the panniers they arrived at the Merrion Hotel in Dublin, from where they could explore the city on foot, walking through St Stephen's Green, see through Michael's eyes his Trinity College, cross over the Liffey by the Ha'penny Bridge, visit Jameson's Distillery and Guinness' Storehouse for tastings, stand in the Aviva Stadium and cheer on their imaginary Irish National Rugby Union Team, tour the world's first purpose-built bicameral parliament house on College Green, bird watch on Ireland's Eye off Howth, go horse racing at the Curragh Racecourse County Kildare, take bike rides into the Irish countryside, to Athlone, Galway, Limerick, Tralee, Tipperary and Glendalough, and race to the top of the Sugar Loaf.

And in Oscar Wilde's House read aloud, laugh and tease each other with some of his quotes of...

I think that God, in creating man, somewhat overestimated his ability. Always forgive your enemies as nothing annoys them so much. The only thing to do with good advice is pass it on as it is never any use to oneself. Some cause happiness wherever they go, others whenever they go. A cynic is a man who knows the price of everything and the value of nothing. There is only one thing in life worse than being talked about, and that is not being talked about. Morality is simply the attitude we adopt towards people whom we personally dislike. How can a woman be expected to be happy with a man who insists on treating her as if she were a perfectly normal human being? Quotation is a serviceable substitute for wit...

And eat and sleep and make love, filling every minute of their wonderful never to be forgotten mi na meala, 'the month of honey' honeymoon.

60

Hannah looked across at David. He was snoozing in his chair relaxing. He had been attending to his bees which he kept on the roof of their apartment. With two hives, he could produce up to 100 pounds of honey in a year. Requiring two million flowers to make one pound of honey, his bees worked hard to harvest a variety of nectar from all the parks, trees, gardens and window boxes in the city of Tel Aviv.

He would say to her many times,

"Eighty per cent of plant species require bees to be pollinated. Without bees, there is no pollenisation, and fruits and vegetables could disappear from the face of the Earth. So one third of our food wouldn't exist, and mankind might not survive. I love my bees, and I delight in their honey. They make me think that if people worried more about bees, they would have less time to think about their differences, and more time to enjoy the sweetness of their lives. I want, as it is written in Deuteronomy, *'a good land, a land of brooks of water, of fountains and springs, flowing forth in valleys and hills, a land of wheat and barley, of vines and fig trees and pomegranates, a land of olive oil and honey, a land where you will eat food without scarcity, in which you will not lack for anything'."*

What an amazing life he had had. To recover from being buried alive, to hold high office in Israel, and achieve what he did was extraordinary. Everyone said so. But, of course, everyone also knew, that in the same breath, the name of Ibrahim Abu-Assad had to be included. For it was with these two that peace could finally came between the Israelis and the Palestinians, from a relationship born in a tunnel linking Israel to Gaza, and the freak nature of their survival in a pocket of air trapped with them in their buried space.

61

David and Ibrahim recovered from their induced comas at about the same time. It had been decided for medical and supervision logistics that they would be kept together in the same room in their secret location. There was also a curiosity in seeing how a relationship between a Jew and an Arab, who had shared a near-death experience, would evolve; if they recovered of course. Whilst the background character and nature of David was already well known, that of Ibrahim had to be obtained through the back channels between ISIS and Hamas. From this it became clear that both men were intelligent, educated and principled and so, it was decided, they could be relied upon not to kill each other, but rather participate in a rational way towards their situation and towards each other. Nevertheless, their room was monitored twenty-four hours a day with CCTV. With the signs of recovery, first with Ibrahim and then shortly afterwards with David, as their dose of drugs was reduced the intense nursing care was relaxed, but always with a two-nurse station in their room.

The reason Ibrahim was first to come round was speculated to be because he was found on top of David with his arms about him in a protective way, and so by facing downwards was better able to breathe the available air. The recorded statement describing the position of the two men became a key factor in the formulation of their future relationship, in that David would feel a sense of gratitude towards Ibrahim. And it was this gratitude by David to Ibrahim, and Ibrahim's gratitude to his Israeli rescuers, that was to lead to the deep friendship that grew between them, and how the interdependence of their lives would play such an important part in how peace was capable of being brokered between the Jews and the Arabs.

Of course, none of this would have followed had it not been for the sharp-eyed Israeli spotter who saw and reported the appearance of the Palestinian soldiers from their tunnel, their reappearance later with their hostage to disappear back into their tunnel, the sudden cloud of debris from the tunnel's mouth indicating an explosion, and then, on the instructions of the Prime Minister, the response of the summonsed Israeli sappers to excavate the tunnel and, after much careful digging, find the barely alive Arab and Jew survivors, and the buried dead Hamas soldiers.

When they had both fully recovered physically, whilst still required to share their sleeping accommodation, they were now also given a separate leisure area with easy chairs, TV, table tennis and pool table, games, reading material and soft drink and snack vending machines, and access to private toilet and washing facilities, all of which still CCTV monitored.

This space also had a screened off area for their respective religious prayer rituals.

For David, the Jew, this was for him to recite prayers three times daily, the Shacharit, Mincha and Ma'ariv, with a fourth the Mussaf on Shabbat and holidays, and the prayer of the declaration of faith, the Shema, a Torah recitation from Deuteronomy:

"Hear O Israel, the Lord our God is one Lord!"

For Ibrahim, the Muslim, this was for him to recite prayers five times daily called Ṣalāh, facing the Kaaba in Mecca's sacred Al-Masjid al-Haram mosque, with the act of supplication referred to as *dua*, and consisting of verses from the Quran, professing:

"There is one God Allah, and Muhammad is his messenger!"

They noticed the prayer dedications, to *one Lord and one God*, were both similar and different at the same time, and agreed that the matter of their different religions should be a subject for discussion, and that the breaking of the cycle of hostilities between the Jews and the Arabs could only be achieved if there was a different attitude towards their separate ownership of the history of the land and of their Gods.

They were wary of each other. But in time they became aware of the statement agreed by the religious leaders in Rome and how it could apply to them as they developed their budding relationship of co-existence through the common ground of goodness. In truth they became part of the 'we' in:

We are prepared to sacrifice our lives for the goodness of the world.

And then there was the Balfour Declaration, which the two men agreed should be their reconciling point, a public statement issued by the British government during World War I announcing support for the establishment of a "national home for the Jewish people" in Palestine, then an Ottoman region with a minority Jewish population, contained in a letter from the United Kingdom's Foreign Secretary Arthur Balfour to Lord Rothschild, for transmission to the Zionist Federation of

Great Britain and Ireland published in the press on 9 November 1917.

It read:

Foreign Office November 2nd, 1917

Dear Lord Rothschild,

I have pleasure in conveying to you, on behalf of His Majesty's Government, the following declaration of sympathy with Jewish Zionist aspirations which has been submitted to, and approved by, the Cabinet.

His Majesty's government view with favour the establishment in Palestine of a national home for the Jewish people, and will use their best endeavours to facilitate the achievement of this object, it being clearly understood that nothing shall be done which may prejudice the civil and religious rights of existing non-Jewish communities in Palestine, or the rights and political status enjoyed by Jews in any other country.

I should be grateful if you would bring this declaration to the knowledge of the Zionist Federation.

Signed; Arthur James Balfour.

The words *that nothing shall be done which may prejudice the civil and religious rights of existing non-Jewish communities in Palestine,* despite the distractions of all that was to follow in the next 100-plus years, still laid the basis for a resolution to coexistence over land that had, and would continue to have indifference to the tribal blood and bones it received.

62

There were two key conversations that helped forge the strong bond between David and Ibrahim.

The first took place following their debriefing interviews with their minders, when they each described their version of the abduction, and were in turn given the details of their rescue. It was the first proper conversation between them, which up to that point had been polite and perfunctory, and it took place in their leisure area following a lunch, which like all their meals was chosen from a special selection of menu items, prepared, delivered and served to them.

David took the initiative.

"It seems that I owe you my life, despite you putting it in harm's way in the first place." He smiled as he said this to remove any rancour, and not waiting for a response continued, "I am aware that you acted as a support over me, doing your best to evacuate the earth around us, allowing me to share the air that was available. I am very grateful for this, and the opportunity to be again with my family and friends whenever this is allowed. And I want you to know that I have refused to accept my own freedom from this place until I have been given the assurances that you will be released to Gaza at the same time."

"How can you guarantee this?" asked Ibrahim. "Surely it would be easy enough for you to be taken out, leaving me here?"

"I have told them that if they separate us, I will tell the world it is against my wishes," said David.

"Does that mean that we are going to be stuck together for a long time?" asked Ibrahim.

"Maybe," said David, "for a while at least. It seems they don't know what to do with you. So I have suggested that both of us are included in the discussion, to find a solution that we can all agree on. In the meantime, perhaps we should get to know each other better and see what we have in common."

And so started their one to one conversations, part background history, part present-day problems, and part future aspirations, so that when the round table talks did take place they were already beginning to forge an alliance over what needed to be negotiated for their joint release.

There was also the question of third-party mediation to help consider an unresolved issue in the future.

"Our Islamic and Jewish shared histories with Jerusalem also include Christianity's. So perhaps the answer lies there," suggested Ibrahim.

The second followed their release twelve weeks after their rescue. The release conditions agreed with both David and Ibrahim were that there would be no conditions, and that they would be allowed to tell the story of David's capture, his and Ibrahim's rescue, their rehabilitation, and what their plans were for continuing their dialogue between their two families, to better understand their needs as people who want a better life for themselves, their children, and their children's children, and what they would be prepared to sacrifice to achieve this peacefully.

This conversation required the attendance of David and his wife, and Ibrahim and his mother, as Ibrahim was still single, and took place at a designated crossing point into Gaza, in a neutral room supervised by the Red Cross, and from which the Jew and the Arab would have unfettered access into their own countries at the end of their meeting.

Coffee and dates were placed on their round table. The flags of Israel's blue Star of David hexagram on a white background between two horizontal blue stripes, and Palestinian's tricolour of three equal horizontal bands of black, white, and green from top to bottom, overlaid by a red triangle issuing from the hoist, were presented with their poles joined at the base and colours splayed to hang away from each other, Palestine to the left and Israel to the right.

The room was filled with flowers, light blue irises, deep purple dark-eyed delphiniums, white and red hibiscus, and green olive branches, with hanging black fruit.

There was a carpet of scented herbs, including camomile, jasmine, lavender, lemon balm and sage.

The four of them were nervous. It had been agreed that Ibrahim would speak first.

"First, may I introduce my mother, Shadia," he said. "This is my friend, David, and his wife, Hannah. We have saved each other, and we now wish to save our people."

He looked at David, who spoke, "We have agreed to dedicate our lives to finding a peace, one that is for the common people. We think we should start by creating a joint weekly blog of the daily lives of our two families, and by showing what we eat, what we wear, what we do and how we think, how similar we are."

"Who will write this blog? Who will pay for it?" asked Shadia.

Hannah came round the table and took Shadia's hand. "We will. It's not expensive. We will share any cost," she said.

It was agreed that the opening sentence of every blog would have the 'peace' words of shalom and shalim, and that these two words would be repeated as:

Shalom-Shalim-Shalom-Shalim-Shalom-Shalim.

It was noted that the difference between the two words were the 'o' in the Jewish shalom and the 'i' in Palestinian shalim, the fourth and the third vowel of the five English vowels, which when added together became seven, which in numerology is:

The seeker, the thinker, the searcher after truth who doesn't take anything at face value, always trying to understand the hidden truths, knowing that nothing is exactly as it seems and that reality is often hidden behind illusions.

As they drank coffee and shared the dates, the atmosphere relaxed between them, and their conversation moved onto the mundane, about family and children, holidays, favourite meals and the weather.

Food had been provided by Shadia and Hannah, and held in an adjacent room, ready to be brought out by helpers.

It had been agreed that the world's press would be invited into the meeting room to take one photograph of the four of them, smiling, holding hands together in front of their flags.

No questions could be asked. There would be no statement, just the posted message on a white board that simply said:

'Read the Shalom Shalim Peace Blog.'

At a sign from Shadia the food was brought in, and the four of them served the press corps, thanking them for their attendance.

All front pages carried the smiling photo, and the entreaty to, 'Read the Shalom Shalim Peace Blog.'

Most included a headline, the most notable of which asked:

'Is this a Quiet Road to Peace?'

The Shalom Shalim peace blog, as it became known, was huge. It would lead to both David and Ibrahim entering and eventually holding high office in their respective assemblies; for David the Knesset, the unicameral national legislature of Israel with its members elected from a single nationwide electoral district, and for Ibrahim, the Palestinian Legislative Council, a unicameral parliament of the Palestinian inhabitants of the Palestinian territories with its members, elected from the electoral districts of the Palestinian National Authority in the West Bank and Gaza Strip.

Now that the survival of David Schiff and Ibrahim Abu-Assad was common knowledge, the bodies of the dead Palestinians were quietly returned to Gaza, draped in their Palestinian national flags.

63

When Hannah, who had been sworn to secrecy over David's rescue, was finally made aware of his recovery the first call she made was to his sister Ruth.

"Ruth dear," said Hannah when she got Ruth on the line, "I have some incredible news. David was rescued from the tunnel alive, and has now recovered. It has all been a big secret, and I have only just been told. He wants to see you. Can you come to us, and bring Michael and the two Patricks? We will delay the celebration party until you are here. Oh, and the silver chain with your mother's ring now hangs around his neck."

She waited in the stunned silence finally to be broken by Ruth's shouts of:

"Oh my God is this true? I can't believe it!" And then more shouts of, "How wonderful! How wonderful! We will come as quickly as we can."

The Irish press, ever alert to the doings of their favourite daughter Ruth, were soon on the trail of a story that would gather the world press and follow her family to Israel, to a celebration with the families of her brother and Ibrahim Abu-Assad, leading to the breaking of a worldwide story that connected the Shalom Shalim peace blog to the fated Vatican religious leaders' message of sacrifice for the goodness of the world.

With the frenzy that followed, other copycat peace blogs were set up between areas of dispute, with the theme that no matter what the differences of human beings, their colour, their sexuality, their language, their race and traditions, their financial circumstances, they still needed the basics of food, water, shelter, energy, protection from disease and the opportunity to live a life to a full potential without fear of oppression.

Nothing new of course, except for the expression of a universal desire now promoted so vociferously through social media, that to be 'fair' one needed to 'share'. Nothing easy either, but the understanding that to move the mountain a beginning not only needed to be made, but the effort repeated again and again, and never stop. And all the while the commonness of daily life should be able to continue through peaceful means, and its participants enjoy the best possible of years.

Handmaidens
64

For Ruth, the finding of her brother had to be tempered with the loss of her father. And so, as this story began with the inexplicable death of her mother, it would always continue with death of another, and that life must always end, and grief will always pay the price of love. But whether the loss of life was deliberate, by accident, unintended consequence, or bad luck, it was always a loss, and that the loss was not just the loss of a life to be mourned, but the loss of time in the fulfilling of any potential possible between the one that had passed and those that remained.

So it was that Michael took Ruth to Chamonix, to experience the Alps by climbing Mont Blanc, beginning her excitement with some facts of this great mountain.

Mont Blanc, (the French name), or Monte Bianco (the Italian), both meaning White Mountain, is the highest mountain in the Alps and the highest peak in Europe outside of the Caucasus range. It rises 15,800 feet above sea level and is ranked eleventh in the world in topographic prominence. The mountain lies in a range called the Graian Alps, between the regions of Aosta Valley in Italy, and Haute-Savoie in France. The location of the summit is on the watershed line between the valleys of Ferret and Veny in Italy and the valleys of Montjoie and Arve in France, with the border passing through the summit making it both French and Italian.

The first recorded ascent of Mont Blanc was on 8 August 1786 by Jacques Balmat and Michel Paccard. This climb marks the start of modern mountaineering. The first woman to reach the summit was Marie Paradis in 1808.

Michael's plan was to climb from the French side, the Miage Bionnassay Mont Blanc crossing, over the three days it took, and described in the guide books as a 'magical expedition of ice and snow arêtes at great altitude'.

The route begins from Contamines-Montjoie, with the first night spent in the Conscrits cabin. The following day, the 12,000-foot Dômes de Miages is crossed and the next night spent at the Durier cabin. The third day proceeds over the 13,300-foot l'Aiguille de Bionnassay, its route comparable to the Traverse of the Liskam summits near Monte Rosa, perhaps a bit longer with more rock climbing in the lower sections, and then the 14,100-foot Dôme du Goûter, with the last stop at the Goûter hut, then reaching the summit of Mont Blanc via the Bosses ridge, before finally descending the traverse to l'Aiguille du Midi to take the cable car back to Chamonix.

Their journey included a flight from Dublin to Paris, a romantic stay in a small boutique hotel overlooking the Eiffel Tower, at the top of which Michael took a series of panoramic selfies over the Paris skyline, a surprise pre-booked dinner in Le Petit Prince de Paris on the rue de Lanneau in the Latin Quarter, on the left bank of the Seine near the Notre-Dame Cathedral, and then the first-class train to Chamonix taking about seven hours, during which they would cat nap, and chat about the exciting climb to come.

Their son, Patrick Michael, would be taken care of by Norah, who was overjoyed at the prospect of having him all to herself.

For Ruth, who had only ever seen snow-clad mountains from the window of a plane, to have the close intimate experience of them underfoot and viewed from the different perspectives of the valley to their summit was thrilling. She had been well prepared by Michael for their Mont Blanc assault, with the fitting out and two-day practice use of her necessary kit, and a briefing on what to expect. They then met up with their guide and the other group of climbers that would make the climb. There were six of them in two strings of three. She was in the second, roped second, with Michael her rope leader.

The ascent to the Durier dormitory cabin from the Conscrits cabin took a gruelling seven and a half hours. After a cold, uncomfortable second night, the two groups left the hut in the early morning dark, arriving at the Summit Ridge traverse of the Aiguille Bionnassay as the sun was breaking, shafts of white light touching the snow on its arête contrasting with the grey black valley spaces below, its sharp mountain ridge with a purity of line perhaps unequalled in the Alps.

The crest of the Bionnassay is indeed a desolate place; its steep long north face under the left foot dropping 4,000 feet to the French Glacier de Bionnassay and, under the right, another breathtakingly steep drop to the remote Italian Glacier de Bionnassay. If ever there was a snow climb traverse that could be described as 'exposed', this was it.

The climb of the Bionnassay itself includes both rock and ice climbing. The rock although not particularly difficult, when climbed in the cold of early dawn, and crampons were often worn when on the snowy rock. The most difficult part of the route is its very narrow crest, where a cool head is essential. It is here where it is not the climbing difficulty that demands the attention so much as the great exposure from the narrow crest. This is where confidence, skill, concentration and conditions that are not too icy must combine together if risk is to be kept to a minimum.

And then none of this was a problem for Michael.

The description of what occurred was not clear to Ruth until several days after it had happened. During that time, she was in shock, unable to grasp the reality of it. What she could remember was the horrified look in Michael's eyes as he disappeared from her sight, and his receding shout of, "Ruuuuth!"

The facts were these. With the inexperience of some of the climbers, including Ruth, it had been decided that, despite perfect weather conditions, crampons should be worn by them for the traverse. The two groups of three had caught up with one another at the Bionnassay's arête traverse.

As Ruth's rope took up its position to cross, Ruth shouted:

"Michael! Take my photograph!"

In order to retrieve the mobile camera from his back pack, Michael unbuckled himself from the rope, put down his ski pole and ice axe, removed the pack from his shoulders, found the camera, and then to improve his position to include the incredible mountain range top of the world backdrop view, moved onto the arête leaving Ruth and the third climber still roped waiting to straddle the crest. He took his picture.

And then the inexplicable happened. He dropped the camera whilst attempting to put it back into the backpack. As he grabbed at it, the backpack which had been slung over one arm whilst he took the pictures slipped out of his grasp dropping just behind him. As the pack began to slip down the steep slope, he instinctively stooped to stop it, lost his balance, fell over and started to follow it in an unstoppable slide, which without his axe, pole and now useless crampons to brake himself, became a headlong rush to a certain death thousands of feet below.

Ruth, who had just finished her smiling for Michael, watched him disappear from her view. She made to reach him, became tangled in the rope and had to be restrained by the third climber.

The first rope, that had started its traverse, and were pausing for the second rope to make ready, saw what happened, and under the direction of the lead guide retreated to join the first, take control of the wide-eyed shaking Ruth, and secure themselves whilst the awfulness of their situation and their shock reaction took hold.

Meanwhile the offending mobile phone, dumb witness to the tragedy, still lay where it had fallen, and ironically would now to be used to alert the mountain rescue. And then later when it was eventually returned to Ruth it would have the cruellest reminder of the tragedy, a picture of her silly happy smiling face at the exact moment when the hand of death would snatch away her happiness.

So, within a matter of five years Ruth, would know the bliss of love found, the joy of new life, a returned life, and the satisfaction of making and belonging to her very own family, for which she would have to pay the price of grief for a lost father, and now the gravest pain; her loss of the shared time with her man, her partner, who had said, "I will love you forever with every fibre of my being".

But worst of all she was aware that Michael would have had the time to know as he fell the thousands of feet, that he was about to die never to see his Ruth again, and that she would be cursed to repeat this deliberate self-infliction of pain, by counting down the many seconds it must have taken for his fall, before he suffered the appalling shock of his body's catastrophic impact on the hard rock of the Bionnassay.

And it was all her fault.

65

The year was now 2058.

Time has treated the two women differently.

For Ruth, with her two weddings, her son and two deaths she was intensely aware of the value of family lost and of family to come.

For Hannah, the almost widow, she needed to live each day as a celebration to the lives of her family and the land that nourished them.

Whilst Hannah had survived intact, she was showing the signs of the weathering that a life in the hot Mediterranean subtropical sun had given her. She was now a plump grandmother, delighting in her grandchildren, and still able to enjoy her fading years with her David, in an apartment in a suburb of Tel Aviv.

Ruth, on the other hand, despite a double mastectomy, still retained the essence of her beauty with her hair now a halo of silver grey to the strong features of her face, living her time within a climate of mild wet changeable oceanic weather in temperatures between 0° and 25°C, in coordinates of 52°N 8°W.

The faded cross blemish on her forehead had now all but disappeared.

Over the years, Ruth and Hannah would meet, sometimes in Israel, sometimes in Ireland, and compare family notes. To lighten the mood this would always start with how David was progressing in the Knesset, how their beautiful brown children of Avishag and Aryeh were doing in school, sports and their musical interests, and how the Shalom Shalim peace blog was doing.

"We are thinking of having another child," Hannah had said. "We can afford it now that David is doing so well." She knew it was insensitive, but then she desperately wanted to share with Ruth, and anyway, when she finally did become pregnant, she would not be able to hide the fact of the baby.

Then it would be Ruth's turn, to talk about how Patrick Michael was doing. Since the passing of Michael, she always referred to her son as Patrick Michael, even insisting on the use of both names after he started school, until the matter was taken out of her hands when his classmates abbreviated it to Pami.

"He's got lots of friends," Ruth would say. "He keeps saying that he wants to be a climber like his da, which terrifies me. But he is clever like Michael. Perhaps he will follow him to Trinity."

But it was a long time before Ruth was able to talk about family without the dark cloud of remembering what she missed, even if the counting of the seconds had finally ceased to fixate her imagination.

Since she had retired from the intelligence service to commit herself full-time to Patrick Michael, with a little research work for Michael on the side, there had been no other children, and she had softened into her role of mother and public community service involver.

Now, as she had done many times over the years, she picked up her long-life graphene battery mobile and rang her son. It went to voicemail, but she knew he would ring back when he could. The modern transmitters, woven into the collars of clothing programmed to emit a mobile call waiting signal, would ensure that.

It didn't take him long.

"Hullo Mammy," he said when she answered. As she looked at his face on her screen, she marvelled at how advanced free mobiles had developed, how easy they were to use, how universal they had become in her lifetime. She doubted if there was anyone on the planet who didn't have one who wanted one and was able to use it.

"Hullo my darling boy," Ruth answered.

"Everything all right?" he asked.

"Yes," she said. "I was thinking of your grandpa and your da, and I just wanted to look at you and hear your voice."

"It's been nearly twenty years since we lost Da, and it still feels like yesterday."

"And another five for Grandpa," Ruth added.

A silence passed between them.

"Will we be seeing you for Friday supper?" asked Patrick Michael. "Deidre would love to see you."

"That would be grand. Give her my love. I will bring your favourite apple cake for tea." Ruth's pleasure at her impending visit had already started.

Meals with her son and daughter–in–law were always a special time for the O'Briens, and certain rituals were observed.

There was the passing and the breaking of the soda bread served with full cream Irish butter, "the best butter in the world," Ruth would say to remember Norah.

When they had sat down, they would hold hands around the table, and Ruth would select someone to say the 'Grace of Gratitude and Remembrance'.

Looking across the table today she asked Simon:

"Will you say Grace?"

Simon, who was also called Peter, had come into Ruth's life many years before, answered

"I would be so very happy to have this honour."

66

Peter, who was now called Simon had bought the *Mary Bell*, along with the fishing trip business when the boat had been offered for sale following Patrick the father's death. He then found a place to live near Cork, where he remained invisible to Ruth until a decent time had passed following the death of Michael. He had continued to ply his intelligence craft, watching over Ruth while she mourned, and it was only by 'a planned' accident that they bumped into each other at Blarney Castle.

He saw that she was shocked to see him.

"Have you come to kill me?" was all she said.

His heart missed a beat as he looked at her.

He smiled nervously and said:

"It is true that you can never leave Mossad, unless by death. But Mossad can leave you if it so chooses and it does choose to let you go, for you have been a loyal and faithful servant. My bond will guarantee your safety. I have been permitted to live in Eire as long as I took over your father's role. I now work closely with G2. I bought his boat and live in a small village outside Cork. If we hadn't met today, I would have continued to stay away from you, although I am pledged to be mindful of your interests."

Ruth gave him a long look.

"I knew someone had bought *Mary Bell*. I didn't know it was you. But I am pleased it was, and that you are here to look after me. What should I call you?"

"Call me Simon," said Peter.

"Peter called Simon, or Simon called Peter?" queried Ruth.

"Not 'Christ's Fisherman' but the Hebrew name for 'God has heard'," replied Peter.

"What did God hear?" questioned Ruth.

"He heard that 'I would always be there for you if you needed me'," answered Peter, "And now perhaps you do. So would take pity on this lonely bachelor and let me share a family Shabbat meal with you?"

"I would love that. I have got into the habit of following Catholic tradition of fish on Friday, so it will be a pleasure to enjoy a Jewish one instead," replied Ruth. "I like the idea of mixing the Jewish and Christian traditions at meal times."

"Do you mean in the way the Shalom Shalim words were mixed and linked together for the peace blog?" asked Peter.

"Of course," answered Ruth. "For is not the family meal accepted worldwide as the greatest harbinger of celebration, and opportunity for the sharing of peace and goodwill amongst fellow human beings?"

"Might I dare to think that you would prepare latkes cakes?" questioned Peter.

"You mean the grated raw potato, eggs, flour and seasoned pancake recipe, served with apple sauce, sour cream and chopped spring onions in the Hanukkah tradition?" smiled

Ruth. "They were a particular favourite of Michael's, and it would be a pleasure to make these again in his memory."

What Simon called Peter kept from her, were the circumstances behind the death of her father. How it had not been an accident, but a deliberate Mafia hit to ensure his silence over the knowledge he had acquired and the faces he had seen.

How he could never tell her that he had been aboard on that fateful voyage, locked below in a secret compartment in the cabin, to be let out by the mate when *Mary Bell* docked, only to discover later the whole truth from the mate himself after he had bought the boat and had had to deal with the mate's threat of having his own accident if he didn't comply with the mate's wishes for continued smuggling.

How, when Peter had learnt everything he could about sailing the *Mary Bell* from the mate, he had dealt with him permanently, confirming to the Irish coastguard the mate's accidental death by drowning whilst drunk despite his best efforts to drag him back on board by his safety line to save him, and how later he had got his own message to the Mafia via G2 to never come calling again.

Simon knew the words of the grace by heart.

"Thank Father Time for this moment we share, the food we shall eat and the water we shall drink, and let us remember the goodness of those still here that we love, and those we have loved who have gone before us into eternity."

Then there was the meal itself, which Deidre said included one of Ruth's meat-free favourites.

"We will start with potato and leek soup, followed by 'wait and see' main courses and deserts, finished with goat cheese, figs, dates and coffee. Then a walk perhaps?"

They all laughed, for this is what Deidre always said.

And as they walked, Ruth remembered how Norah had been such a friend to her, always available to Pami until she passed away quietly in her sleep not so long ago, and who was always remembered through her potato soup recipe with its secret ingredient, a bay leaf from her father's bay tree, added with the cream to steep and then removed after much tasting before the serving.

And she looked across at her Pami and said to him,

"I see that the hockey ball wound to your forehead is healing nicely. It's going to leave a bit of a scar. Now that you are going to be a da, should you not be thinking of giving up such a dangerous sport?"

"What, now that I am on the verge of being picked for the team, and could play in the 2058 World Cup and then possibly the 2060 Olympics? Away with ye!" But Patrick Michael knew he had been lucky to recover so quickly from the impact of a blow that rendered him unconscious, and would leave him with its ragged cross-shaped mark that required twelve stitches.

Finally, when they returned from the after-lunch walk with Lady, Ruth's loved and lovely, black with white throat blaze cross collie bitch rescued as a puppy from ill treatment, who had squatted and peed in fear when Ruth's hand first reached out to stroke her before becoming her loyal darling, and the throwing of her ball into exhaustion, there would be the home-baked apple cake with their Darjeeling pot of tea.

And as she mused on the pleasure to come, she twisted her mother's ring that David had insisted she take back, and altered to wear on her wedding finger, whilst he had kept the chain and the blood stained Herkimer 'diamond' dolostone, and remembered Michael's *Marking Time* words:

"Nothing is more beautiful than love

That weathers the storms of life
And knows the truth a new day brings.

"Nothing gladdens my heart quite like your smiling face
That takes my early morning kiss
And welcomes me.

"Nothing awakens more my memory sense
Than the blue grass smell of you
That takes me back to our beginning.

"Nothing contents me more than sight and sound of you
When I return home and know
That you will greet me well.

"No one can fill the place
Your pretty form and softening face can make
On all the days that I have yet to know.

"No one can be what you have meant to me
A thousand, thousand breaths of lucky time
That lived and lives so long a while in mine.

"You are the one that marks the time with me!"

Reckoning
67

On the anniversary of the Peace Convocation held every year to reinforce its commitment to the religious leaders' pledge that '*We are prepared to sacrifice our lives for the goodness of the world*' the assembled group, still representing the different faiths but now with only a few that had been present at the first, were gathered in its new location. The meetings, having already been held in Europe, Russia, Africa, Asia, Australia, South America and now in North America, this year it was the turn of Montreal in Canada. As with the first meeting representatives were dressed in golden-coloured gowns to emphasise solidarity, with the chairman chosen from amongst them now in white. Because of greater interplay between faiths and the established precedents for travelling and accommodation, security measures were not exceptional.

What was particular to the Montreal Convocation however was that this year's annual guest invitation sent to Jack Connelly and Ruth Cochrane had been accepted by them for the first time. Further, their acceptance had not been just coincidence as Jack had made his intention to attend quite clear to Ruth in advance of her reply. His unexpected call when Ruth answered her phone explained everything.

"Hello," he said giving her time to recognise his voice. "I have decided to attend this year's Convocation. I think it is time to spring another surprise. Will I see you there?"

"Hello to you too Jack," she replied letting the memory flood back from the last time they had spoken. It had been just before the doors had been opened for the second time, when the religious leaders and the chairman had risen from the dead and, looking about, had seen her standing by the locked doors and then hearing Jack shout out:

"We've done it! My friends we've done it!" and moving from his seat begin to embrace the leaders while saying:

"This is a great day for the world, a great day for the well of goodness from which peace must come."

On reaching Ruth he clasped her and said:

"Thank you. I could never have done this without you," and then he was moving again, his eyes lit up with excitement, to be surrounded by the leaders as the doors were unlocked by Ruth and people rushed in, then halted, confused by what they saw, before being pushed from behind into the chaos of happy smiling faces, allowing Ruth to squeeze past and escape to make her call to Michael and then flee to him in Wales.

So the reason for Jack and Ruth's acceptance to their first repeat Convocation and how it could turn out should be of special interest to the reader because of deep-rooted convictions, convictions that are based on both good and bad reasoning, the bad dangerous and very difficult to eradicate even if the possible good might yield benefits for the many.

Think of the dandelion, the common name from the French *dent-de-lion*, meaning 'lion's tooth', its leaves lobe-shaped forming a basal rosette above the central taproot with pretty yellow to orange flower heads which open in the daytime and close at night, maturing into spherical seed heads called blowballs or clocks. Does one not remember picking a stem, carefully so as not to lose any of its single-seeded fruits attached to a pappus of fine hairs, a fluffy 'parachute' which easily detaches from the seed head enabling the wind to disperse them, unless of course one is there first blowing on them until they are gone and counting the blows to tell a time. Oh, such fun!

You may also think of dandelions as valued for their medicinal qualities in treating inflammation, swollen lymph nodes, cysts and abscesses as well as a diuretic in detoxifying the kidney and liver, or because they are rich in vitamins A, C and K and a good source of calcium, potassium, iron and manganese. And for their culinary uses coming from the same family as lettuce and endive, their leaves sharing the bitter taste when eaten in salads, their flower petals used to make dandelion wine, and the ground-up roasted roots used as a caffeine-free dandelion coffee. Oh, so good!

But then think of dandelion pollen causing allergic reactions when eaten, or adverse skin reactions in sensitive individuals after handling from the latex in the stems and leaves, and then of the roots which, as a common weed, spread easily from their root fragments and can take forever to get rid of by digging out up to two to three feet deep. Oh, just get rid of it with weedkiller!

Ruth did not really want to go. She was done with intelligence work, contented with her life with Simon, her son Patrick Michael and his family, and her dog Lady. Her response to

Jack would be as it had been every year to the Convocation committee, a polite no, were it not for his wanting to 'spring another surprise'. His last surprise, she was sure, had masked a deadly intent to be superseded by the hoax, because of the lack of support from Jonas Burden with his supply of 'sarin'. Other than the anonymously sent news clipping with the cryptic handwritten note, obviously from JC, she had had no contact whatsoever with him. Neither had she ever wanted to, content to let the memory of their association slip like a receding tide into the past. But here he was, still free to move about and in demand by the very people Ruth knew he loathed. And now even more dangerous with his stubborn rooted hate. How could she not go and keep an eye on him? So she had said she would check her diary and get back to him knowing that whatever else she was committed to she would have to say yes. Her problem was how find out what was in Jack's head and then what did she have to do to neutralise him. And this time kill off that root for good.

As a precaution Ruth sought council with Simon. After all, Simon was still in touch with his intelligence channels and would have an opinion on the risks involved and precautions necessary. Sitting together later and having been told of her conversation with Jack, Simon said:

"I am certain of one thing. You should not go. However, I do agree that there is some danger to his presence at the Convocation. So I will talk to my friends, check out what Jack has been up to and how likely he poses a threat. In the meantime, tell him you will be going. You can always pull out later. OK?"

Ruth's call back to Jack was interesting in the questions Jack asked about Ruth and the little he had to say about himself.

"Hi Jack. I have freed up my diary and so will be happy to come. So how have things been with you and what has triggered your 'special' interest in going?"

There was a hesitation to the word 'special'.

"Montreal is not too far for me to go and I have some academic friends in McGill's School of Religious Studies. If you don't mind student digs, I could probably fix you up with accommodation." Jack sounded relaxed.

"That sounds like a good idea, text me the details. So I see you are still in with God's crowd despite your atheism?" Ruth teased.

"I've mellowed a lot over the years and my religious teaching needs to pay the bills," Jack answered. But there was change in his tone and he shifted the conversation back to Ruth.

"Still attached to the CIA?" Jack asked bluntly. "I suppose that connection never lets you go."

"No, I am well out of that, just a retired middle-aged woman." Ruth could see where Jack wanted the conversation to go. Next he would be asking her about the security arrangements.

So she finished the call.

"Got to go. Let's talk again nearer the day," and hung up.

Simon's enquiry into Jack's past had failed to reveal any controversial activity. He had been in a long-term relationship with a male partner, now deceased, and his gayness appeared to have been accepted by his contemporaries. But it did produce one interesting piece of news. He had been treated for the human immunodeficiency virus, or HIV, and there was some talk that this had recently developed into acquired immune deficiency syndrome, or AIDS, which the US Department of Health and Human Services' website reported that people so infected had a life expectancy of around three years.

"So," said Simon, "despite undergoing antiretroviral therapy on a consistent basis it should never have progressed to the AIDS stage, and Jack could be an angry man if his time is running out. And if he focuses blame on the Catholic Church's position on HIV/AIDS prevention due to its opposition to condom use, the coming Convocation could be a perfect place for him to exact some form of revenge."

"Well, I will have to go then," said Ruth emphatically.

"I have another idea," interjected Simon. "Why don't I go? I am not known to JC and could watch him and take him out if he acts dangerously."

"But you have no idea of what he intends to do?" questioned Ruth.

"So I will have to find out," said Simon. "But in any event you will not be going, and that's final."

68

The facts reported by the English-language *Montreal Gazette* are these:

The extraordinary fire that burnt out a McGill University Campus meeting room appeared to have been caused by cleverly concealed incendiary devices planted under the meeting room table. Eyewitness accounts from delegates able to escape said that following a whooshing sound, fireballs erupted from beneath the table, setting fire to the gowns being worn by the delegates. Those that managed to escape the room and remove their gowns have a chance of survival. The intensity of the heat was such that identification of those that perished was going to be difficult. This included the ex-Chairman who this year was reprising his infamous part in the hoax perpetrated at the first of the Peace Convocations for Religious Leaders in Rome.

The world has entered a state of mourning for the dead and the injured, with prayers being said in churches and temples in every country affected.

How the devices were able to be planted, and why the gowns were not made with fire retardant material is under investigation.

Ruth sat in front of her television set staring at the screen, her eyes barely focusing on the images that flicked before her. How could this be happening to her for the second time? Simon was not Michael to be sure, but he had been her 'first', and now very likely her last. How vividly she remembered his final call.

"*Hello Darling*," he had begun. He was forever calling her Darling whenever they met or Dearest Darling if he wrote or texted. "*I will be going into the meeting shortly, disguised in a golden robe as one of the religious representatives. Although security is tight, I have been included in the arrangements to keep an eye on the inside of the room and so have a pass to enter. I have watched JC and have been assured that there has been nothing untoward in his room and body searches. He has been very social to those around him and seems very pleased with the small part he has been given with the proceedings. I gather from my contact that he has enquired about you and was satisfied with your last-minute excuse for not coming.*"

"*Oh. I really should be there with you*," she had replied. "*I really feel it should be me taking the risk.*"

"*Don't worry Darling I have got everything covered, and when this is over, I will be hotfooting it back to you and Lady.*" She visualised Simon smiling into the phone.

"*I hope so*," she had sighed. "*Please take care.*"

"*I will. Must go*," and he had hung up.

"*God protect him please*," she thought.

Ruth patted the seat beside her, and Lady who had been lying at her feet jumped up pushing her head into Ruth's lap. Moving her hand to rest it on Lady's body, Ruth said aloud:

"He's not coming back Lady. He's not."

Perhaps the whiteboards' promise would now come to pass.*

*It is astounding that we know exactly
when the passing moment takes place.
Exactly when to release, and when to hold.
To instinctively trust the transfer
through a fragment of space and time.
And so precise is this skill ingrained
in our very being that it just happens
as if by telepathic communication
from the moment of our birth
when we pass into the world
to be held for the very first time.
And incredibly this passing is repeated
again and again without consideration
as to the how and the knowledge
as to when we first acquired the magic.
So no matter what the happening,
whether ethereal or mundane,
whether unique or commonplace,
this exchange will continue unto death.
And even then the salt will still be passed.*

*So pass me the salt my darling one,
And I will take the time,
To savour now the moment come,
Then store the moment fine.*

*Pass me your love my darling one,
And I will take your hand,
To go towards the endless sun,
And share the promised land.*

Post Script
1

You know the Shalom Shalim peace blog is a figment of my imagination at the time of writing. For it to be real, special interests would have to become subordinated to general interests, and sacrifices would have to be made. Something must be given for something given. But if the value of peace were to become priceless beyond imagination and for a time without end, the particular gods must become universally good, and the sense of place that draws living things like a magnet to find a home must also find a place in the heart to share a space. And in that space precious life must be preserved.

Perhaps all that is needed to trigger a beginning is not for a god to create the heavens and the earth, but for a human just to do a good thing and for all humans to combine, as suggested by the archbishop, to *fill the well with goodness*.

"Yes," the Archbishop answered. "I am suggesting that it is in human beings' self-interest to do good, however small, and with each small good combining to replenish the well of goodness. I call it 'The Practical Philosophy of Incremental Goodness'."

So as my story of *The Go(o)d Year* comes to its end with the idea of 'The Practical Philosophy of Incremental Goodness' offered to become the path to mediation between the Jews and the Arabs, it is also offered as to how to live a life, and as that includes my life, perhaps I should confess my secret and how it has led to my becoming a joyfinder.

So there is Jesus who sacrificed himself for the good of the world and, depending on your belief, was a man-made god by rising on the third day after his death, two thousand years ago, to enter heaven, and to whom I have given a fictitious extended life after his crucifixion in my book *The Fisherman's Story*, with his seed passing from that story through many generations to become the twins Ruth and David of this fictitious book, *The Go(o)d Year*, both books allegories for my secret.

I say 'there is Jesus' because I was brought up a Christian, and his New Testament story helped form me with his teaching of love, still relevant to me today.

But then there is me who wrote my books as figments of my imagination with an idea that joins them to this chapter by the common thread of my secret, my atheism, my conviction that there is no God, that the world would be a better place without belief in a God, that in another time I would be a martyr to my conviction and you, the reader, would have to test the strength of your opinion by accepting the responsibility in deciding whether to 'strike the flint' to set fire to the kindling at my feet, as I stand tied to the stake waiting for a choking death by smoke inhalation as flames burn my feet and cook my body and I cry out involuntarily against the searing agony of white-hot pain.

But I cannot change what I have become and I must endure.

I am an atheist, *who disbelieves in the existence of a deity* as defined in the Oxford Dictionary.

And further, as a rebel who knows there is no God, I cannot accept the word atheist with its illogical meaning.

For how can one disbelieve in something that does not exist?

So I have changed the word atheist to joyfinder; the substitution of a pointless word for a word I have made up to describe my joy when I realised that God did not exist, in 2000, when I was sixty.

But it is not my intention to debate the many faces of God. Instead, I will pose a question of what I think lies at the root of a need for faith; a question that does not rely on an answer to come from the ether or the abstract but from the here and now.

The question is:

What is the point of life?

Well, I say the answer is in the word joyfinder. I say it is to become a joyfinder and accept that all that counts is life in the here and now, and the trying to do *a good thing* during that life for its own immediate reward, and not to procrastinate and delay to gain benefit in a hereafter.

So I say the first step is to give up God and reliance in God and open your mind to consider the implications, not just for you in your body but for all humanity, for all of us that are warm blooded and that when we bleed, the colour of our blood is red.

I wrote a poem for our fortieth, ruby wedding anniversary in May 2003. The poem is in the shape of the clasp setting for the ruby stone ring I gave to my Dearest Darling Dawn, my DDD.

It is also relevant now because of its association with blood. It's called:

Red

Red is the colour of my love
Rich and warm and flowing thick as blood
A crimsoned ribboned stream of life, a line
Through seasoned time, linking beginnings new
With now and then
Perhaps a gem of captured rubessence
In brilliant presence, a glowing praise
For forty blessed wedding days in May
Hurrahs that seem as soon as yesterday
And then again
Before the rain a painted morning sky
To wonder by or set the coming night
To give delight and stain the words I've said
The colour of my love to red.

So I say again: give up God and think instead of the common blood bond that links all human life and in so doing offers us a common interest in *doing a good thing* through just living.

I wrote a poem to try to explain this.

Just Living

If there is no God
Then there is no heaven and no hell
And the life lived is all there is.
If there is no God
Then there is no need to speculate
Beyond the grave.
If there is no God
Then the reasons for the human condition
And the inequality of opportunity for human beings
Must be explained in the context of human existence
Justified by human values and what's possible with change.
Since change is part of the very existence of life
Its random consequences are inevitable
Subject to the uncontrolled and controlled forces of nature.
Fairness and rights do not exist
Unless wanted and granted by the will of humanity.
This will is influenced by selfish rewards and disadvantages
Both material and of the conscience.
Excess of the material leads to saturation of need
And so to disadvantage.
Whilst the conscience has an insatiable appetite
For the reward of appreciation
The greatest appreciation must come
From influence on the quality of life itself.
From this all things that are possible for benefit
Are up to the wit of mankind and so possible to achieve.
For fairness the rights of all must be acknowledged
And enshrined into a universal law
That will be observed by all mankind
Whatever the group or individual selfish interest.
If there is no Go, then mankind
Must grant to all the opportunity
To make the most of every living moment.
If there is no God there is no second chance.

2

Now you may ask, where is the justice in some lives being long and ending in a peaceful death whilst others are finished before they have hardly begun or are painfully and randomly cut short through the unexpected, without a heaven to go to?

Well, I say there is always value in the residue of love created by the life that has passed and that the incremental goodness in living a life, however long, will contribute for the benefit of all for infinity *to fill the well with goodness*.

Think of the Higgs boson or Higgs particle, an elementary particle in the Standard Model of Particle Physics with its main relevance of being the smallest possible excitation of the Higgs field, a field that, unlike the electromagnetic field, cannot be turned off, but instead takes a constant value almost everywhere. Named after Peter Higgs, one of six physicists who, in 1964, proposed the mechanism that suggested the existence of such a particle. Also called the 'God particle', a nickname disliked by many physicists including Higgs, who regarded it as sensationalism, the description nevertheless might begin an imaginative link between faith believers and non-believers through joyfinders; my name for atheists, in case you have forgotten.

So in the beginning God created the heavens and the earth, Genesis 1.1, or there was the Higgs boson, or in time something even smaller. Either way intelligent life must begin somewhere and with it an evolving understanding for *Homo sapiens* of goodness as the quality of virtue.

My very imperfect life has tried to measure up to the ideal of *doing a good thing*. So I wrote a poem about it, called:

POW

'50/'58 UK Boarding Schools
'58/'60 Eire Trinity College Dublin
'60 UK Labourer
'60 Canada Montréal Medical Orderly & Textile Shipper
'61 Canada Calgary Labourer & Lifeguard
'61 UK London Trainee Clark Weddle & Co
'62 UK Dunster Trainee Hotelier Lutterel Arms Trust Houses
'62/64 UK London Trainee Hotelier Savoy
'64/67 Kenya Nairobi Ass Manager Norfolk & New Stanley
'67/69 UK London Staff Manager Claridges
'69/70 UK London Training Officer Savoy Hotel Group
'70/71 UK Reading Catering Consultant Henry Smith
'71/72 UK London Catering Area Manager Kardomah
'72/75 UK Catering General Manager Ring & Brymer
'75/77 UK Operations Director Little Chef
'77/79 UK Catering Director Ring & Brymer
'79/81 UK Restaurateur John Dory & British Schooner
'81/83 Hong Kong Catering Controller HK Jockey Club
'83/86 UK Catering Director Letheby & Christopher
'86/87 UK Catering Director Graison
'87/90 UK Torquay Catering Consultant Better Sales
'90/12 UK Devon Tofu Factory Dragonfly Partner with DDD
'12/Present UK Devon Retired Poet Author and end time player

I may have been a POW, a Prisoner of Work, but I was a happy one, liking my work and lucky to meet wonderful people during my many jobs. You see, I am by nature an open yet private half-glass-full type of person, sentimental, find it hard to hate, but abhor violence. My health has held up and I have been contentedly married for fifty-five years and counting, now living in a beautiful part of Devon after two working experiences of about twenty-five years each, one for others in the hotel and catering industry in the UK, Kenya and Hong Kong, and one shared with DDD here in Devon, making tofu.

And now there is my retired writing time in my seventies, with three books finished, one of poems published by Spiderwize in 2016 called *Fortunes of Love*, and two novels published by Olympia, *The Fisherman's Story*, 2017, and this book to be published in 2020, with its Post Script and the thread that I mentioned, a distillation of my thinking in *The Practical Philosophy of Incremental Goodness* to reach an answer to the question:

What transcends the summit of all life experiences?

Something that is relevant to all living things and lies within the gift of all intelligent life. Something that by its action produces only fulfilling rewards for the benefit of all, without a precondition in the giving or as to the outcome of the effort made; the one thing we would wish to be remembered for. A question with the answer:

"Do a good thing and fill the well with goodness"

3

So I have come up with a formula:

$$WG^{00<} = (LH^0 \times GA)\ HI^2$$

Where:

$WG^{00<}$ = Well of Goodness infinite size
LH^0 = Lifetimes of all Humans
GA = Good Actions
HI^2 = Human Intelligence potential growth

Of course this formula is pure invention and a bit of fun, but on a serious note it is based on Einstein's mass–energy equivalence formula $E = mc^2$. I have created it to try to express, in a pseudo-scientific way, what it would take *to fill the well with goodness*, even if the well is infinitely large and will take the lifetime of all humans to fill it by *doing good things*.

So, let me see if I can hook you to this idea, by including some scientific connections that I have researched and am using to empower my thinking.

4

On 15 February 1564, Galileo Galilei was born. He lived for seventy-eight years, dying 8 January 1642.

Galileo was a polymath, a central figure in the transition from natural philosophy to modern science and the transformation of the scientific renaissance into a scientific revolution. Galileo championed heliocentrism, where the Earth and planets revolve around the Sun at the centre of the Solar System, and Copernicanism which positioned the Sun near the centre of the universe. He studied speed and velocity, gravity and free fall, the principle of relativity, inertia and projectile motion, inventing the thermoscope and various military compasses, and using the telescope for scientific observations of celestial objects.

His contributions to observational astronomy include the telescopic confirmation of the phases of Venus, the discovery of the four largest satellites of Jupiter, the observation of Saturn's rings, though he could not see them well enough to discern their true nature and the analysis of sunspots.

Known for his work as an astronomer, physicist, engineer, philosopher and mathematician, Galileo has been called the *'father of observational astronomy'*, the *'father of modern physics'*, and the *'father of science.'*

So, Galileo's connection to the selected scientists that follow help to advance my assertion that human beings intellect develops over time, and that the outcomes from new ideas for all human beings *do a good thing*.

On 25 December 1642, Isaac Newton was born. He lived for eighty-four years, dying on 20 March 1726.

Newton was an English mathematician, astronomer, theologian, author, and physicist, recognised as one of the most influential scientists of all time. His book Philosophiæ Naturalis Principia Mathematica or Mathematical Principles of Natural Philosophy, first published in 1687, laid the foundations of classical mechanics. It was he who would ask why an apple must fall downward from the tree and not sideways, when anyone picking an apple off the ground would only be concerned whether it was ripe, maggot-free, and ready to eat.

In his memoirs of Sir Isaac Newton's life, William Stukeley recorded a conversation on 15 April 1726 with Newton.

"We went into the garden and drank tea under the shade of some apple trees. Amidst other discourse, he, Newton, told me he was just in the same situation as when formerly the notion of gravitation came into his mind. 'Why should that apple always descend perpendicularly to the ground?' thought he, occasioned by the fall of an apple as he sat in a contemplative mood. 'Why should it not go sideways or upwards, but constantly to the earth's centre? Assuredly the reason is that the earth draws it....'"

So, think of an apple as a good thing, and that with gravity, it is drawn to another good thing that, combines as a collection of apples to fill a basket, as all *good things* will combine to *fill the well with goodness*.

On 12 February 1809, Charles Darwin was born. He lived for seventy-three years, dying on 19 April 1882.

Darwin was an English naturalist who developed the theory of biological evolution by natural selection. He established that all species of life have descended over time from common ancestors, introducing the scientific theory that evolution resulted from a process that he called natural selection.

So, think of the evolution of goodness as human intellect that must evolve towards having *to do a good thing*.

On 14 March 1879, Albert Einstein was born. He lived for seventy-six years, dying on 18 April 1955.

Einstein was a German-born theoretical physicist who developed the theory of relativity, one of the two pillars of modern physics, alongside quantum mechanics. His work is also known for its influence on the philosophy of science. He is best known for his mass–energy equivalence formula $E = mc^2$. This formula states that the equivalent energy (E) can be calculated as the mass (m) multiplied by the speed of light (c), (c = about 3×10^8 m/s), squared.

However, taking Einstein's formula, for my purposes (E) is the Well of Goodness, (m) is a good thing, and (c) is the human intelligence growth potential. Therefore, I contend that humans are hard wired to *do a good thing*, and by freeing themselves from *the idea of separation* and widening *their circle of compassion*, they can influence the size of the well and the speed by which it is filled.

On 8 January 1942, Stephen Hawking was born. He lived for seventy-six years, dying on 14 March 2018.

Hawking was the former Lucasian Professor of Mathematics at the University of Cambridge and author of the international bestseller, A Brief History of Time, with his science standing on the shoulders of Einstein, Darwin, and Newton. His scientific works included a collaboration with Roger Penrose on gravitational singularity theorems in the framework of general relativity, and the theoretical prediction that black holes emit radiation and shrink to singularity before melting away, perhaps to be repeated. He was the first to set out a theory of cosmology explained by a union of the general theory of relativity, and quantum mechanics. He was a vigorous supporter of the many-worlds interpretation of quantum mechanics. He did not rule out the existence of a Creator, instead asking in A Brief History of Time:

"Is the unified theory so compelling that it brings about its own existence?"

The possible repetition of black holes appeals to me because it links with Swami Vivekananda's idea of the inhalation and exhalation of the Great Breath recorded in his book *Inana-Yoga* in June 1964, given to me by Herbert Gantes fifty years ago.

So Stephen's life search for the beginning of time, in spite of his struggle with amyotrophic lateral sclerosis was *a good thing*, even if my journey has reached a conclusion that what matters is just the getting there and *filling the well with goodness*.

Then there is me, Simon Boreham, born on 14 March 1940, by coincidence Einstein's birth and Hawking's death dates, and still living at the time of writing.

So, whilst time, matter and ideas connect Galileo, Isaac, Charles, Albert, and Stephen with their science of Astronomy, Motion, Evolution, Mass–Energy Equivalence, and Black Holes, I have dared to produce my own speculated truth:

That within the corrupt bodies of human beings that follow Darwin's survival imperative there is another, and that is that we are bound to strive *to do good*, even if there are bad apples in the barrel that bring bad outcomes for some. Yet on balance, we must *fill the well with goodness* for the benefit of all humankind, and that this is the point of intelligent life that has resulted from the big bang, whenever that was.

5

The first thing you need to understand is that, in just surviving day by day, you are already involved in *doing a good thing*, but perhaps not to the extent that you could be. Remember, there is no limit to *doing a good thing*, never too much, or too little. Even *different good things* done by one person or *small good things* done by many people can add up to become a massively good thing. Because *every good thing matters* whether it is initiated by the most important leaders of countries, or the humblest of individuals in them.

The second is that your involvement is just that. It's just you, all on your lonesome with no need for anyone to help you, no divine inspiration required, no luck involved, no practice run, no matter how much or how little effort you have to put in. It doesn't matter how you feel, what you are thinking, or what situation you are in. You too can *think a good thought*, *do a good thing* and appreciate *a good act*, but you need to get a grip on your potential if you really want to get the feel-good response that will come with a better attitude, and a little more effort to get the reward.

Remember it's not just your reward, it's everybody's. It's a share in:

The Well of Goodness.

Although there is no barrier to *doing a good thing*, this is written for responsible minds, or anyone at any age who thinks he or she has a responsible mind. Those who haven't got one, too young, too infirm maybe will need consideration, support and help.

So, once you are in charge of the moment, you need to get in the zone, and a good way is to think of something wonderful, something that will make you smile with the memory of it. It could be a person you really care about, a musical sound, a beautiful picture, a delicious taste, a fragrant smell, a silken touch, a magnificent view, a sense of place, fine words and so on. It doesn't matter what, just that it gives you delight at the thought of it.

For me, for many years, it was the knowledge that I would be seeing my Dearest Darling Dawn, my DDD, when I was returning home from my day's work and would be sharing an evening meal with her. Now that I am retired and rarely separated from her, the pleasure thoughts are very much in the moment. Waking to the dawn's chorus in the spring as the days grow longer and watching the birds cross our horizon from our elevated bedroom window that looks over the Vale of Galmpton. In particular, the house martins that return every year to rebuild their nest in the roof eaves, and on the wing streaking back and forth to catch insects that rise up in the thermals. It's Dawn reading aloud to us from our latest book with our early morning tea in bed. It's hearing the happy shrieks of children at play at our local primary school when I stroll down to our local post office and general store most mornings to get our daily newspaper, and greeting Kay and

Gary and all of their friendly staff. It's holding Dawn's hand when out walking, and being greeted by our children and grandchildren with a hug when we next meet

Of course, it goes without saying that if you are full of anxiety and anger, or just having an off day, as we all do, you will need to make an extra effort to refocus your thoughts, but you must try to do this even if life is treating you harshly and unfairly. You must break the curse of negativity by switching to a happy thought, and you must practice this until it is second nature, an automatic resetting habit.

Now, having written the words *do a good thing*, I find I am using them to put the break on my own bad thinking, whenever bad thinking tries to take control, to calm down and find a good thought once again.

So take a moment now to reflect on this, because it will change your life and the lives of others, and you really will find yourself *filling the Well of Goodness*.

6

So, let's consider just what *doing a good thing* is. Let's say it's anything thought or expressed that makes us feel a bit better, and at the same time, possibly someone else. I say possibly, because *doing a good thing* could be just for one's self. It should not be offered as a trade-off per se, but of course reciprocal goodwill benefits increased goodwill and the contribution of the value to *the Well of Goodness*. As I have said, a *small good thing* has value because it doesn't take much effort, adds up, and like laughter, is infectious and spreads.

Let's have an example from my experience. When I go for my newspaper, I pass people coming and going, some I have seen before, and some I have not. No matter what the weather, I always make a point of giving everyone I meet a smile with my greeting, which almost always gets a similar response. It makes me feel good, and I hope it leaves a good feeling with the responder, however little it might be. This simple recognition of one human to another is so easy to do and yet so often denied, with the loss of the chance for goodwill to be created.

We all have our own small good thing we can do more of, don't we? So what's yours? Can't think of one? Can't be bothered? There has to be something, and giving it your consideration is as good a place to make a new habit, find a better outlook on life, and *fill the Well with Goodness*.

This good thing is easy. It's not trying to save the world as a superhero might. It's already in your life, even if you are deaf, dumb, blind and confined to a wheelchair. Even if it is just a smile, a nod, a touch, or some response that acknowledges your grateful presence to another. Even an anonymous good thing counts as long there is a satisfaction return for you. It all adds to t*he Well of Goodness*, and as a joy pebble dropped into a well, it will produce a ripple effect, spreading and combining with all the other joy pebble ripples. The result will be to give a cumulative benefit to *doing a good thing*.

As for the well, it is a suitable vessel that can refill itself from a source that, like spring water, replenishes itself from the depths of the bountiful earth, just requiring rain to *do its good thing* and fall upon the ground.

And perhaps if and when you realise that your time on earth is coming to an end and you wish that there was a heaven to go to, a place of beauty where one can experience the most wonderful colours, scents and sounds and reunite with all those that you have loved in an atmosphere of peace and harmony, then your imagination can become your heaven on earth in a *joyfinder's Well of Goodness.*

7

There was a route for me to the idea of *Incremental Goodness* leading to *The Practical Philosophy of Incremental Goodness*. It required a distillation of all my experience, my knowledge and my instinctive thought. It required me to take a leap into the dark and test my primeval belief in superstition.

Now take a breath, for what I am about to write will go against the grain of the majority, but it must be considered if the separate God reservations of religions are to be removed for everyone to do *universal good things*.

For me, it started with my 'God was not working' realisation, then 'God did not exist', then 'there is no God just us' and then 'God was a human construct' invented to excuse humanity from the consequence of its actions.

That being the case, I must be an atheist, even if I didn't like the word because, as I have said, 'how can you have disbelief in something that doesn't exist?'

During the process of rejecting the idea of God, I wrote my first novel, a fictional love story called *The Fisherman's Story*, suggesting that Jesus didn't rise up to heaven but survived his crucifixion to live out the remainder of his life sharing a physical love with Mary Magdalene with whom he had a child.

Early in this 'The Go(o)d Year' novel, I have argued that 'God' should become 'good' and suggested that, as Darwinian self-interested life evolves to survive, human self-interested intellect evolves for us to be better humans.

Simply, human beings are predicated to think and do good and *The Practical Philosophy of Incremental Goodness* idea is a positive way of living a life that exhorts:

Do a good thing and fill the Well with Goodness.

So, this idea is about hope but not from a God that doesn't exist, because it is about responsibility and attitude. It is about self-help, and it requires something from you. It is an adult way of looking at life, starting with the need to strip away all superstition, including the reliance on a non-existent God, leaving one dependent on nothing more than the skin one lives in.

It starts with a request to consider that we are as the day we were born, naked and needing the charity of others, and then, as we grow up and break free, accepting the Reinhold Niebuhr Serenity Prayer used by Alcoholics Anonymous to aid alcoholics.

I have altered the original prayer from a longer version so that the words can flow more easily from the tongue:

Let me learn to accept the things I can't change,
Have the courage to change the things that I can.
Let me learn to accept things no matter how strange,
Have the wisdom to know the place where I stand.

This is not said to stifle ambition for better, rather than to learn to enjoy contentment when enough is enough.

8

My route to writing started with the idea of giving up God, of being an atheist, but as I said, I didn't like the word atheist, so I have changed it to another word that I do like, 'joyfinder.'

What may surprise you to know is that there was energy in making the change, which came in two ways at once. One was elation, elation at the discovery that I was free of the hold that God had had over me, my moment of joy, the other anger, anger at the blind faith attachment that human beings had for a God, and then through religion perpetuated.

My realisation came about as a result of questioning the necessity for faith, and forcing me to face the consequence of finding an alternative. In understanding that, despite all the imperfections that there were in living my life, there was a core value that was truly a 'joyfinder' for me, the potential for knowing joy no matter how small, and in *doing a good thing* I could find joy and contribute to *the Well of Goodness*. And that what was true for me must be true for everyone whatever the circumstances of their lives, irrespective of their attachment to religious history and practices that I do not wish to denigrate, but that there was always an opportunity for everyone to contribute to and share in *the Well of Goodness*.

Reading both my books will help you in understanding me. Both follow my journey into atheism, a disbelief in something that does not exist, to becoming the word I want to substitute it for, my joyfinder. However, if you haven't, no matter. You will just have to pick up the thread from here.

So, I will say it all started with the idea of replacing God with the word 'good' that had been forming in my mind since my Damascus moment when I became convinced that God was not working, not for me anyway.

I was brought up to believe in Christianity, attending church, becoming a choirboy and being confirmed, so I am familiar with its forms and practices, which I must say I liked. However, belief in a God was always difficult, as my logic asked how it was possible for an invisible God to have influence over human behaviour, when humans had a choice to be good and practice goodness, or not as the case may be. Then there was my Damascus moment, when doubt became certainty and the question that 'if God was not working, did God exist anyway?'

For those unfamiliar with the Damascus story, let me refer the reader to the Acts of the Apostles 9 (1:19), when Luke wrote of Paul and his realisation of Jesus, and how such a complete realisation could be achieved in a moment of time, as it then did for me in reverse about God in my moment.

I don't remember the actual summer day in 2000 I had my realisation, but I remember what I was doing. I was driving to work to our Dragonfly tofu factory and, having left our village home, I passed a beautiful oak tree in the right-hand field, which had already inspired a poem that I had enjoyed writing after a previous commute and which I love reading again and again, with the title:

Tree Secrets

Oh tell me tree oh tell me please
The secrets of the summer breeze
That rustles thoughts amongst the leaves
And fills my head with dreams of ease.

Oh tell me tree oh tell me why
The secrets of the autumn sky
That calls songbirds to southward fly
Leaves falling tears of dreams gone by.

Oh tell me tree oh let me know
The secrets of the winter snow
That rests in branches leafless hollow
To hide the truth of dreams tomorrow.

Oh tell me tree oh tell me when
The secrets of spring's scented rain
That swells leaf buds to bursting strain
Will release my dreams to dream again.

Oh tell me tree oh tell me how
The secrets of the season's flow
Locked in the heart of ancient yew
Can share those dreams of paradise now.

Now, remembering the *Tree Secrets* poem, the certainty that there was no God came to me out of the blue and with the same breath-taking awareness. As this realisation settled over me and I continued on my way with this astonishing discovery, I began thinking about its ramifications. I realised I would need to test my new conviction, which I then started to do when I returned home by writing the first of four verses of a poem with the title:

Superstition Reason Life Love

Superstition
There is no God there now it's said
So go on God strike me dead
Or strike the nonsense from my head
And leave me be to see instead.
But there is good!

Reason
But there is good if understood
In nature's mud and human blood
In future's seed and man's kind deed
So in the sod I say that's God.
Then earth is all!

Life
Then earth is all a wonder ball
Of life in thrall with time on call
To seeking find a peace of mind
So in the sod lives thought of God.
So sod is God!!

Love
So sod is God let it be said
And in that sod the knowing dead
Their fertile presence in my head
To guide me free for love instead.
And sod is good!

Of course, ninety-nine per cent of me knew that this was not how God would work if he, she or it existed, responding to threats, but one per cent still clung to a superstition that I was tempting fate, and so it would be some time before the lingering doubt finally left me, and by then I had started to think of how to explain (to myself) the consequence of eradicating God within the great teachings of Christianity, and further, if there was no God for Christianity, there could be no God for any religion.

During this period, I played blind justice's advocate, arguing that if God was to have value God must produce a benefit, but because God was invisible, God required blind faith to believe that its particular benefit could be aspired to with prayer, fulfilment opportunities, better human behaviour outcomes on earth, and rewards in various afterlife options. However, in achieving this, I reasoned that this invisible God was not working. The world was in turmoil. Religious self-interest came before that of other faiths, and granted prayer wishes, better human behaviour, and the rewards after death had yet to be proved, at least to me anyway.

So better to dispense with an invisible God that cannot exist, and to start considering a human alternative, say based on Darwinism. Consider then, that as nature evolves towards better survival opportunities, human beings, with the benefit of continual development of scientific knowledge, will also evolve to better serve their own interest. In this, they would avoid mutual self-destruction by producing an altruistic understanding that as nature will fend for itself, godless human behaviour must also serve the interests of others, leading mankind to the advantage of sharing in the universal benefit of *the Well of Human Goodness.*

So, I asked myself, why is belief in an invisible God perpetuated? Well, my view is that religions' belief in a God was to blame, and in particular those persons that control religion's purposes and purses by peddling the fallacy of the king's new clothes, the deceivers of mankind with their self-interest in keeping the status quo through unquestioning blind faith.

Since religions are the link between humans and their God belief, with their human spoken and written words, rituals and artistic representations, nothing changes if belief is not seen as a figment of human imagination and that gods are, and always have been, a human construct. As I still believed in Jesus' teachings, there was now the need to explain away the Resurrection, the Christ becoming the embodiment of God in heaven on earth. So fifteen years later in 2015, I wrote my first book written in the gospels' simplistic style, *The Fisherman's Story*, with the introduction from the Gospel of Luke (24:2-3) giving me the perfect entry:

And they found the stone rolled away from the tomb, but when they went in they did not find the body.

And, because it was my fiction, I gave *The Fisherman's Story* its tongue in cheek title for the one that got away. I also gave it a hook ending link to this, my second book, set 2000 years later *The Go(o)d Year*, with its own particular challenge to redefine the meaning of God as a sub-text to an exciting story that would, hopefully, keep the reader interested to the very end, a hook ending which would became its introduction:

Two thousand years have passed since the birth of Jesus, and the many generations that have followed the birth of his child in the year thirty-five. The face of the world has changed, but Jesus' message of love and hope remains if precarious against the will of other prophets.

So, the logic of my reverse conversion is that what was good for Paul was also good for me. My blinding light however, with the realisation that God did not exist came from within me, and that I, as a human being, was responsible for

327

providing goodness as it is only humans that can be good and practice goodness.

Furthermore, my absolute conviction has remained as strong now as it was when it began in 2000. In fact, it grows stronger the more I think on it and develop my arguments on why it is better not to believe in a God that does not work, not just for me but also for everyone that suffer the divisions of mankind. Indeed, it would be better if the world accepted that whilst there is value in religious history and its wonderful manifestations, there is no God at its root, just extraordinary human beings who have developed religion's philosophies and practices and created the need addiction over time.

Better still, without an invisible God to blame, praise and explain the human condition, human beings must take responsibility for their behaviour, particularly those who control and earn from keeping their religion alive. Further, they must now justify their religious teachings against the standard of 'goodness' that their religion brings, not just to their followers but to all humankind.

Keep God, and the divisions between peoples and the consequences of disagreement remain. Nothing changes. Accept that there is no God, then it is up to human beings to take responsibility, make the world a better place, a place where goodness conditions behaviour and when loving one's neighbour as one's self is truly understood and aspired to.

As St Gregory of Nyssa, a mystic who lived in Cappadocia in Asia Minor around 380 AD, said of Jesus' Beatitudes:

Beatitude is a possession of all things held to be good from which nothing is absent that a good desire may want.

Furthermore, making sense of God is impossible unless one accepts 'blind faith.' Without it, there can only be human explanations for everything ascribed to God and aspired from

God. The buck of reason and expectation cannot be passed, but must be taken back, with human beings accepting responsibility for their own thoughts and actions.

As 1 Corinthians (13:11) states:

When I was a child, I talked like a child, I thought like a child, I reasoned like a child. When I became a man, I put the ways of childhood behind me.

A child must give up childish things when stepping into adulthood. Acceptance of this is the first rule, and that however unfair life's chances may be, they can only be altered by human beings themselves.

So, the question for self-interested human beings is:

Why bother about others if there is nothing in it for themselves?

Well, there is, and the human imagination that created the idea of God proves it. The very success of God manifested religions, the practice, the power, the art, the wealth, the community of fellow membership proves that individual self-interest spreads through the osmosis of mutual benefit. Within mutual benefit, there is the satisfaction of sharing, of friendship and of companionship. There is the understanding of love, and with this, humanity's contribution to *the Well of Goodness.*

This is my theory of 'intellectual evolution' that must run in parallel to Charles Darwin's *On the Origin of Species* biological evolution.

My argument about faith of course will not be black and white for some, but require life's imagination to see Newton's sevenfold spectrum of rainbow colours

red, orange, yellow, green, blue, indigo and violet

I wrote a poem based on a line that came into my head, and excited me with its movement, becoming obsessed with producing a poem that went from night time to sunrise, celebrating the beginning of a new day.

This developed into a day breaking over Dartmoor, a beautiful wild open area of Devon countryside, near where we live between the sea of Torbay and the granite of the Tors, linked by the river Dart, which flows from Dartmeet on the moor to Dartmouth on the coast. Here it is:

Black and White Time

Slowly slowly comes the light
On the edges of the night
Fading black time into white
That spreads its rainbow colours bright
From violet deep to crimson height
Along rays scenting air to flight
Bird song on silent ear's blind sight
And touch life's eyelids closed sleep tight
Still spinning dreams escaping fright
Till new dawn's sunshine fresh delight
Can witness Dartmoor's mystic might.

And because I am on a bit of a roll, I want to tell you about one October afternoon when, knowing it was going to be a beautiful sunset on Dartmoor, me and D jumped in our car, dashed onto the moor to a spot overlooking Widecombe, parked the car, and clambered up to a perch below Bell Tor. There we stayed until it was dark, starting to rain, and our bodies were stiff and cold. It was quite fabulous, and we sang 'Uncle Tom Cobleigh' at the top of our voices as we drove home. If ever you visit, learn the words and find it if you can.

I just had to write a poem about it, called:

Dartmoor Sunset with Dawn

We watched the sun going down on October Dartmoor
With our backs to the granite of rocky Bell Tor
And heard the rooks calling out their evocative cor
As they settled to roost above Widdecombe's floor.

We saw the sun slip from silver to an orangey blur
And the skies fade to silence with night time azure
Split by the bark from a fox on a musk laden spoor
And the hoot of an owl poised with ravenous claw.

We felt bat's air brush a cheek unnoticed before
Making gooseflesh creep and chapped lips sore
As cold dropped the curtain on daylight's encore
And the stars started glimmering in a galaxy galore.

We sat still and tingled until clouds did obscure
The moonlighted secrets of nature's harsh law
When the weak turn to jelly and then into gore
And resolves turns to water as rain starts to pour.

We ran for safe shelter behind the car door
Chasing and laughing not knowing what for
And sang the glad song of Tom Cobleigh and all
Between Bone Hill, Chinkwell and Honey Bag Tor.

9

When I was twenty, because of a stammer that crippled me during the oral part of mandatory French classes necessary for my degree I flunked out of university after two years. That was my excuse anyway much to the great disappointment of my doting parents. In running away, I emigrated to Canada, spending eight months in Montreal as a medical attendant in a mental hospital, and then textile shipper, before going to Calgary for four months as a labourer, and swimming pool life guard.

I travelled out by sea sharing a cabin for the seven days and nights with a man a little older than me (I regret I forget his name, but Francis seems to present itself). He confessed to me that he had suffered from acute shyness until he took a Dale Carnegie course on 'How to Win Friends and Influence People', and his routine habit of speaking into a mirror:

'Every day in a little way I get better and better!'

It had changed his life and indirectly effected mine knowing that positive thinking could change one's attitude to negative behaviour, and although it would be another three years for my stammer to cease to blight my life, with the help of DDD it did.

So now I would like to restate the Dale Carnegie mantra for *doing a good thing,* making a daily habit of thinking:

'Every day I get better and better in doing a good thing!'

What is the reward for *doing a good thing*? Well, for the smallest bit of *a good thing* given to me I feel good, even if only for an instant. For a grand gesture, I have observed that I can get a welling of emotion that makes me want to cry, but then I do cry easily. It takes practice to be a happy blubberer, but the particular tears I want to describe are not those that come with grief and sorrow. They are those that come from joy when one's heartstrings, the cord-like tendons that connect the papillary muscles to the tricuspid valve and the mitral valve in the heart, become figuratively linked to one's inner feelings, and are tugged by the emotion of a loving touch, fine words, a kind gesture, a grand vision, or lyrical music. Then the hair rises on the skin, tears prickle eyes, and goodness flows through the body.

Filling the human *Well of Goodness* first requires a commitment to do good as any dry well that needs to be filled first needs a water source, and then a continuation of doing good to replenish what is needed to satisfy the thirst of all living beings drinking from *the Well of Goodness*. It is the repeating continuance of life that begets life and the value of the incremental offer as practised by the cyclist coach, Dave Brailsford, with his idea of Marginal Gains; if you broke down everything you could think of that goes into riding a bike and then improved it by one per cent, you would get a significant increase in performance when you put them all together, showing how everyone's little good will combine together to keep topping up *the Well of Goodness*.

Of course, *the Well of Goodness* may also receive the acid poison of hate and have to be neutralised with the alkaline of

333

love. But if hate must express itself, then a Macbeth's witches' brew curse poem delivered by the Four Horsemen of the Apocalypse might have to suffice:

Zombie Curse

You,
Yes you,
Who are
The damned few,
That visit pain and grief
And sorrow for a memory store
Filled now with lingering sadness blue.
You,
Yes you,
Who twist
The truth anew,
To suite a false belief
From self's corrupted store
Of poisoned foul rank stinking stew.
You,
Yes you,
Who marks
A pristine view,
That stains a virgin leaf
From blemished vision's store
With bloodied tears of weeping yew.
You,
Yes you,
Who are
The damned few,
Who will without relief
Be cursed from victim's store
Of hate stirred molten witches' brew.

10

So, to a 'Guide to Goodness', starting with an agreement that what is good for me is going to be good for you, as long as the giving and receiving of goodness results in making everyone happier with the result.

Doing good is about attitude and behaviour, thinking that it is the right thing to do and doing the right thing again and again and again, no matter how small or unimportant that thing may be, making the right thing a habit so that it influences one's outlook on life.

I know it's easy to say, and for some who face hardship and injustice, very difficult. But when all is said and done, it's worth the effort, remembering that *the Well of Human Goodness* will always receive the smallest gift of doing good and will always be available to respond to a human request for assistance.

As Matthew (7:7-8) says:

Ask and it will be given, seek and you will find, knock and the door will be opened. For everyone who asks receives, whoever seeks finds, and to the one who knocks the door will be opened.

I would like to offer my poem *Light on the Path*, written before my conversion to atheism, which although obscure, should touch the reader's hidden place if allowed to reach there, as it did and continues to do for me whenever I re-read it. It's called:

Light on the Path

Before the eyes can see beyond the earthly grave
The tears of life must dry
And fall like withered autumn leaves.

Before the ears can know the sound that silence makes
The drum must pause
To hear the flowers bloom on lily lakes.

Before the voice can speak the wordless truth
The lips and tongue must seal
A yearning kiss with peaceful proof.

Before the soul can stand before the master's gate
The stricken heart must bleed
And wash the path the feet will take.

Suffice to say it is still as powerful for me today as my introduction to the text of the book of the same name nearly half a century of life ago, with its subtle command to see, hear, speak and stand, to understand that life's suffering is a doorway to bliss through just *doing a good thing*.

For anyone interested, this poem is based on the four preparations required of disciples attending to the rules stated in *The Light on the Path*, written down by Mabel Collins, published by Blavatsky Study Centre, and compiled by W Q Judge and A Keightley. Mabel was a theosophist, and author of over forty-six books. She was born 9 September 1851 in St Peter Port, Guernsey, and died 31 March 1927.

I was introduced to the book by Herbert Gantes in 1968 when we both worked in Claridges Hotel London, he as Billing Controller in his sixties, and me as Staff Manager, aged twenty-eight. We would often have lunch together in the hotel's basement staff dining room, adjacent to the main kitchen and my staff office, followed by a walk in Barkley Square when we would discuss the meaning of life and I would listen to his wise words. To think that in drinking Coke, diet now because of my diabetes, I am reminded of him and that he worked for Coca-Cola in Egypt.

He also introduced me to *Inana-Yoga* by Swami Vivekananda which he gave me, but he told me, that as a condition of ownership, I had to find and buy *The Light on the Path*. I found a 1968 copy, price six shillings, but because of its apparent profound content, I delayed reading it for two years, keeping it with me nevertheless until finally I was ready to do so. It had a profound effect on me, and I have kept it close by ever since.

Now, *The Practical Philosophy of Incremental Goodness* has come out of me and been written, and in so doing has also had a profound effect on me, believing as I do, that it contains a simple rule for all human beings living a worthwhile life:

Just do a good thing and help fill the Well with goodness.

I am also including a poem, first written for C&C as an exhortation for their journey through life, and then for all those who strive to overcome life's trials and tribulations by understanding the value of sacrifice. Formally titled 'Bittersweet', I renamed it following C's idea to use the strapline headline 'Know Hope' to describe her business.

I centred the lines and found the cup shape, which in turn gave idea to the form of "the Holy Grail" for the image:

Know Hope

Oh how I grieve for yesterday,
That day, when all that ever could become,
Of joy and satisfaction, spent,
And gone, forever lost because
I could not see beyond myself,
And know the priceless treasure
Of the moment, so rich in opportunity,
To give and to receive the love of life,
The very breath of every living being,
With all the sweetness possible
From sight and sound,
Of taste, and smell,
And touch,
Oh God,
How much
I miss that
Which is past.
But then, perhaps,
If I can just hold to,
A moment still to come,
I may yet get to know, to find,
The truth of now, and savour full
With every bristling pore,
With every heightened sense,
With every draft into my very self,
What I did grieve for yesterday.

11

As I said, I have chosen to be a joyfinder, because of the joyous release I felt from dispensing with the illogical burden of God. I could finally see life for what it was, and try to understand it and make the most of it. That's not to say that my association with various religious paths, and the way they led to their version of paradise, haven't helped me with my journey. They did, but now I had also discovered a way without the need for blind faith that also offers a reason for living through the simple task of *doing a good thing*, and contributing to *the Well of Goodness*.

However, a test for me has yet to come. That is if I go before my Dearest Darling Dawn, my DDD, or she goes before me, the terrible feeling of knowing that we would never see each other again, ever! I wrote a poem:

Waiting for Dawn

So when I'm gone and memory's all that's left belong,
To you I've loved and breathed my song,
I'll wait distilling peace upon,
Your aching beating heart still strong,
Until your time must come along,
And you join me, however long.

Whenever I read this poem, I commence to grieve at the inevitability of death for D and me, and my heart begins to break until I can know her presence once again. I cannot imagine living without her, or of the thought that I might leave her to live on without me. If only I could believe that death was stepping into the light where all soul mates were reunited. But I am cursed to know that God does not exist, that the time we have is all there is, and that the great lesson to be learnt is that one must make every moment the best possible, not only for oneself, but for all living things that one comes into contact with. Of course, the greater the love experienced, the greater the pain of loss that must be endured when the object of that love is gone, and all that is left is the memory.

And while I wait I can remember a poem:

Ago

I love you as we were ago,
When you and I would sigh and sigh
From lovers' breathless kissing slow
Our thirsty parting lips aglow.
I love you as we were ago,
When you and I would lie and lie
From lovers' senses sated so
Our empty drifting dreams a flow.

I have lived with the thought of a possible permanent separation from D ever since writing my first poem for her, *Tofu Wo(r)k* when I was fifty and we were starting on our extraordinary tofu making adventure in 1990. This poem is all about Dawn spending one day, 2 January 1990, on her own, without me, making tofu with Lindsay and Graham, the third owners, to decide whether we should buy the organic wholefood business 'Dragonfly' that she had found advertised in the Thursday 23 November 1989 copy of the Western Morning News classified section offering for sale:

"ORGANIC WHOLE FOOD Manufacturing Business in idyllic riverside position near Totnes, producing Tofu, Healthy t/o Tel..."

She returned tired out said 'yes' and we completed in June 1990.

The poem is called;

Tofu Wo(r)k

Dawn is on a journey
To make tofu,
Although I'm not going with her,
My love is
Too!

We moved house to release the funds needed and became the fourth owners of a business established in 1984. After a two-week handover to learn the basics, D and I started to make tofu with two part-timers, continuing to do the production work ourselves without a break, save a two-week maintenance break at Christmas, for the next seven years. We lasted twenty-two years in two factories and having grown Dragonfly twenty-four times in the UK and into Eire, France and Belgium supplying health food stores and supermarkets we sold the business debt free in 2012.

A sort of poem for those years:

Dragonfly

1990 Staverton Devon Factory Riverside Unit
1991 Soil Association organic certification
1991 London Marigold listing
1994 Buckfastleigh Devon Factory 2a Mardle Way Unit
1995 Computerised forecasting
1996 French Distriborg own label listing
1997 Trademark 'beany' and 'insider'
1997 First Factory Manager
1997 HRH Prince Charles UK National Organic Tofu Award
1997 Sheila Dillon's BBC Radio 4 Food Programme
1998 UK Independent Health Food Market Distribution
1998 Which? 1998 Veggie Burger Review
1999 Logo Design www.dragonflyfoods.co.uk website
2000 Trademark 'tatty'
2002 Trademark 'soysage'
2001 Sainsbury UK listing
2003 Trademark 'tofupot'
2004 Trademark 'appleheart'
2005 Trademark 'soysweet'
2005 Japan visit to purchase Takai production equipment
2006 Factory expansion 2a+b+c Mardle Way Units
2010 SALSA quality assurance standard
2011 Holland and Barrett UK listing
2012 Sell Dragonfly

To assuage my fears about our future, I wrote her a poem before our first day at the tofu factory, just in case we didn't survive the experience, which then lasted for the next twenty-two years:

DDD

If anything ever happens to me,
And you are left undone,
Remember this dearest one that I shall always be
In the sweet night air bird songs you hear
And the golden rays of the sun.
If anything ever happens to me,
And the journey seems too long,
Remember this dearest one my love will cover thee
And tread the path that you must take
As though our lives are one.
If anything ever happens to me,
And the pain is hard to bear,
Remember this dearest one that I can make you free
By sharing memories of the past
Until there are none to fear.
If anything ever happens to me,
And you need to know the why,
Remember this dearest one my dearest darling D
That I live on forever
In every breath you sigh.
But if I am spared and you leave me,
And I am left alone,
I shall remember dearest one with every day I see
The light we shared the joy we had
The times we were at home.
So as you survive along with me,
And we are given time,
Remember this dearest one to prepare for eternity
Our living spark must fuse with love
And our golden threads entwine.

And then later, to bolster myself up when the remorseless routine became hard to bear, I wrote her the poem *Round and Round* to remember that I had told her often that I loved her:

Round and Round

Round and round and round we go
Hello goodbye goodbye hello
Breathing unconscious rhythms flow
The air that fickle seasons blow
Hot summer clouds cold winter snow
As earth turns sun day moon night glow
When sleeping fires wake hope's rainbow
And changes sown make chances grow.

Round and round and round we go
Fingertip welcome farewell tiptoe
Live happy quick dead weeping slow
Glad joyful love sad tearful woe
Close friendship spent earns lonesome foe
Ask why the why and never know
Tomorrow becomes today's ago
Our turn in time must end in sorrow.

Round and round and round we go
From seminal milk to bucking roe
Life is just more than H_2O
More than two cents on dice a throw
A feast to feed a carrion crow
Life is the link that links tomorrow
With sky above and earth below
Our bonding guarantees it so.

Round and round and round we go,
But did I say I loved you so?

12

Great value is given in religious belief to the soul's state after death, what is in it for the departed, and how the offer of a life after death can be a balm for those that remain. I have no intention to comment on that which is held dear by believers, but I can offer three poems about dying, the first called:

Exit

Oh, masters of the universe
Bring me my lover's song,
To break the broken-hearted curse
Of riven lovers gone.
Cast me a spell from memory's purse
For lovers left undone,
And ease my half heart to rehearse
My exit line alone.

The second takes from:

Psalm 23 King James Version
"The Lord is my shepherd; I shall not want. He maketh me to lie down in green pastures. He leadeth me beside the still waters. He restoreth my soul. He leadeth me in the paths of righteousness for his name's sake. Yea, though I walk through the valley of the shadow of death, I will fear no evil for thou art with me, thy rod and thy staff they comfort me. Thou preparest a table before me in the presence of mine enemies, thou anointest my head with oil, my cup runneth over. Surely goodness and mercy shall follow me all the days of my life, and I will dwell in the house of the Lord forever."

The Burial words from the 1559 Book of Common Prayer said while the corpse is made ready to be laid into the earth:
"Man is born of a woman, and has but a short time to live. His life is full of misery. He comes up, and is cut down, like a flower. He flees as if he were a shadow that can never continue beyond the day. His days are as for grass, flourishing as a flower of the field. But as soon as the wind passes over, he is gone, as dust, and the place of his presence no more."

The first Epistle of Paul the Apostle to the Corinthians words for courage taken from the Original 1611 KJV Book of 1 Corinthians Chapter 15 55:
"O death, where is thy sting? O grave, where is thy victory?"

My poem is centered to shape the genie in the lamp.

Simply Death

Listen,
Listen to me,
Listen to what I have to say.
Whilst dying may well be painful, death is not.
And since death is inevitable, fear of death should not be.
However, fear of death alone, and for those left behind is
real.
So whilst the opportunity for a heaven thereafter, may fail to
satisfy,
The knowledge of continuity of life through a gene pool,
Or the continuation of lives that have been touched,
And influenced by the life that is finished,
Should give comfort and meaning
To both those that will remain,
And those that must depart.
So fear not,
The passing of the countless lives before
Lights the way into the valley of shadows.
This is the genie in the lamp.

The third expresses my thinking that at the end, the memory of the departed is all any of us have left to remember and to pass on, and what better epitaph can there be than that the loved one *did good things* and helped *fill the Well with goodness* in their lifetime. It's called:

Soul

Soul is the memory of life
However led.
It is elixir or poison strife
To thought about the dead.

For those remaining yet to pass
Their genie on to future's mass,
This lasting message theirs to find
For some a salve to peace of mind
Of worthy souls most precious kind,
For others cursed and left undone
By wicked souls boasting death's drum,
Pain to endure till mercy comes
And fades Cain's mark until there's none.

Soul is the memory of life
However led.
So pass this moment free of strife
And bless the memory of the dead.

Within my soul there is a poem I wrote in 2003 for Dawn, as a memory jogger to celebrate forty ruby years of married life, and included in my first poem collection *'so far so good'* dedicated to David Gerrard, our lost first born son.

It is written in lower case to reflect the movement of time as a river that flows to the sea, with its surface coma rippled by memories of places, faces and other traces shared. Although it will not mean much to the reader, I offer an extract for those who may be curious, perhaps don't keep a diary but might wish to consider copying the idea for a legacy. It is between meeting DDD and Dragonfly, called:

Places, Faces and Other Traces

'62 fiat 500, somerset, dunster, lutterel arms thf trainee, bridgette, meet ddd, odell-court hellfire club bar, derek & dodo, ray charles can't stop loving you, dunkery beacon first kiss, chris & mac, valley of the rocks picnics, osteopath con mahroni, south african franz, pallet knife painter george deakin, minehead pier farewell tears, dusseldorf pallet paintings flop, london retreat, pringles savoy introduction, cezerini interview, savoy training, miss barnet, river room restaurant, gondoliers private room, pinafore photo crocker & me, table roses post ddd, d regent palace interview, miss brandreth head housekeeper, kensington flat hip bath overflow, 101 church road wimbledon, mike & sybil, michael & elizabeth higginson, i ching, dr no chocolate melt, doing a good job to staff caper, spearman staff manager, frank furlong trainee pal, putney, 142 upper richmond road, mackeson, gooseberry wine, escofier cook book, knife set, trompeto grill head chef, chelesa pub proposal to d, us, birmingham, quinton, 49 max road, harry & elizabeth, ask harry, val, peter, duntisbourne, mick & val, bill & stella, dressed salmon, morden registrar 18/5, burford bridge honeymoon, box hill climb, david gerrard, st. teresa's, shirodkar, dg 25/9 rip merton, jack b, heathrow,

'64 farewell uk, kenya, nairobi, airport, park, jomo, uhuru, block hotels, norfolk, courtyard bird cage, 2 bedroom veranda blinds, rains smell, jacaranda tree blue flowers, frangipane tree scent, henry & fay & eileen, joginda sing aa, ford anglia, manager tom, delamere bar, asante sana sampson, sweetie thing angelo, laundry stan, jimmy fernandes & lui, sunday beer & curry kip, nile perch, boac capt harry, cliché cramb, mary aspinal, racecourse, fat anna, navasha flamingos, hippo path, princess elizabeth hospital, catherine 17/7, angela godmother, python skin, safari, hunter george, safari, george & michael, eric, capt, Kilimanjaro, mount meru, arusha, n'goro-goro, seringetti, leopard hide, siafu camp ants, outspan, ricky & evy, sigona golf, judo, theka drive in, lilly of the fields, wogmorie, jason 17/3 coarctation, guiness, dr. zhivago, modelling, new stanley, thorn tree, brian & jenifer, peter & anthea, paul & bernice, colin, willie, masai man & sunflowers, westlands, james kikuyu, pat menu,

'67 england, bibury, osbournes, coblers, harry rip max rd quinton, great ormond street, bonham-carter, tadworth, claridges, hanson, bonnington, herbert, fulham, bishop mansions, park gardens, david & roma, valerie, malta, reading, henry smith, peter & john, humphrey-reeve, sonning common, 10 priory copse, piano, swing, wendy house, mini clubman, betty, dennis & heather, pete & diane & susie, lisa & henry, christof, bambi, niel & marge, peppard common, school, church, mrs stagpole, mother ivy's bay, mrs beeton, brandy & ginger, trust houses forte, kardomah, ron, ring & brymer, sandown, neville, john & queenie, kempton, colin, bob, peter, larry, mike, newbury, frank, keble, rose bowl, ruby, henley-on-thames, red house, catherine & graham, little chef, hackbridge, stan, ernie, norman, michael, david, vivian, peter, great gran, bond, bookham, dunglass farmhouse, billericay, lady, albufera, villa sybilla, faro hospital, wardrobe key, sardines, constantine, jc superstar, burford, sibsy 18/11 rip cottage hospital, cafe royal, royal festival hall, mervyn, sinatra, earls court, dillion, talk of the town, eddie, nicky,

ascot, lobsters, chapel farm, burnt foot, maggie, newcastle cc, ozzie, rocco, press club, parkside, soar mill cove, hawkward dell, easton court, torquay, vane hill road, herbie,couch, 9 park hall, jibset, michael, ian, john dory, lisburn square, meadfoot, bluebells, teneriffe flats, richard, peter, lyn, michael, brixham, british schooner, ian, janet, cat stevens, john & barbara, st. margarets, carmina burana, donald & dora, st. wilfrids, trinity, tim, new barkley,

'83 hongkong, jockey club, locking, archer, joe, derby room, tulio, happy valley, lee gardens, sha kwong do, percy, armon, hc yeung, mat, paul, rosemary, to fat, jimmy, i.club, ben vereen, sean & sirpa, jim & sheila, jellyfish junk, sixth furlong, larry, gym, trams & taxis, macao, dr sunyat-sen, lantau, kowloon, starferry, shopguide, ikebana, chinese, victoria peak, repulse bay, stanley, shatin, oi seun, jimmy, tango, beas river, tedford, ocean park, star ferry,

'85 england, grand met, 27 berkshire road, jp sibford, cr devon & exeter, letheby & christopher, theale, kit, regatta, glyndebourne, goodwood, dick, clock, glyn cemetry gates, mecca, michael, lords, saab, suppers, goring, mike 8/2 rip battle hospital, st. lucia, snowdon, wellswood manor, roy robinson, wellswood, greystones, ilsham marine drive, exmouth, elizabeth balloon ride, phyllis rip, john, crete, elounda, silver, laurentian, patsy, staverton, totnes, dartmoor, dragonfly'90, suzuki, honda, wo(rk), tofu, shurtleff & aoyagi, basil, lindsay & graham, sue, malcolm, kiri, david, chris, gus, flood, soil assoc, seasons, parvis, best of the west, nigel, riverford, ben, guy, basil, peter tanner, demelza, essential, marigold, patrick, galmpton, vale close, ddd, 4 stoke gabriel road, greenway, dartmouth, phil, judas tree, red arrows, oldway manor, sarah, joshua, crispin, berry pomery, pastoral, paddy, liz & mike, pam & tony, gp, wedmore, mrs muscova, quarry house, emily, insider, buckfastleigh, 2 abc mardle way, clive's pies, sue & keith.......

13

I hope that my story will help shape the way you are as a human being, how you think, how you feel, how you behave, how you are going to face your death, a certain death that is coming faster than you can grasp, so fast that the very air you breathe and take so much for granted, is going to be denied you in an instant leaving you with nothing but empty space and a legacy of crumbling bones unless, unless you squeeze out fear and understand that the value of everything can be found where joy resides in the bliss of *doing a good thing*.

So two poems, a reflection on David Shanahan's cross-legged Indian beggar painting and a thought on life's cycle:

Am

Oh you sitting man
Sitting, waiting
Until I can
Sit and wait
And be I am

Old Wrinkly

Birth.
When I was born unready at days demanding dawn
Thrust sightless cold and naked into harsh lighted room
And strangely held aloft and curiously looked upon
All sticky haired and scared and desperately alone
Gasping breath mouth open wide in muted shocking swoon
Before wailing flailing limbs will struggle all forlorn
New wrinkled skin of virgins that I have hardly worn
All pain and pleasure feelings for me yet still to come
I longed for a return to that empty thought-free home
The dark wet pulsing warmth of mother's loving womb.

Life.
My time began too soon and soon my time was gone
Amid a blur of memories real and sometimes memories spun
From ups and downs in places and journeys to and from
Of telling secrets kept and broken promises sworn
To know a love that's lasted since loving time began
To taste success that's busted the appetite of man
Old wrinkled skin life polished that I have badly worn
So sipped and slipped my days beneath the ageless sun
And now at home I shrink from thoughts filled with return
To the dark wet rotting sod of mother's earthly tomb.

Death.

So, will you strike the flint?

14

The book was meant to end with *Old Wrinkly*, but felt there is a need to introduce my poetry and my writing.

Up to the age of fifty, I mainly worked for others.

Up to the age of fifty, it never occurred to me that I would write poetry. Despite early thoughts on the meaning of life, I became too preoccupied with following an ambitious twenty-five-year career in the support of family. This career was to come to an unexpected end, and I was cast adrift. In the same year, my father died. So we fled to Devon for the second time, and there in 1990, after a pause, my life partner, 'Dearest Darling Dawn', discovered Dragonfly and the art of making tofu, and we commenced a working partnership that was to engage us for the next twenty-two years. From a life that began in Uganda in 1940 and having travelled far and wide, I now found myself in a place I treasure, close to the sea and the moor, with people I love, have loved, will always love, and who are available for my wellbeing, my feel good spell.

How lucky am I!

I also started to write poems (two hundred to date) which opened a door to a potential for me to communicate through poetry. The poems, never very long, were always born with effort, needing their final outcome to satisfy me with the words, sometimes their shape, to settle finally on the page.

The poems included in this book are a selection of poems from my *Fortunes of Love* Light and Dark shaded Pocket Books collection published with Spiderwize. I chose the title because of the various forms of love expressed, whether just mine for the words and the subject of them, or for the love that can be found within them. In doing so I have come to realise the extraordinary nature of that simple four-letter word, and that there is very little that cannot be included within its orbit of powerful influence, provided the expressed intention is honest.

The poems are about legacy, a lasting print about anyone or anything that has touched me and I have been able to capture with words. But whilst poetry has its own agony and ecstasy, writing novels is more about learning, discipline, hard work, editing and knowing when one has said enough.

I conclude with a poem on 'letters' to say how important words have become to me and how essential they are as one of the means of communication for all life in expressing their wants. Think for a moment, and take any living thing, animal or vegetable, to test whether any does not use some sense, some sound, some colour, some artifice, whether instinctive or deliberate, to get attention for a selfish or mutual benefit. For humans, words can be signed, written and spoken, to be felt, seen and heard. For me, they have opened a new world into my imagination, allowing me to articulate the feelings of my heart. It's called:

Letters

Letters matter for fine words to form
And carry the love from a heart still warm
And the word I want to be remembered by is joyfinder.

Finally, as I complete 'The Go(o)d Year' and it is autumn, I am reminded that every September, for nearly thirty years, geese congregate in their gaggles in fields we overlook from the bedroom window of our Devon home. They fly in, in skeins of varying sizes, honking to each other, announcing their arrival, hardly giving us time to trace them and watch, thrill and rejoice at their presence.

When the weather is right, they go, leaving us to mourn their absence.

I have always been drawn to geese. My father, shortly before he died, spoke to DDD of a dream he'd had, of me riding the back of a goose. If only that were possible!

I wrote a poem to celebrate their departure and to think of him Mike and then my mother Sybil who bore me:

September Song

The geese are on the wing
As September draws the summer in
With golden sunlight threads that trailing catch
A gentle autumn wind.

The geese are on the wing
Calling my heart to follow them
To different climes and times and then perhaps
Return to me next spring.

The geese are on the wing
Oh how I love their honking din
That urgent bonding song whose echoes scratch
Upon my gooseflesh skin.

And because it is autumn, two poems to sign off:
Fall

Shudder wake to chilled air
Morning
Frosty sundrenched green leaves
Turning
Sugar sweetened sap filled
Bursting
Yellow golden amber
Burning
Flames that rustle gently
Curling
Copper beaten burnished
Glowing
Skyline blaze with senses
Flowing
Breathe to catch the east wind
Blowing
Cold on pulses slowly
Slowing
Time to feel the changes
Calling
Break the grip of still life
Stalling
Autumn's ochre ready
Falling
Falling into winter
Mourning.

Autumn Leaf

A fallen leaf tumbling in the wind,
Blown hither and thither with no one to mind,
Whether this way or that way is certain to find,
The answer to autumn's golden shaded design.

Some Definitions with Comments

God: *an abstract superhuman being worshipped (by humans).*
To have belief in God human beings must have blind faith.
Faith: *trust, unquestioning confidence and belief.*
To express faith human beings must believe in a religion.
Religion: *a particular system of faith and worship.*
Human beings must record a particular religion's content.
Good: *having the right qualities.*
Human beings must have defined the right qualities.
Goodness: *having virtue, excellence and kindnesses.*
Only human behaviour can manifest virtue.
Incremental: *degree of increase.*
From the concept of aggregation of Marginal Gains.
Abstract: *separated from matter.*
Separation from matter requires human imagination.
Atheist: *someone who disbelieves in the existence of a deity.*
My word for Atheist is 'Joyfinder.'
Soul: *Spiritual or immaterial part of human beings.*
My idea is that soul is the memory of a life lived.
Conspiracy: *plot of silence.*
By Religions to protect their own God beliefs.
Responsibility: *accepting to be called to account.*
The first responsibility is for one's own thoughts and actions.
Philosophy: *seeking after wisdom.*
I am not sure philosophy is practical, but I like the idea.
Intellectual: *being enlightened.*
Anyone can be enlightened even if they are not intellectual.
Wisdom*: experience and knowledge.*
I like the idea of aged common sense.
Bliss: *perfect joy.*
Available to Joyfinders.

THE JOYFINDER
(j)

You will not be surprised to learn that the title of my next book is THE *JOYFINDER*. It is a non-fictional account of my life. As the title implies, there is the central theme of my atheism to be considered, with the story of my life to the time of writing at seventy-nine plus, being the background to, and fertile ground for, my becoming a joyfinder, a frame of mind that believes passionately in the preservation of life, the seeker of wellbeing from *doing a good thing* in the form of joy, with the ability to knowingly contribute to and receive from that inexhaustible reservoir of sweetness that lies within us all, *the well of goodness*, and truly is the answer to the question:

What is the point of life?

Note. You will see I have included the symbol **(j)** to represent joyfinder. Perhaps there is a better one, but it will have to suffice for now. The purpose of this is to try to give the word joyfinder the universal power of a logo, as with the peace logo.

Dear Friends,

Now that you have read THE GO(O)D YEAR, I hope you will accept my offer of friendship, join me in being a joyfinder with my message to do a good thing, fill the well with goodness and shout out THE GO(O)D YEAR to all your friends, both face to face, and through your social networks.

Perhaps the simple idea of doing a good thing, however small, will cross all barriers and become a universal way for peace and harmony to be added to and shared from the limitless well of goodness.

Remember there is never any regret from doing a good thing when all that remains is the imprint of love.

Simon Boreham

Doing a good thing makes sense in any language.

(Apologies for missing languages and inaccurate translation)
do a good thing-ānidi melikami negeri yadirigu-doen 'n goeie
ding-bëj një gjë të mirë-afeal shyyana jydana-lav ban ara-
yaxşı bir şey edin-ekati bhāla jinisa ki-gauza on bat egin-
zrabić dobruju reč-uradi dobru stvar-pravi dobro neshto-
kaunggsaw aararko pyu par-fes-ho bé-buhata ang usa ka
maayo nga butang-zuò yī jiàn haoshì-fà una cosa bona-činiti
dobro-dĕlat dobrou vĕc-gør en god ting-doe iets goeds-faru
bonon-tee head asja-gumawa ng isang magandang bagay-tee
hyvä asia-faire une bonne chose-faga algo bo-k'argad
gaak'ete-mach eine gute sache-kánoume éna kaló prágma-
sārī vāta karō-fè yon bon bagay-yi abu mai kyau-e hana i kahi
mea maika'i-achchha kaam karo-ua qhov zoo tshaj plaws-
csinálj jó dolgot-gera gott-mee ezi ihe-lakukan hal yang baik-
déan rud maith-fai una buona cosa-Yoikoto o yaru-nindakake
perkara apik-olleyadu māḍi-jaqsı närse jasañız-thveu rueng l-
oh-eun il-eulhaela-tiştek baş bikin-jakşı eç nerse kıla-hed
singthi di-non est bonum-darīt labu-daryk gerą dalyką-eng
gutt saach-napravi dobra rabota-manaova zavatra tsara-déan
rud maith-oru nalla kāryam ceyyuka-tagħmel ħaġa tajba-mahi
i te mea pai-eka cāngalī gōsta karā-sain züil khii-kaunggsaw
aararko pyu par-rāmrō kāma gara-gjør en god ting-zrób coś
dobrego-faça uma coisa boa-Ika cagī gdèan rud math-ala
karō-face un lucru bun-delat' khoroshuyu veshch'-faia se mea
lelei-uradi dobru stvar-etsa ntho e ntle-ita chinhu chakanaka-
hoňda deyak karanna-robte dobrú vec-počni dobro-samee
wax wanaagsan-haz algo bueno-ngalakukeun hiji hal anu
alus-kufanya jambo jema-gör en bra sak-ita chinhu
chakanaka-kori xube kuned-oru nalla visayam-mañci
visayamē-thả šìng thì dī-iyi bir şey yap-dobre robyty-Yaxshi
ish qil-làm một việc tốt-gwneud peth da-

361

Previously Published Works:

The Fisherman's Story (2017)
ISBN: 978-1-84897-948-2

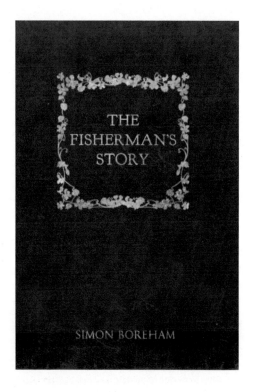

Two thousand years have passed since the birth of Jesus, and the many generations that have followed the birth of his child in the year thirty-five. The face of the world has changed, but Jesus' message of love and hope remains if somewhat precarious against the will of other prophets.